CELG

S0-BFF-233

MAR - - 2017

THE ALLIANCE

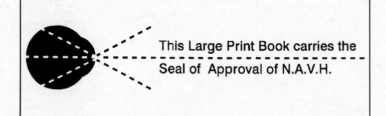

This Large Print Book carries the
Seal of Approval of N.A.V.H.

THE ALLIANCE

JOLINA PETERSHEIM

THORNDIKE PRESS
A part of Gale, Cengage Learning

Farmington Hills, Mich • San Francisco • New York • Waterville, Maine
Meriden, Conn • Mason, Ohio • Chicago

GALE
CENGAGE Learning®

Copyright © 2016 by Jolina Petersheim.

Some Scripture quotations are taken from the *Holy Bible*, New Living Translation, copyright © 1996, 2004, 2015 by Tyndale House Foundation. Used by permission of Tyndale House Publishers, Inc., Carol Stream, Illinois 60188. All rights reserved.

Some Scripture quotations are taken from the *Holy Bible*, King James Version.

Thorndike Press, a part of Gale, Cengage Learning.

ALL RIGHTS RESERVED

The Alliance is a work of fiction. Where real people, events, establishments, organizations, or locales appear, they are used fictitiously. All other elements of the novel are drawn from the author's imagination.

Thorndike Press® Large Print Christian Fiction.

The text of this Large Print edition is unabridged.

Other aspects of the book may vary from the original edition.

Set in 16 pt. Plantin.

LIBRARY OF CONGRESS CATALOGING-IN-PUBLICATION DATA

Names: Petersheim, Jolina, author.
Title: The alliance / Jolina Petersheim.
Description: Large print edition. | Waterville, Maine : Thorndike Press Large Print, 2017. |Series: Thorndike Press large print Christian fiction
Identifiers: LCCN 2016040617| ISBN 9781410495617 (hardback) | ISBN 1410495612 (hardcover)
Subjects: LCSH: Mennonites—Fiction. | Interpersonal relations—Fiction. | Large type books. | BISAC: FICTION / Christian / General. | GSAFD: Christian fiction.
Classification: LCC PS3616.E84264 A79 2016b | DDC 813/.6—dc23
LC record available at https://lccn.loc.gov/2016040617

Published in 2017 by arrangement with Tyndale House Publishers, Inc.

Printed in Mexico
1 2 3 4 5 6 7 21 20 19 18 17

*To my husband, Randy, without whom
this story — and my life —
would be impossible. No hero I write
can compare to you.*

ACKNOWLEDGMENTS

One of the things I love most about writing is the way it takes me on a journey of discovery, particularly discovering God and who I am through him. *The Alliance* has been my most challenging writing "journey" so far, but through its creation, I've learned that without Christ's anointing, I am a wordless vessel. I've also learned that the body of Christ can work together as the perfect community, if we allow ourselves to be of one mind and accord through him.

Our family went through a challenging season in the winter of 2015, and Tyndale House somehow knew exactly what I needed and when, offering me both support and space to heal. I am grateful for each member of my team: Karen Watson, who offered to come to Wisconsin to rock my babies, Stephanie Broene, Kathy Olson, Shaina Turner, and Maggie Rowe. You all have become so dear to me. Thank you for your patience and kindness and — Kathy — for allowing me to do an extra round of edits, even though it added more work to your plate.

I am also thankful for Wes Yoder, my agent, who shares my love for homegrown carrots, family history, and working in the dirt. Your quiet steadfastness has been crucial for me during this publishing journey. Thank you.

To my readers: thank you, *thank you,* for your support. You cannot know how much comfort it brought me to receive your care packages, to read your messages, and to feel your fervent prayers surrounding us. You have become more than my readers; you have become my friends.

I want to thank my parents, Merle and Beverly Miller, for loving me even after I moved their granddaughters twelve hours away. Your care packages, Mom, are the materialization of children's dreams. I love you and Dad very much. I love you, too, Josh and Caleb. Sometimes a girl needs brothers to help counter all her sparkle and pink; God knew I sure needed mine.

Thank you, Mom Betty and Dad Rich Petersheim, for all the work and love you poured into us — the winter of 2015, especially. Thank you, also, for the unconditional acceptance of our dreams. We couldn't have made this move if not for you both.

Joanne Petersheim, sis-in-love, thank you for speeding through the night to reach the hospital, watching my babies, cleaning my house, making me tea, crying and laughing with me during that dry-bones winter. So glad God gave me you.

Misty, my beloved best friend: thank you for traveling twelve hours to bring me two Bantam chickens, birthday cake, and books for my girls; and for sharing late night walks, talks, tea, and period dramas on *BBC*. Despite the distance between my farm and yours, I know we'll always be close. I love you so much.

To my daughters, Adelaide and Madeleine. Right now, you're sitting on the couch with your wonderful "da-da," and I can't help but stop typing to watch your

9

smiles and listen to the soundtrack of your mischievous joy. You two make my world. My chest aches with love for you.

To my husband, Randy: thank you for encouraging me to dream, to live without fear, to hold fast to the promises of God. This past year, more than any other, has made me feel like we are truly one. I cannot imagine this simple, beautiful life without you. I am relieved and overjoyed that I do not have to try. I loved you; I love you; I will love you. Always.

To my heavenly Father: Thank you for this faith-filled journey, which helped me face one of my greatest fears and discover that — even while I was in it — you were always by my side. I know that I can trust you with every aspect of my life and with the lives of my family. I love you. Thank you for loving me even when I was unworthy and still calling me your child.

CHAPTER 1

LEORA

Buffered by grassland, the collision is strangely quiet. Dirt sprays as the small plane scrapes away the top layer of Montana soil, coming to an abrupt halt in the middle of our field. Black smoke billows as fire leaps to life on the front end of the mangled plane. Standing for a moment in shock, I leave my sister, Anna, eating cold peach *supp* at the table and run out the open back door. The corners of my mouth stretch as I scream for Jabil, who is down the lane, working beneath the pavilion. I cannot see him, and I doubt he will be able to hear me. But over the din of the devouring flames, I do not hear anything. Not the whine of the saw blades that sometimes soothes my sister's tantrums. Not the fierce roar as Jabil and his crew power-wash bark from the once-standing dead trees that will soon become the walls of another log house.

On the back porch, I grab a piece of firewood left over from winter and leap down the steps. I cross through the gate and wade into the meadow and see that, around the plane, a diameter of grass is seared by the heat of the fire. I scream for Jabil again, and then I scream for my younger brother, Seth, who is working down at Field to Table at the end of the lane.

I run up to the plane and stare into the cockpit. The windshield is shattered. The pilot is slumped over the control panel. Blood trails down half his face like a port-wine stain. For a moment, I think he is already dead. Then I see his fingers twitch near the throttle.

"Can you hear me?" I yell. The man groans and tries to look at me without turning his head. I use the butt of the log to hit the door handle, because the handle itself is too far off the ground for me to reach. When it won't budge, I try to break the side window, thinking it'd be better for the pilot to be cut by the glass than burned to death. But the glass is too thick and the window, same as the handle, is too far off the ground for me to put any leverage behind my swing. "You have to help! I don't know how to get you out!"

The pilot says nothing. His deep-set eyes

close as he loses consciousness, his jaw slackening beneath a tangled beard. I hear a sound over the crackling flames and turn to see Jabil and his logging crew charging down the lane. Some of the men are still wearing hard hats or protective goggles, and the sawdust from their work sifts from their bodies like reddish sand. Their uniform steel-toe boots stamp the meadow as they surge toward us — about ten of them — and create a circle around the wreckage. Jabil is carrying a crowbar; his brother Malachi carries a shovel; Christian, a fire extinguisher; and the *Englischer,* Sean, a bolt cutter.

They did not need me to scream for help because, of course, they would have seen the plane crash on their own. The entire community must have seen it. I keep holding my worthless piece of firewood to my chest and watch the crew extinguish the fire and pry open the cockpit door; then Jabil tries to lift the pilot out by his arms. The man falls toward him, but his feet remain lodged under the crumpled floorboard. Jabil uses the crowbar to work the pilot's feet free. Christian tugs on the pilot's shoulders, and he slides out into the waiting loggers' arms. The plane's metal ticks and acrid smoke from the charred engine burns my throat and eyes. I back up from the plane in case it catches on fire again.

Jabil turns to me. "We take him to your house?"

"*Jah.*" I gouge the wood with my nails. "Of course."

Jabil Snyder has been foreman of the logging crew since his father's sudden passing last year, when, literally overnight, Jabil became the wealthiest man in the community. At twenty-one, he is only two years older than I, but next to his uncle, the bishop, he is also the most revered. Therefore, when Jabil calls out commands, the men respond in unity. They move across the meadow as one, the pilot's broken body borne by their work-hardened arms. Running in front of them, I open the gate and prop it with an overturned wheelbarrow. I dart up the steps into the house, and Anna looks up from her bowl.

"We need the table," I say in Pennsylvania Dutch. "You'll have to move."

My sixteen-year-old sister continues watching me with the eyes of a child, her smile serene despite the bedlam outside. "I mean it," I continue, because sometimes she understands more than she lets on. I take her bowl of *supp* over to the countertop. Anna frowns and stands to retrieve it, as I

16

expected she would. I drag the chairs away from the table and remove the tablecloth and quart jar full of weeds Anna picked and arranged like flowers.

Knowing the pilot's appearance will upset my sensitive sister, and the small crowd in our home will upset her even more, I carry the *supp* bowl, cloth napkin, and spoon into the back bedroom we share.

"Read to you?" Anna asks, glancing up at me with an impish smile. What she really wants is for me to read the book to *her*.

"Later," I promise.

I tug my sister's dress down over her legs and kiss the white center part of her twin braids. Closing our bedroom door, I hurry down the hall and see Jabil is supporting the pilot's head and shoulders and Malachi the legs as, together, they maneuver his body onto the table. His clothes are singed, and blood from his head wound stains the grooves of the beautiful pine table that — like most of the furniture in this house — was crafted by my *vadder*'s skillful hands.

"You have scissors?" Jabil asks. I withdraw a pair from the sewing drawer and pass it to him. Touching my hand, he meets my eyes. "Sure you want to be here for this?"

At my affirming nod, he turns and cuts off the pilot's *Englischer* clothes by starting at the breastbone and working his way down. His thick, calloused fingers are so confident and swift, it seems he's been performing this action all his life. My face grows warm as the T-shirt falls away, exposing the pilot's chest. Besides my younger brother, I have never seen a shirtless man, as such immodesty is prohibited in the community.

The pilot is smaller-boned than Jabil, who, along with his brothers, I once watched lever a main barn beam from horizontal to vertical without breaking a sweat. But the pilot is still muscular and lean. A thick silver band hangs from a chain around his neck, engraved with the words *Semper Fi.* A cross, ends elongated like spears, is tattooed from the pilot's left clavicle down to his pectoral — biology terms I recall from the science book I borrowed from the Liberty Public Library, back when I had time to spend studying, simply to absorb knowledge, and not to prepare for the tedious classes I did not want to teach.

I turn and see that Jabil is extracting a pistol from the holster on the belt threaded through the pilot's jeans. I pivot from the sight — and the fear it evokes — and wrap my arms around my waist. "Has somebody tried calling 911?"

Sean, the *Englischer,* says, "Tried ten times. My cell wouldn't work."

I dare a glance over my shoulder, being careful not to look at the table where the pilot lies. "Did you try the phone in the shop?"

Malachi says, "We tried that, before we came here to help. It didn't work either. Electricity's all messed up. Our equipment shut down too."

There's the clunk of soft-soled shoes dropping to the hardwood floor.

"That doesn't look good," Jabil says.

Willing myself to maintain a clinical eye, I turn yet again and walk to the end of the table. The ball of the pilot's right ankle is distended. I cradle the pilot's foot in my hand and gently rotate it to see if the ankle is broken or just strained from the men wrenching him from the plane. The pilot's eyes fly open, and he yells, the force of it whiplashing throughout his body. The cords of his neck stand out as he bites down. Concerned that — in his panicked state — he is going to hurt himself, I do not let go, but keep the ankle braced between my hands.

"It's all right," I soothe. "You're safe."

The pilot's eyes meet mine. They are the color of Flathead Lake in summer, the clar-

19

ity only slightly muddied by the haze of his pain. Then he closes them again and the foot in my hand relaxes. I hear the back door open. My thirteen-year-old brother, Seth, strides across the kitchen. He takes off his straw hat and wipes the sweat from his hairline with his forearm.

Leaning over the table, he peers down at the pilot's head wound. "Was he trying to land?" Seth turns toward Jabil. "Did you see anything?"

"No, just the crash."

I look down at the pilot's right foot, feel the knot of his stockinged heel cupped in my palm, and for some unknown reason it brings me comfort. "We need to get him to the hospital," I say. "We have no idea what injuries he has."

"I don't know how we can get him to the hospital." Seth straightens and looks at me. "The electricity at Field to Table shut down and none of the customers' cars will start. And with him being in this shape, it's too far to take him to Liberty by buggy."

The logging crew stops speaking among themselves. The silence draws attention to the dripping faucet and rhythmic snoring of *Grossmammi* Eunice, napping in the living room.

I ask Seth, "Why won't the cars start?"

"No clue. The *Englischers* are trying to figure out how to get home, but they can't get ahold of anyone because their cell phones won't work. Bishop Lowell and the deacons are asking everyone to meet at the schoolhouse so we can come up with a plan."

I glance down at the table, where the bleeding stranger lies. The pilot's in no condition to be moved, because we don't know what is broken. But neither can he just stay here in our house unsupervised. "You all go ahead," I say. "Take Anna. I'll stay here with him and *Grossmammi*." I look over and see that Jabil's eyes are trained on the gun, glinting on the table. The smooth, polished weapon appears so out of place — almost vulgar — among our rustic, handcrafted things. "And take that with you."

"You're sure?" Jabil asks me again, motioning toward the pilot. And I cannot tell if he's asking if I'm sure that I want to remain behind, or if I'm sure that I want him to take the gun.

"I'll be fine," I say. "Just leave me here."

The strident tone of my request rings in the uneasy quiet. Without a word, Jabil turns and leaves through the back door.

■ ■ ■ ■

Hearing the tapping cane behind me, I turn from the sink and see *Grossmammi* Eunice. She must be having a good day. She has taken time to put her dentures in, which she keeps in a jelly jar beside her recliner, and to tidy her hair beneath her *kapp*. Her sparse eyebrows are also jauntily cocked behind her pince-nez glasses, which serve as little purpose as mine, since she's legally blind but still too stubborn to admit it.

"Have a good nap?" I ask, drying my hands. "You look rested."

Grossmammi harrumphs and moves into the kitchen, using her cane like an extension of her arm. Her eyesight is so poor, she doesn't notice the shirtless male lying on the table beneath a sheet. She pulls out the chair and sits across from him, waiting to be served her tea. I stand frozen in the kitchen — bucket and rag in hand — not sure how to tell her about all that's happened during her nap without causing my grandmother to drop dead from fright.

"Ginger and rose-hip blend?" I ask, buying myself some time.

Grossmammi nods. "*Jah,* and some *brot,* if you have it."

Setting the bucket down, I splash hot water from the cast-iron kettle into a mug and fill the strainer with a scoop of *Gross-mammi* Eunice's favorite tea blend, which I set in the liquid to steep. I pray she keeps her doll-sized hands in her lap rather than on the table, where she would inadvertently touch warm flesh.

"Would you like your tea in the living room?" I ask. "You might be more comfortable there." She harrumphs again. "It's just that —" I rack my brain for a valid-sounding excuse — "I'm about to mop the floor, and I know you don't care for the Pine-Sol fumes."

She pushes up from the chair. "Why didn't you do it while I napped?"

"I should've; you're right." I would agree with about anything, just to get her out of here before she discovers the pilot, or — worse — he pops up from beneath the sheet like a jack-in-the-box. I hurriedly slice off a heel of bread and slide it on a tray, along with a knife and two small pots containing butter and jam. I stride across the floor with the tray, trying to herd my cantankerous, eighty-pound grandmother back into the living room.

She shifts her whole body to glower at me, though her milky eyes are missing their mark, scorching the wall over my shoulder. She takes the tray from my hands and backs into the living room. Setting it on the coffee table, she pulls the door closed between us with something akin to a slam. My whole body deflates with relief. All in all, I got off easy.

Carrying the bucket back to the table, I prepare to clean the pilot's head wound, like I'd planned before my grandmother's interruption. My hands shake as I dab the hair matted with so much blood, it appears ruddy. But once the water's tinted copper, the hair reveals its hue: pale blond, like Silver Queen corn in summer. The strands are also just as fine as corn silk. I watch the pilot's eyes skitter back and forth beneath the pale lids. His jaw is coated with beard, but his upper cheeks and nose are speckled with freckles that make him appear boyish, despite the tattoo on his chest and another on his bicep, though I cannot decipher the latter's design.

In our community — which adheres to a strict set of rules resembling a hybrid between Mennonite and the more conservative Amish — the pilot's beard would be a symbol that he's married. But he would have to remove the mustache, which Amish leaders deemed too militaristic back during the Civil War, when full facial hair became a symbol of combat and control. Therefore, Amish men were forced to shave their mustaches in order to set themselves apart as pacifists who would never raise arms against another man.

I'm continuing to inspect the pilot when the sheet covering him flutters at the movements of his bare chest. I scrape my chair back across the floor, my own breath short. I look toward the living room door and wait. I hear only the tinkling of china as my grandmother enjoys her tea. Before the loggers and Seth left, we debated moving the pilot to the couch in the living room, where he would be more comfortable. But we did not know if that was wise. We have no way to gauge whether his neck and spinal cord have suffered injuries as well, which could have been exacerbated by the force the loggers used to free him from the cockpit. Plus, I imagined that if *Grossmammi* Eunice awoke to the presence of a half-naked man asleep in our living room, she might have a heart attack and fall into her cross-stitch pattern. I never anticipated the fact that *she'd* wake up before he did.

My stomach taut with anxiety, I place two fingers against the side of the pilot's jaw to check his heart rate. The hairs of his beard are rough against my fingertips, and the throb of his blood beneath the pad of my index finger makes my own pulse speed up. I have almost counted to a minute when the pilot comes to and bolts upright, clenching my hand. Choking on a scream, I struggle to free myself, but the pilot won't let go. He draws me in closer, his strong hand still clamping mine. I can smell the tang of his sweat mixed with the residual blood from his head wound as he rasps in my face, his blue eyes blazing with terror, "Where am I?"

My throat goes dry; my head swims. Swallowing, I command with far more authority than I possess, "Release me first."

The pilot looks down at my hand, as if surprised to see he's holding it. He lets go and reclines on the table. His face whitens, and I can almost see the wave of adrenaline receding.

"Your plane crashed in our field." I point to the door, which Jabil left open, as if that would encourage propriety between me and an unknown *Englischer* pilot who sports tattoos and a gun. "The logging crew got you out and brought you here."

The pilot tries to get up again.

"Don't!" I force his shoulders down to the table. I step back, mortified by my impulsive behavior, but the pilot obeys. He keeps lying there with his hands shuttered over his eyes. "You want some water?"

"Please."

I go over to the sideboard and pour water from the metal pitcher. I carry the glass over to the pilot, but he makes no effort to sit up. "Are you going to be sick?"

He shakes his head. "I'll try drinking in a little while."

"No. Here. I'll help you." Skirting around the kitchen chair, I place one hand on the pilot's upper back and bring the glass to his lips. He drinks greedily, the water trickling down his chin, catching in the strands of his beard. My hand burns where it touches his skin.

The pilot pushes the half-emptied glass away. "Thanks. Can you help me off the table?"

His left pupil looks more dilated than the right — the blue iris a thin Saturn ring orbiting the black — and his breathing is heavy. Possible signs of a concussion? But I don't have the right or the power to restrain a grown man. I step closer to the table and wait as the pilot puts an arm around my shoulders so that he can use my body like a crutch.

He must be around five-ten or -eleven,

since he's only a few inches taller than I am. But I can feel his sinewy power through his arm alone. The pilot winces at the pressure on his hurt ankle and curls the foot up again, balancing on me and on the table in front of him. He seems to think nothing of our proximity; I can think of nothing else.

"Can you tell me where I am?" he asks.

"An Old Order Mennonite community called Mt. Hebron."

"But what state?"

"Northern Montana, near Glacier Falls. Not far from the Canadian border."

"That close."

"You were going to Canada?"

He doesn't say yes or no or offer any more explanation, so I gesture toward the open door and the pilot nods. We hobble together for a few labored steps. Then he leans against the jamb to catch his breath, eyes glimmering. "What's your name?"

"Leora Ebersole." I pause. "And yours?"

He looks at me with those odd, concussed eyes. "Moses. Moses Hughes."

"Moses," I repeat. "Don't know many *Englischers* with that name."

The pilot stumbles and his injured foot touches down, a knee-jerk reaction for stability. He curses, and my eyes grow wide. "I've never known *anyone* with your name," he says. Removing his arm from around my shoulders, he touches the railing and hops over to the edge of the porch. He stares out over the meadow — at his plane that looks like the smoking carcass of an enormous yellow bird — and sighs.

"Where are you from?" I ask.

"What's that?"

"Where are you from?"

"Kentucky," he says, looking ahead, "but I've moved around so much these past few years, I can barely remember where all I've been."

I gesture to his plane. "Looks like you're going to be here awhile. The community's having a meeting at the schoolhouse because the electricity shut down at Field to Table, the community's bulk food store. My brother also said that the *Englischers'* cars won't start. Nobody can go home or even call out on their cell phones. It's like someone —" I snap my fingers — "flipped a switch."

The pilot turns from the porch post and looks at me. I had tried to keep my manner light, but his expression is now so grave that a wave of panic courses throughout my body, raising the fine hair on my arms. "The deacons and bishop are trying to figure out what to do because the *Englischers* want to go home but have no way to get there."

Moses faces the woods again, holding the porch railing. "When did this happen?"

"About two hours ago, I guess. Seth, my brother, wanted to get up here to help right after your accident, but there was such chaos at the store, he couldn't get away."

"And when did my plane crash?"

"Around the same time." I stare at Moses's bare back. Freckles, the color of those on his face, dot his shoulders like paint chips. "Why? Do you think they're connected somehow?"

The pilot sinks one fist into the pocket of his jeans and turns to face me while being careful not to put more weight on his injured foot. My eyes are drawn like lodestones to the cross tattoo on his chest. My face grows hot. I look away from him, but I feel his gaze on me until I am forced to look back. "There's no way to know for sure just yet," he says. "but I think it could've been an EMP."

"What does that mean?"

"An electromagnetic pulse. A special warhead, probably set off hundreds of miles above the earth, gives off this huge electromagnetic pulse that wipes out technology because of how the pulse reacts with the earth's magnetic field. It's harmless to humans and animals, but it can take out the power grid and everything that relies on a computer, throwing civilization back a couple hundred years. I've heard it can be over a few states, or —" he glances out at the land — "it could knock out half of our hemisphere."

"How . . . how do you know about this?"

He shrugs. "I probably read more than I should."

I glance away from him and stare at the field, where his ruined plane is backdropped by the chiseled mountain peaks, piercing through the sea of softwoods as if from a volcanic eruption. "You think this — this bomb is why you crashed?"

"We can't really call it a bomb, because there's no obvious detonation. But, yeah — that's a pretty likely explanation, if everything else is off the grid too."

"How do we fix it?" I ask. "How do we get it all back?"

He turns and I glimpse his eyes again — a brilliant hue that seems to mirror the entire spectrum of the wide Montana sky. "That's the thing. If I'm right, then . . . we don't."

■ ■ ■ ■

CHAPTER 2

■ ■ ■ ■

MOSES

We crest the bend and the log schoolhouse comes into view. Buggies identical to Leora's are tied to posts in the front yard, but the horses are all different shades of brown, white, and black, which seems about the only way to tell the buggies apart. An unpainted wooden swing set and teeter-totter are the only recreational items on the playground. There is no flagpole with stars and stripes snapping in the wind. From what I've read (or absorbed through reality TV), this is an intentional omission. Mennonites, Amish, and Quakers aren't very patriotic, since they don't believe in war. Kind of funny that I landed here, considering I'm a third-generation son of war.

I look over at Leora. "Will you have to introduce me?"

"Think you introduced yourself just fine when your plane crashed in our field."

"I guess I made quite the entrance."

"You could say that." She meets my eyes but doesn't return my smile.

"How old are you?"

She grips the reins. "Nineteen."

"Most Mennonite girls married by your age?"

"No. Least not the smart ones."

Her voice is flat and hard. If I was hoping to see her stammer and blush again, like she did when I cussed, that won't happen. I admit I'm flirting, but I'm not trying to come on to her. I haven't had time for such things in a year. Or even the desire to pursue. All that I left behind before Aaron and I deployed.

Leora suddenly leans forward, her profile blocking the sun like an eclipse. Her eyes are squinted, as if her glasses aren't thick enough or maybe there's just too much light to take it all in. I don't want her to see my face until I've distanced myself from that day in the desert, so I take careful breaths and look out the buggy's window at the long lane fenced in with this slew of cookie-cutter log cabins, except that some are two-story and others — like Leora's — only one.

There are no attached garages, of course, because nobody has cars around here. But each cabin has a barn and chicken coop

36

made from wood treated to match the houses. An immaculate garden also seems part of the communal package — acorn and butternut squash vines spreading across the ground, the fruit's thick rinds ripening to orange; cornstalks decorated with thick, tasseled ears — along with an adobe-style greenhouse that must be used to preserve some of the more sensitive vegetables from the impending frost that my Idahoan grandfather complains can assault this region well before fall begins.

Just before the schoolhouse, on the other side of the lane, a pavilion with a cement base looks big enough to hold a small concert or a roller-skating party. Inside the pavilion, stacked like a giant's Lincoln Logs set, are timbers so massive, a forklift would have to be used to move them. A tangle of power tools — their neon extension cords snaking back to a large generator — are laid out, along with some hard hats and goggles. Beside this, there's what looks like a warehouse. I sit up higher on the bench seat, trying to get a better view of this bulk food store Leora mentioned earlier, which could be so crucial for the community's survival. But I can only catch a glimpse of a tin roof and an assortment of cars and trucks that look out of place, compared to all this treated wood and black canvas.

Leora maneuvers the horse and buggy up to the schoolhouse and around the other contraptions like she's been doing it her entire life. She gets out of the buggy, loops the reins around the hitching post, and knots them with a downward jerk. Coming back, Leora opens the door on my side of the buggy before I've had time to remember about my leg. She stands there, not offering a hand or even a glance, but just waiting for me to clatter down and lean on her — this person who looks like she'd get bowled over in a stiff breeze. My pride would love just to stride right past, leaving her in my dust. The truth is, though, without her help, I'd fall flat on my face within a few feet. So I put my arm around her shoulders.

Leora looks at my arm without enthusiasm and begins leading me toward the schoolhouse's open doors. I try to keep from putting my full weight on her, but the strained tendons in my ankle make it impossible to put any pressure on that foot. The ground is also rutted with a multitude of hoof- and bootprints, making it difficult to maintain balance with my good leg.

She takes a breather before we reach the schoolhouse porch and inspects me like she's going to spit-shine my face. She seems to think my hair and beard are a lost cause, 'cause she just sighs and pulls down the sleeve of the shirt that she let me borrow from someone who I guess is her younger brother or else a very small man. "Keep that tattoo covered," she instructs in this prissy voice, "or they'll not listen to a word you say."

Feeling a fool, I nod and hop over to the edge of the porch with my arms flailing in double time to make up for one bad foot. I glance up. On the front of the schoolhouse, there are two doors — trimmed in green, almost side by side — and a handrail that divides the middle. Leora tucks some stray pieces of hair beneath this white netted thing on her head that reminds me of a miniature Spanish mantilla. She starts climbing the four steps toward the left door, and I go around the dividing rail and begin walking up behind her.

She turns and says, "This is the women's side," like I've committed some cardinal sin.

I think, *For crying out loud, woman, I've got a busted ankle!* But I mind her by hauling myself over to the other side and clomping up the steps. This tall, dark-haired guy about my age is speaking at the front of the room. But he stops when he sees Leora and me coming in through the segregated doors.

He looks at her again, and then at me . . . then back at her. His narrowed eyes keep ping-ponging between the two of us in a way that would be comical if he didn't look so disturbed. I nod at him in a friendly way. He nods back but doesn't seem impressed.

The guy keeps speaking in a low monotone, and my shell-shocked ears have a hard time hearing this far in the back. I hop down the center aisle and note that the men are seated on the right side and the women on the left. Most of the women are wearing plain dresses like Leora's, and their head coverings are made from the same white netted material with untied ribbons trailing down onto their shoulders. The men are wearing collared shirts like the one I'm borrowing. But they are all made in different pastel colors that would look effeminate except for the fact that the men wearing them have these enormous forearms and beards that make mine look like pubescent fuzz. Their massive backs are x-ed with suspenders, and their bowl-cut hair is imprinted with ironed rings from the hats they must've been wearing in the field.

I take a seat at the end of the second row and glance down at the backless pew that is so crude and unsanded, it must be an incentive not to move during the service or risk getting splinters. I spot a few men who are dressed normal like me — or, I guess, like I was — but here they don't look "normal" at all, just as out of place as I feel. I guess they are the *Englischers* who were stranded at Field to Table when the electricity shut off and their vehicles wouldn't start. One woman on the opposite side has short hair and big hoop earrings. I watch her not even attempt to pay attention to the speaker and instead punch away at her smartphone — her fake nails flashing like sabers — but of course, it's not working. I'm glad I came, although my plane crash really left me with no choice. Somebody's got to break the news that technology as we know it might be extinct. For that matter, *life* as we know it might be extinct.

Dark-Haired Guy clears his throat. I raise my head and see he's looking at me. "I assume you're the man who crashed in the Ebersoles' field?"

I smile and wave at the hodgepodge group. "Yeah . . . hey . . . my name's Moses." They don't smile back, but stare at me goggle-eyed, the person who survived the plane crash. They should know that even if I wanted to, I couldn't die. That was obvious a year ago and confirmed again today. The blessing of existence has been transformed into a curse, a reminder of all those who died in my stead because I couldn't do what was required of me.

Dark-Haired Guy continues speaking, arms crossed. "And do you think that your plane crash might have something to do with our power failure?"

Is he trying to imply that I might be the cause of this mess? How could I have brought something like this to a little backwoods community? I didn't even know it was on the map. I doubt many know it's on the map, which makes it a perfect place for me to hide until I can escape. I push off the bench and try rising to my feet. Then I remember about my ankle. I wince, being forced to put pressure on it because I don't have anything to prop myself up.

"This is far beyond me," I say, and then point to the speaker. "And this is far beyond *you.*" I turn and look at the crowd. They are fixated on me, but then I guess my wild hair does make me look like a cross between a hobo and an Old Testament prophet. If I hadn't crashed in Leora's yard, they'd probably think I fell from the sky. "This is, honestly, beyond all of us."

Dark-Haired Guy doesn't say anything for a second. Instead, he's looking at the crowd and I crane my kinked neck, trying to follow the direction of his gaze. A white-haired guy with this long, pointed beard like a wizard's is sitting in the same row as me. He's got these chapped red hands — as square and solid as bricks — that he rests on his black pant legs. I notice that the toes of his boots barely brush the floor.

White Beard nods once, and Dark-Haired Guy says, "Moses, would you like to come up here to address the congregation?" But there's not a lick of invitation in his voice.

I shake my head and smile, repelling whatever hostility's bouncing off this guy. "I'm not getting around too great at the moment. All right if I talk from here?"

"Of course." He walks over to the first bench and takes a seat.

I hobble around to face the group, since more are behind me than in front. "I believe that what we're experiencing right now may be the result of an electromagnetic pulse. . . ." I go on to explain everything, like I explained it to Leora less than an hour ago. The four *Englischers* — three men, one woman — appear concerned; the Mennonite men and women in the congregation appear skeptical. But Dark-Haired Guy's and White Beard's endorsements at least keep them from looking at me like I'm crazy. Or at least not *as* crazy as I am.

Then (isn't there *always* a "then"?) this gigantic lumberjack, with a brow line like a hammerhead shark, asks how I know about the EMP. My eagerness to provide validity weakens my resolve not to tell anyone about my past, and I find myself giving the congregation a grain of sand on this shifting coastline called truth. "I come from a distinguished military family. I was drilled and educated in such scenarios from birth. Trust me, I know what I'm talking about."

White Beard turns on the bench to inspect me. Since he's the one who granted me and Dark-Haired Guy permission to speak, I assume he is the leader of the community or something close to it. I am being watched by countless eyes, but his are the ones I feel boring into my skull like drill bits. "So you think this EMP may affect our daily lives for a while?" His voice is an aging growl that would be intimidating if I hadn't grown up with someone like my father.

"Yeah," I say. "Possibly more than you or I can wrap our minds around right now."

Dark-Haired Guy pipes up, like he doesn't want me to forget he's second in command. "Can you tell us, then, what you see ahead for our community?"

I take a quick inventory of the room, noting the few children who are in attendance.

The younger ones are sitting in their mothers' laps, gumming stretchy necklaces made from bright blue or green beads twined around their dimpled, drool-covered fists. The older children are sitting as quietly as the adults: boys on the right and girls on the left, just like their parents. I bet if they move a muscle, they'll get pinched. That's what my mom used to do if Aaron and I acted up during Mass.

When he sees me looking at the children, White Beard says, "Do not worry about talking in front of the *kinner*. The little ones do not learn English until they go to school. They won't be able to understand much."

I nod, wary. "Okay, I'll tell you what I see happening if there's really been a widespread EMP attack. It sure isn't good or pretty, and I don't wish to put fear on everyone, but . . ." I clear my throat and have to fight against the urge to sit down and rest my ankle, which is throbbing with every pump of my heart. "What I see happening is this: the cities will get hit hardest first. Food will run out in the grocery stores in a day or two, and there'll be looting and crime almost instantly. Most Americans are so reliant on fast food or stopping at the supermarket after work, they don't have enough stored in their pantries to last even a week, to say nothing about months.

"People in the city don't have room for gardens like you all do — and most wouldn't even know how to keep a garden if they did. So when things go haywire, they're going to want out of the city, and there's going to be this immense, chaotic exodus. I imagine they'll try packing their belongings on bikes or even in grocery carts, trying to move as much as possible as quickly as they can. If this is really what I think it is, it's going to be a very hard and dangerous time, starting whenever people realize the power's not coming back on and the grocery stores aren't going to be restocked.

"There will be a whole drove of them, and they'll probably start by walking down the interstates. The roads will be pretty much deserted, except for the cars that were stranded after the EMP. Eventually gangs and criminals will start patrolling these interstates and stealing from the people, the refugees, trying to escape. Conditions will get worse and worse and continue to deteriorate. It will look like what you've seen about civil war in third-world countries."

I pause and stare out at the community, picturing the honest faces hollowed by relentless hunger, coal-dust shadows ringing their weary eyes; the babies' smiles wiped from their rosebud mouths and replaced with cracked lips and wailing. Time and time again, I've witnessed a society's infrastructure crumble on foreign soil, even as we tried to rebuild it our way without really knowing what we were doing or, sometimes, why we were there. But I never believed it could — or *would* — happen here, the land of the free and the home of the brave. And it's obvious our government also believed we were invincible, or they would've taken the measures to ensure we were protected against an EMP attack.

For the first time, I think that maybe it's a good thing this community's remained so isolated. Maybe, in this draining hourglass of disruption, this silted earth can provide the last measure of peace. For they are some of the only ones left in this country who know how to survive when our corner of the world's been reverted back to the Stone Age.

I exhale. My eyes twitch with nerves. "Clean water will become more valuable than gold," I continue. "Starving refugees will begin looting homes along the interstates, trying to find food for their families. They'll become a frantic swarm of locusts, devouring everything in their path. Violence will increase. And then, because everyone's too weak to bury the dead, disease will increase. If studies are correct, in six months' time we could lose 60 to 90 percent of the population affected by the EMP."

For a second, nobody moves or breathes. And then one of the chubby toddlers — with this mound of blond curls — erupts into a stream of meaningless chatter, drawing us back to the present with a heartrending contradiction of cheer as we consider such sobering words.

"So . . . what do we do to protect ourselves from 'the locusts'?" The blonde-haired woman asking me the question actually puts air quotes around *the locusts.* But at least she's given up on resuscitating her phone.

"I'd say we have a few days, a week tops, before people start realizing the power's not kicking back on and their food's running out. A week, maybe two, until the *real* panic sets in. That's when they'll begin their exodus and branching off the exits to find food and shelter with country people like you all — which is really to say, when they'll start rampaging.

"In the meantime, I think we should set up a perimeter. Think of it like the boundary wall around a compound that would secure the location and keep track of who's coming in and out — scouts, hunters, et cetera. We should place armed guards at strategic locations around this perimeter. It's going to be difficult to protect your bulk food store, since it's right along the main thoroughfare that will eventually be traveled by the refugees. We can either ration the food throughout the community, so it's not all sitting in one place, or make sure it's guarded at all times. Either way, it's crucial that the assets at Farm to Table — or whatever it's called — are protected. This food could be what keeps you and your families alive.

"I know this all sounds hard to believe, and maybe even downright crazy. But I said that I'd give you my opinion of what to expect, if we *have* been hit with an EMP. And so, there you have it . . . my honest opinion."

I take my seat. White Beard strides to the front of the schoolhouse on short, bandy legs that appear undersized for the heft of his torso. Dark-Haired Guy follows on his heels, like a dog that has outgrown his master. Both men turn to look at the congregation. Then they put their thumbs in their suspenders, turn, and stare at me, their identical gestures emphasizing their matching expressions of fear, skepticism, and outrage.

"We will *not* fight these — these locusts, as you call them," White Beard declares, holding his hands up. And I realize, absently, that he's missing all but his pinkie and his thumb on his right hand. "Fighting back is not our way and is certainly not *Gott*'s way. Our people have been practicing nonresistance since the 1600s when we were persecuted for our Anabaptist beliefs. If these strangers come — as you say they will — and they need food, we will feed them; if they need clothes, we will clothe them; if they need a place to stay, we will house them, just as the *Ausbund* declares:

"To be like Christ we love one another, through everything, here on this earth. We love one another, not just with words but in deeds. . . . If we have of this world's goods (no matter how much or how little) and see that our brother has a need, but do not share with him what we have freely received — how can we say that we would be ready to give our lives for him if necessary?"

White Beard turns after reciting this from memory and addresses his congregation. "Perhaps our *Gott* has allowed for this to happen, so we can share with our brothers and sisters the peace that passes all under-standing . . . even in this time of unrest."

The lumberjack, the one who asked how I knew about the EMP, rises to his feet. "And what about us? I can't just sit back and twiddle my thumbs while bands of looters are trying to steal. I don't got a family, but I still think it ain't right for a man not to fight to protect his own."

White Beard looks at the *Englischer.* "You and others like you are more than welcome to live within the community until you can make your way home. But if you are living here —" and I can see that, though he is old, this man's not someone you want to mess with — "you must abide by our rules. If that is a problem, anyone is free to leave at any time."

Lumberjack snorts. "I read about this EMP quite a bit myself, and I thought the same thing when my truck wouldn't start, my cell wouldn't work, and I went inside to use you all's phone and everything was down." He points at me. "And then you have the fact this here guy's plane fell clean outta the sky." Putting skillet-size paws on his waist, he says, "I've been expecting a crash like this for years. Now that it's hap-pened, I'm telling you, all your peace and love ideas sound real fine. But when those locusts come in here, steal your food, and violate your women and children, I hope you remember we talked about a different way."

So Lumberjack's a prepper — one who's been preparing for the apocalypse since long before Y2K — which probably explains why he was at Field to Table, buying bulk food, in the first place. Already I can tell his survival knowledge might be handy to have around. As for what he said about standing up and fighting, I agree with him there. These people have no clue what they're about to face.

Not able to take the pain any longer, I put my throbbing foot on a six-inch space on the bench in front of me. I'm sure this is as taboo a move as playing AC/DC in the sanctuary, but these Mennonites are going to quickly learn that in the wake of an EMP, they're going to have to compromise some of their religious ideologies. And this is when it strikes me.

Taking my foot down off the bench, since I don't want to draw any more negative attention from White Beard, I call out, "What about a compromise?" Everyone from the riled lumberjack to Leora Ebersole looks at me. White Beard frowns, so I talk fast. "What if, over the next few days, we work together on securing the perimeter and prepping the community? We can kind of split up into two teams. The men of the community can take care of the community itself — like food, water, sanitation. The *Englischers,* like —" I point to the lumberjack, and he shrugs, looking down at the floor, apparently self-conscious getting singled out in a crowd that, a few minutes ago, he'd been addressing like he was at a town hall meeting.

"Some call me Charlie," he says.

I smile. "All right. Thanks for introducing yourself, Charlie." I turn back to the group. "The *Englischers* like Charlie here can help protect the perimeter of the community from infiltration. If somebody can spare me a good set of crutches, I should be able to help out too."

Dark-Haired Guy says, "What do you mean, 'protect the perimeter'? Would you use guns?"

"We'd have to *carry* guns, but that doesn't mean we'd have to *use* them." Even *I* know how ridiculous this sounds. "Think of it like border patrol. You all could be in charge of taking care of basic needs and helping the people, and we would more or less be in charge of keeping the property secure and protecting all the assets. You won't be able to help anyone if you don't have anything left to help them with." Still, Leora and the rest of the community look at me like an outsider calling the shots — which is exactly what I am.

I glance over the group, squinting at the other *Englischer* guy with sunken gums and a dirty fleece hat. And then we've got Miss Technology, who looks like the hardest thing she's ever done is file her nails. I inwardly sigh; we don't exactly have a militia. "Members of the community would not have to participate in the border patrol," I conclude. "But it's also unfair to ask us, who don't believe the way you all do, to give up our lives just because you don't agree with taking up arms."

A woman's sob cuts through the room. We all turn and look. Miss Technology is the one crying, her chin on her chest. I can see the perfect alternating streaks in her dyed-blonde hair, and the diamond rings that capture the light filtering through the schoolhouse windows, casting prisms on the plaster above. "I just want —" she sobs again — "to see my family."

"And where are they?" Leora asks beside her, in a remarkably kind tone.

The woman uses a Kleenex to dab the skin beneath each eye. "Estes Park. Colorado. I was on my way home. I saw the sign for the community. I just wanted . . . produce."

I don't say anything, but I'm sure my silence — *everyone's* silence — says enough. Without transportation, this woman's detour has turned into a dead end. I don't want to tell her now, yet there's a very high chance that she might never see her family again. Or that she might die in the process of trying to make it back to her family, like so many other refugees whom I have unintentionally designated as the locusts.

I rise to my feet, shifting my weight to my left foot. I look at everyone again and ask, "So — is an alliance possible?" It feels callous to keep forging ahead while this woman is mourning the loss of her family. But I also know we have no time to lose.

The community says nothing; they just look at me, their faces as blank and white as the ceiling. The two *Englischer* men are nodding. Miss Technology is crying too hard to respond.

"We will discuss this with the community," White Beard says. "I do not think a decision like this needs to be made in haste."

"Forgive me," I reply, "but isn't it necessary to decide in haste when time is of the essence?"

"Bishop Lowell, why don't we ask the *Englischers* to leave while we take a vote?"

Bishop Lowell, who is now no longer just "White Beard," nods and repeats the request as if we haven't heard Dark-Haired Guy say it. Lumberjack Charlie huffs, and the older *Englischer* guy in the fleece hat gets up from the bench and walks down the center aisle. But I remain where I am.

"The Mennonite women don't have to be present for this either," Bishop Lowell adds, making sure he's heard over the drone of conversation. "The fathers and husbands can represent their families."

"And what about those of us who are fatherless?"

I turn to look, along with the entire Mennonite population clustered together in that tight-fitting room, beginning to stink of body odor and trapped air. Leora Ebersole is the one who, upon feeling the pull of our gazes, rises from the sea of people like the figurehead on the front of a ship. With her quiet voice and habit of avoiding people's eyes, she strikes me as someone who would try to blend in with the crowd. And yet, here she stands.

Leora's skin is candle-wax pale except for two burning circles pressed high on her cheeks. Jet eyes gleam behind the wire-rimmed lenses of her glasses. Her body vibrates with anger, like a divining rod trying to establish its energy's source. But I have no idea at whom this anger is directed.

Dark-Haired Guy steps forward. Our gazes all shift from Leora to him. He looks at Bishop Lowell and lowers his shoulders, meek, like he's approaching a tsar. "I think what she means is that she's concerned for her *familye.*" Clearing his throat, Dark-Haired Guy says, "I will cast a vote for you, Leora."

I look at her. The burning circles on her cheeks have spread down to her neck. She reaches up and twists a crimson pinch of skin. "How — how can you cast a vote for me?" she asks, her voice trembling. "You are not my *vadder,* and you are certainly not my husband."

Before the words have finished resonating, Leora whirls and flees the schoolhouse. I glance at Dark-Haired Guy's face, as colorless as Leora's own, and feel a twinge of sympathy. But it's still not enough to keep me from getting up from the bench and hobbling down the aisle behind her. I don't bother going out through the segregated door, but through the same one Leora just exited. It's time to change some of these old-fashioned rules.

■ ■ ■ ■

CHAPTER 3

■ ■ ■ ■

MOSES

The *Englischer* guy in the fleece hat turns to watch my progress — one pasty gray eye shooting off to the left, one fixed right on me. He smiles, showing a gap where his front teeth should be, but doesn't offer me any support. He just lights a cigarette and leans against the side of the schoolhouse with his right boot propped up on the log siding behind him — the outline of his face chiseled rough like an arrowhead, his smoke twisting in the late-summer breeze.

Meanwhile, Leora walks over to the cedar fence enclosing the yard and paces, her hands set into fists. That knowing grin from the guy in the hat makes me understand how desperate I look, falling all over myself, trying to reach somebody who doesn't want me around. And I don't blame her; she doesn't know me from Adam. So I shamble over to the playground and sit on the wooden swing, which is even rougher than that bench inside the school.

Wrapping my hands around the ropes, I prop my hurt ankle on the knee of my good leg and scope out my surroundings. The Mennonite women are coming out the correct side of the segregated doors. They have their hands so full, trying to wrangle their kids down the steps, that they don't seem too perturbed by the exclusion from the meeting. Someone inside the schoolhouse draws the doors closed. At the sound, Leora turns from the fence. She's taken her glasses off, and when she sees me studying her, she pauses. Her face looks vulnerable, and softer, without the frames.

Perhaps aware of this exposure, she turns from me and holds the wire frames up to the sky to inspect each lens carefully before slipping the glasses on and pushing them with one finger onto the sloped bridge of her nose. Then she stands there, her back to me, before moving across the grounds, her granny shoes imprinting the dirt. I don't let myself believe that Leora's really coming over until she gives me the smallest of smiles and takes the swing next to mine.

I smile back at her, and she closes her mouth over faintly lapped teeth and looks away. Together, we watch the mothers huddle beneath the mature line of pines shading the east side of the schoolhouse. They feed their babies pieces of sandwiches and cookies they must've wrapped in cellophane and packed in the black purses that look as cumbersome and outdated as their shoes. When they return our stare, they stop clucking at their kids long enough to give Leora a disapproving look.

But Leora ignores them. Lifting her chin, she pulls back on the ropes of the swing and pushes off the ground. She pumps her legs in and out until the swing rises and her cotton dress fills with wind, revealing black tights with a run trailing along the back of her left calf.

I observe her — suspended in midair, nearly weightless. I am unable to look away, although I sense that in their culture, as in most cultures, it is considered rude to stare.

Leora's swing slows, and she stops it entirely by placing her feet on the ground at the same time, causing the pieces of loose hair to fly toward her face. She wraps her arms around the ropes and clasps her hands together and rests them between her knees, the weight holding down the fabric of her dress. "Tell me. How certain are you that the EMP is really what happened?"

I think about telling her I'm a hundred

percent certain. But if there's one thing I've learned over the years, it's that it is almost impossible to be fully certain about anything. Even faith, even love. "About 75 percent," I admit, not meeting her eyes. For some reason, I feel more deceitful telling the truth than I would a lie.

Leora leans back from me, as if shocked by the lower percentage, when earlier I pretty much guaranteed that if we don't start moving now, lives will be lost.

"Look at it from my viewpoint," I say. "If I'm right, it's a huge benefit that everyone will be prepared when things really get tough. If I'm wrong — and I doubt that I am, but if I'm wrong — what's the problem with running people through a drill of worst-case scenarios?"

"The problem *is*, Moses," Leora snaps, "that they're in there right now, voting on using armed guards to protect us, when we have never taken up arms in our lives."

"But I already told you, the *Englischers* would be doing the protecting part. You all would just be like . . . the community's tenants."

She shakes her head in disgust. "We will not become mere 'community tenants' of the land and food that we own."

"We are not asking for even *half* an acre

of your land. We are simply hoping to establish an alliance that will benefit all of us. We can provide protection, and you all — in exchange — can provide food and shelter."

"We do not *need* your protection. Our *Gott* is plenty capable of taking care of us."

Only then do I comprehend that Leora Ebersole has not come over here to separate herself from the rest of the Mennonite women and to show solidarity with me. Because right now I know that she does not agree with anything I've said, and I can feel there is an even larger chasm between the two of us.

"Oh, really?" I turn in the seat of the swing so that I can lean closer to her without putting pressure on my ankle. "You think you don't need protection because God will take care of you, but I bet you've got health and home insurance in case of an emergency, right?"

Leora's lips curve in triumph. "Actually, we don't use insurance, but take care of our medical expenses within the community. We believe this is the way it should be, so don't dismiss my culture just because you do not understand it."

"And don't dismiss mine. I've seen what rises to the surface when the infrastructure of society falls apart. Have *you*?"

She continues looking at me — *absorbing* me — her eyes so intense on my face that it's hard not to look away. "No," she whispers. "I haven't."

"Lowlife scum is what rises to the surface, Leora, the very worst of humanity . . . the likes of which you've never seen. Especially not back here, in this community. It is an evil that is very hard to even imagine." The two of us turn to peer across the playground — over to the children who are frolicking so happily, oblivious to the dangers that lurk on the horizon — and then we look at the snowcapped mountains behind them, behind us, that are no longer just a postcard of panoramic beauty, but a symbol of all that remains hidden, unseen.

"These people shouldn't even be called 'people,'" I continue. "They're like locusts that feed on other people's misfortunes. These locusts don't have any qualms about what they've got to do to stay alive. They are ruthless, without a tidy conscience like yours to keep their actions in check. Do you think any of the families leaving the city are going to stand a chance against these low-lifes?"

"No," she whispers again.

"You're right. They won't. Maybe in the

beginning, if they're in groups, they'll be okay. It's kind of like herd immunity. But they will run out of food and water and they can only go so far without rest. Besides, most won't even have a clue as to where they're going. They'll just be trying to get out of the city and find help. The locusts will form gangs and will prey on the desperate folks fleeing. They will take from them the little that they *do* have and leave them for dead. There will be no safe place."

I stop speaking and look at Leora. She has taken off her glasses to peer blindly at the grounds. Some of the women have moved away from the pine trees and are now letting their barefoot babies toddle along in the grass. I see that young blond boy again, who I spotted in the congregation, chewing on a piece of clover. The mother chides him in their language and pulls the weed gently from his fist and mouth. He plops down on the grass — worn bare by the amount of foot traffic — and smacks his hands against the earth, stirring up puffs of dust.

That's the thing with kids. It doesn't matter what's going on with the rest of the world; they are so oblivious that it's hard not to laugh at their antics, even when it feels like everything around you is falling apart. Behind the kids, the guy in the fleece hat keeps chain-smoking cigarettes in a long stream of shaky fingers and nicotine. The mothers draw their kids away from him, as if his addiction can be ingested along with secondhand smoke. The lumberjack, who introduced himself as Charlie, stands beside the fleece-hat wearer. His large arms are crossed and bottom lip jutted out with a wad of snuff. In a way, they already look like displaced people, like refugees from a war nobody can really see or name, only hypothesize at its origins as I have done.

Leora remains silent while I observe the grounds, but I can feel her staring. The children's laughter flits across the wind, making me smile despite it all.

"But don't you think that *Gott* can protect us?" she asks. "I saw the cross tattoo on your chest. . . . Do you believe in *Gott*? Are you a man of faith?"

I turn to her and see her eyes are wet; she is begging me for the kind of comfort I can't provide. Paralyzed, I block her out — I block *everything* out: light, touch, and sound — viewing instead where I was a year ago, as if I am back there right now. A dark, guilt-ridden place that I keep trying to escape from through every medium in my power, but always find myself returning to.

"I'm not a man of faith," I rasp. "I don't

know what kind of man I am."

From my peripheral vision, I look at Leora and see that she's put her glasses back on, like a veil. I am wearing my own kind of veil. But I guess, in a way, we all are. One of the benefits of something as catastrophic as an EMP is that these veils are stripped away and true countenances are revealed. Soon we will know who we can count on and who will only wait until our guard is down to stab us in the back. The most surprising aspect of all is that, more often than not, these divisions of character are not as black-and-white as you might expect.

"I understand that you've seen more than I have," Leora says. "And I'm sorry. I understand, too, that you think I'm just a sheltered Mennonite girl who looks at life through rose-colored glasses. Well, I'm not. My *vadder* walked out on us two years ago. Or he disappeared two years ago. The result is still the same. We were penniless. Broke. My *mamm* and younger brother had to go work at Field to Table, and my *mamm* died not long after that. So without meaning to, I became like . . . the patriarch of the family. This is why I don't care to be excluded from the community's vote. Protecting my siblings is the highest calling I have. My greatest responsibility. This is why your words hit me so hard. I do not want to see my brother and sister suffer, but I also know —" Leora nods toward the schoolhouse — "that what Bishop Lowell said is true. We can't take up arms to defend our lives at the risk of extinguishing a soul."

She pauses, looks at me. "Ever heard of *Martyrs Mirror*?" I shake my head. "It's this compilation of stories about Anabaptist martyrs. Regardless of what they faced — and death wasn't always the worst — they never took up arms to defend themselves. *Martyrs Mirror* was first published in 1660, and it's still our most revered book, next to the Bible."

"I can tell you're upset with me," I say. "Only a few short hours ago, you helped saved my life, and here I am . . . trying to change your community's ancient beliefs."

"Yes, I'm upset. But not only at *you*. I'm upset by the fact that one of the most cataclysmic events in our community's history is taking place right now, and I cannot take part because I'm a woman who can only have a voice through her father and husband when I have neither to my name."

I smile, trying to add some levity to the conversation. "That dark-haired guy seemed pretty eager to give you his name."

"Jabil?" Leora sighs. "He might want to

give me his name, but I'm not sure I want to accept it."

"I'd think about it if I were you. You'd be safer having a man like him beneath your roof when things get hard."

Leora rises from the swing, her once-waxen skin flared with color. "You sound like everyone else. And I hope you know I'd rather *die* knowing there is a possibility of love than live in safety without it."

Then, without another word, she walks away from me and stands beneath the pines with her people, her face as unyielding as if she's crossed a line in the sand.

LEORA

One of the schoolhouse doors opens. I turn and see Jabil standing there, his arms positioned on either side of the jamb. He scans the yard — searching for someone — and then his eyes alight on me. He nods, but I can tell he's uneasy, powerless to understand what happened between us in the schoolhouse. I am unable to understand it myself.

Jabil lowers his gaze and withdraws from his pocket the first decree ever drawn up by the community without the Lancaster County bishops' consent. "May I have your attention," he calls. The entire group —

both *Englischers* and Mennonites — angles toward him. "The Mt. Hebron Old Order Mennonite Community has agreed to an alliance with the *Englischers* already gathered in our midst by means over which they have no control. The *Englischers* will hereby provide protection for our families, bulk food store, gardens, livestock, homes, and barns. We will set up blockades on the lane and around the perimeter of the community that will be guarded at all times. But we agree that we will offer water, soup, and medical care to the refugees who are walking past the barrier.

"However, to protect our community from disease, we will not allow them to come past the Beilers' *dawdi haus,* which — from this day until a new day dawns — will be transformed into a hospital to the best of our available knowledge and supplies. Though firearms may be used for intimidation and control of outsiders who wish us or our assets harm, *Englischers* will agree not to fire the weapons unless fired upon first." Jabil stops and looks up, scanning the assembly. "If anyone shoots an unarmed person, he will be expelled from the community without delay."

The Mennonites peer across at the *Englischers* who are lined against the side of the schoolhouse like they're expecting a firing squad to materialize in a place where no one takes up arms. Counting Sean, the *Englischer* who's been working with Jabil's crew, and the pilot, Moses, there are five altogether: four men and the sole woman from Colorado. There are over a hundred of us Mennonites, and almost half are children. I struggle to comprehend how such a small group can provide protection for us at these different locations. It's impossible; I can see that already. The only way any of this is going to work is if some of the Mennonites can act as watchmen, who — if they see anything amiss — can notify the *Englischers* to defend the land.

But if a Mennonite is aiding in the callous taking of another man's life, even if he does not pull the trigger himself, does that mean he has still adhered to his nonresistant ideals? I think not. So that only leaves us with the option of taking in more *Englischers* — more refugees who are going to need housing and food, despite our not knowing how we are going to feed ourselves once our storehouse of canned goods and dried goods runs out. And how are we supposed to trust these outsiders around our families and our homes? We have no idea of their life history, and yet we are placing in their hands the means — albeit cheap hunting rifles — to take us over instead of offering us protection. Are we going to have to protect ourselves from the ones in the alliance who are supposed to protect *us*?

I must not be the only one mulling over these questions. Neither side rejoices nor protests, but it's obvious that both feel trapped by this arrangement that might change not only our future, but our daily lives. The children seem subdued as well, standing beside their schoolhouse yard, which for once cannot provide amusement. They quietly play with floral chains made from entwined red clover and tussocks of orchard grass, and do not bicker among themselves when Anna, my sister, takes Jane Stoner's chain from her lap and drapes it over her own braided hair like a crown. My brother, Seth, turns and studies me with perturbed brown eyes, as if asking, *Why aren't you watching her?* Adolescence has made him concerned with what other people think of him and of our family. So I am comforted that he's been oblivious to the community's opinion of us until now. We are the only orphaned home in Mt. Hebron, and we were the only broken home before our *mamm* died. Therefore, whatever attention we have garnered has been sympathy at best.

Acknowledging Seth with a nod, I move from beneath the pines and clasp the back of my sister's elbow. She wrenches away and gasps, "No!"

The sound stuns the group from silence.

The *Englischer* Charlie says, "Let me get this straight: we're supposed to protect the property, but you're telling me that we can only walk around here like robot rent-a-cops while we got people with sawed-off shotguns wanting to kill us and take everything we got?"

He exchanges glances with the older man in the floppy hat — whose name I still don't know — and Sean. I'm startled to recall that, just this morning, like so many other mornings, Jabil was cutting timber beneath the pavilion, and I was standing at the sink, spooning fruit from a jar of last year's peaches, the juice running down my hand. And now here we are, compromising our ideals because our lives may be in danger.

I look over at Jabil and see the pigment has all but drained from his face, drawing attention to the small pink scar dividing the cleft of his chin. I am proud of him for maintaining his composure, even if I know it is a front. "Now, listen —" Rifling in his pocket, Jabil extracts the edict again and reads: "Though firearms may be used for intimidation and control of outsiders who wish us or our assets harm, *Englischers* will agree not to fire the weapons unless fired upon first."

He holds the paper at the top and taps the crease with the fingers of his opposite hand. "All I'm saying, Charlie, is I don't want innocent people, who are only trying to find help, killed because they happen upon your perimeter. There will simply be *no* firing unless fired upon."

"That's the stupidest thing I ever heard."

The man in the floppy hat grunts in agreement with Charlie, flicking his cigarette to the ground. With his shoe, he scuffs the lit end in the dirt. I look over at the pilot, Moses, who is still sitting on the swing. His face is twisted with repugnance. But I am not sure if it is directed toward Charlie's insolent manner, or if he is as irritated as the rest of the *Englischers.*

Jabil's shoulders square, and though his expression remains impassive, his voice is far from it as he says, "Another ordinance you must obey, in order to live under the protection of the community, is to attend the Sunday services at the schoolhouse. Also, everyone who is able-bodied must work on every day but the Lord's Day, or else they won't eat. This goes for both *Englischers* and Mennonites alike. Trust in our Savior, patience with one another, and a hard work ethic are the tools we need to survive."

"Sounds like Jamestown," someone quips.

I turn toward the voice and see that Moses has made his way over to the schoolhouse and is leaning against the siding with his foot resting lightly on the middle step. We stare at each other, and then he lowers his gaze, his brows furrowed. Whatever kinship we established earlier today — when we were standing close together along our back porch railing, staring at the smoking carnage of his plane — has all but disappeared. I miss how it felt to have him speak to me like an equal, as if I had a say in the matter. A mind and a will of my own.

The man in the floppy hat lights another cigarette. Holding the smoke for a second, he expels it through his nose and says in a graveled voice, "I'd rather starve than live like this."

Jabil stares at him, jaw working, and then addresses the entire community so the older man does not feel singled out. "It is easy to say you want to leave when you are well fed, but there is a benefit to being shielded within the community. You can help offer us protection, yes, for which we are grateful. And in exchange, we can teach you all how to live without the modern conveniences to which you are accustomed. We can teach you all how to preserve meat and vegetables, gather seeds for the next harvest, sew, can, bake, prepare tallow for candles and soap, and a thousand other skills that most *Englischers* forgot generations ago.

"Some of these practices, even we Mennonites have forgotten due to the convenience of purchasing items ready-made. But there are no convenience stores now. Or according to the pilot, they soon will be destroyed by looting. Moreover, if this EMP truly exists —" Jabil halts midsentence. My stomach clenches at the touch of his eyes upon my skin. "If this is what we think it is . . . then we are going to need to cultivate a whole new way of life. So I would think carefully before anyone says he will not agree to the community's edict. Without the community, you all will probably not survive. That being said, we must all get along and work together, even if we come —"

Charlie interrupts, his face reddening. "And without us protecting *your* hides, you all'd be dead the first time someone comes up that lane with a gun."

Moses pushes off the side of the school-house and tries to use his body as a barrier between Charlie and Jabil. But I am not sure, in his condition, what he could do if a defense were needed. Jabil holds up his hand and shakes his head, letting Moses know he's all right. And I find it odd that such disparate men are — for the time being, at least — functioning as a team.

"Charlie," Jabil intones, "as Bishop Lowell mentioned before, you are free to walk away right now. But if you decide to stay, then we must maintain a civil tone with each other."

Charlie doesn't say anything more. Taking his cue, the rest of the *Englischer* men also remain silent. Perhaps we will need Charlie's considerable size as a scare tactic when faced with the people who wish to devour our land. But I do have to wonder if he's going to be more trouble to our community than his brawn is worth.

Jabil concludes his oration and holds up the edict, upon which everything he has said was no doubt written beforehand by the bishop and deacons, who are inside the schoolhouse, almost cowardly awaiting how their words will be received.

"If you agree to this edict," he says, "you can come back into the schoolhouse and sign the paper before the administrators of

Mt. Hebron Community. This will hold you accountable to all our rules and stipulations. If you are discovered to have disobeyed any of them, no matter how insignificant they might seem to you, you will be expelled from the community with nothing but what you had when you arrived. This goes for both *Englischers* and those who have been lifelong members of the community. Our lives must be ruled justly so that — in a time of war — we can be the last modicum of peace."

Jabil turns and walks back into the schoolhouse, holding the community's declaration by the edges like a gentleman, although his hands are calloused and he wears a laborer's shoes. I watch him go, my own thoughts blocked by his words, which were far more eloquent than any the bishop or deacons could have penned. I am astounded by the fact that, though I have seen him oversee his logging crew, I have never seen him lead our people like this. He is no longer just his powerful uncle's mouthpiece, but a stalwart young man with the wisdom to foresee what is coming and, hopefully, protect us from harm.

The whole ride down the lane, Melinda — the *Englischer* from Colorado — perches on the seat between my sister, Anna, and me. Her elbows are tucked in close to her rail-thin body. Her purse and rolling briefcase, which she fetched from her vehicle, are stacked in her lap. She looked so forlorn when she exited the schoolhouse after signing the edict that I saw myself in her and felt it was my duty to invite her home with us. She seemed as hesitant to accept my invitation as I was to give it, but I don't see that she has any other choice.

Five years ago, when I was in the same awkward, peer-consumed stage Seth is in now, I also found myself stranded in a community where the cliques were established, making it next to impossible to fit in. The girls, led by the lovely yet puerile Ellen Mast, made an effort to welcome me by striking up conversation whenever our paths crossed during the community's frequent events. Despite this, I feared they knew why my family had fled to Mt. Hebron and were simply befriending me in an effort to obtain more gossip, so I was averse to participating in the exchange of confidences required in female relationships. No doubt this fear came across as snobbery, and soon the girls did not attempt to draw me into their circle, and I remained on the fringe, telling myself friendship was impossible with those who believe life is filled with light simply because they've never witnessed its darkness. But deep down, I know this is not true. Anna's innocence causes her to approach each day with her arms flung open to the light, and she and I are as close as we can be, considering she can offer neither confidence nor conversation.

The instant I pull the reins back on the horse in preparation to tie it to the hitching post, Anna scrambles out of the buggy and sprints, barefoot, toward our garden. She glances over her shoulder and smiles — one long braid flapping over the front of her flowered dress — watching to see if the stranger will follow her. Which, of course, Melinda doesn't. She is too busy studying her surroundings. And I imagine I can see her features morph into a sneer behind her oversize sunglasses. She climbs out primly, carrying her purse, and there's no hint of her earlier disheveled manner. I secure the horse and pick up Melinda's briefcase, left behind on the seat like I'm nothing but a country bellhop.

Melinda picks her way across the barnyard, the heels of her sandals stabbing themselves into the muck. Her tailored clothes and showy jewelry, not to mention that Mercedes SUV stranded at Field to

Table, reveal her financial standing. I feel embarrassed to open the front door and let her maneuver around me into our home, whose organization and spotlessness cannot conceal our pitiable state.

I tell her, "You're welcome to set down your purse." She glances at the floor, where Seth left his work boots, whose soles are clotted with dirt. Her lips tighten. Her purse remains where it is. Melinda takes off her sunglasses and spears the stems through the sprayed top of her hair.

"I appreciate you letting me stay," she says. "But I'm sure it's only temporary."

I avoid a reply by moving into the kitchen. I pour two glasses of water and take a sip from mine. Standing in the parallelogram of light beaming in from the window, I look at the scarred stretch of grass leading to the wreckage of the plane. My earlier conversation with Moses replays in my mind, when I asked him how we could get everything back post-EMP, and he declared that we could not. I wonder how Melinda is going to fare if this altered lifestyle turns out to be far more than temporary.

CHAPTER 4

LEORA

Four days have passed, and we've not seen anyone besides the two neighbors who have stopped by. But both Brian Mendenhall and Richard Murphy were seeking answers to the same questions we have been asking ourselves. Jabil told me that, with Bishop Lowell's permission, he invited them and their families to join our community. He thought we could benefit by having some *Englischers* on hand whom we could trust, and that the families would benefit by feeling more secure, shielded inside our walls. Mr. Mendenhall and Mr. Murphy, to Jabil's surprise, refused his offer. Also anticipating looters, they said their families must stay and defend their land.

This lull is virtually as debilitating as the fear of seeing masses of people swarming on the horizon. In the interlude, all we can do is brace ourselves for a horror we're not sure exists. So, though it is the Sabbath, we are trying to take our minds off of it by staying busy. *Busy* for the men means siphoning gas from the otherwise-useless vehicles and using it to sustain the generators, so they can run power tools that will help them construct the perimeter at a far more sufficient pace. *Busy* for the women means heeding Moses's advice and scrambling to distribute whatever meats and cheeses are left in the industrial cooler, which is no longer cooling since the backup generator's being used for the construction.

I am the only one who has not been busy by any definition of the word. Anna's routine-oriented nature has regressed a year for every day since the electrical grid stopped working, rendering us post-EMP housebound. Somehow Moses learned why I have not been at Field to Table. Yesterday, when I was sitting on the back steps braiding Anna's hair, I heard a noise and turned to look. Moses was coming around the corner, limping, his shoulders and forearms straining with the weight of two old log-stain buckets crammed with leftover pine boards.

"Found some paint and stuff when I was over at the pavilion looking for nails." He set the buckets against the greenhouse.

"Thought you could maybe make some signs for the perimeter, warning that the property's under surveillance."

"Thought that, did you?" I wasn't sure if my tone was coy or annoyed. Moses didn't seem to know either. He shifted his weight and pushed back his baseball cap. A piece of hair was pasted to his forehead with sweat. Should I be grateful that he singled me out?

Eyes stinging, I lowered my gaze, acting preoccupied with my sister's hair, which I could fishtail braid in my sleep. Anna slapped my thigh as I, again, pulled it too tight around her ears. "Sorry," I murmured, relaxing my grip. I looked back at Moses. He was watching my sister with the bewildered expression I've witnessed many times before. So far he hadn't had enough interaction with her to notice anything other than the fact that Anna possesses our *mudder*'s head-turning beauty. Now he saw the truth.

"She had an accident when she was six," I explained. "Fell from the barn loft. She's never been quite right since then."

A line appeared between Moses's brows. His pupils telescoped in the light. "I'm sorry."

"No need," I reassured him — I reassured

myself. "She doesn't know anything's wrong."

But *I* knew something was wrong; I remembered life before, when she was all right. We went from telling knock-knock jokes while we ate breakfast that morning, to me standing over her pediatric bed in Cleveland Clinic Children's Hospital that night, staring at the patch covering the burr hole in her skull, which the neurosurgeon had drilled to access the hemorrhage on the surface of her brain. That instant was the most defining of my life, for just as there was such a stark contrast between how my sister's day started and ended, I knew the rest of my own days were never going to be the same.

"I guess not knowing anything's wrong does make it easier for her," Moses agreed. "But I imagine it can't be all that easy for *you* . . . to remember how she was before the accident."

I dropped the pretense of studying my sister's hair and met his gaze. He smiled sadly. I found myself smiling in return — amazed that someone I just met could read my mind when no one else made the effort to understand me. Touching two fingers to his hat brim in a halfhearted salute, Moses Hughes left his buckets behind. Did they symbolize a proposal of friendship? Or did his singling me out mean something more?

I dared not hope the latter. It scared me to watch him limp away and realize I did.

MOSES

"Too tall?" Charlie bellows. "You kidding me? We don't want people jumping over the perimeter like pole-vaulters!"

Jabil holds his ground. "All I'm saying is that we don't want to waste logs if we could use them someplace else."

Charlie finally stops hammering. "Someplace else? This is our main defense against bloodthirsty thieves, and *you* want to go build yourself a cabin?"

Jabil sighs. "Don't be irrational, Charlie. Nobody's building a cabin. But if we cut the logs down from fourteen feet to eight, we could use that six feet to build outhouses."

"They can use the woods!"

"We're talking women and children and elderly, Charlie. Not men who could care less."

Charlie steps away from the perimeter. "What you tryin' to say?"

Jabil lifts his hands. "Just that it's time to think of the community's immediate needs for a change, rather than putting all our efforts into a project that might not need to be done."

Charlie's eyes glitter. He stalks across the flat stretch of earth and hovers over Jabil. The difference in height doesn't make Jabil look small as much as it emphasizes how huge Charlie is. He spits, "You haven't lifted one finger doing this 'project,' while the four of us —" he juts his chin at Henri, Sean, and me, who are watching this exchange like it comes with popcorn — "have been out here in the heat, working like dogs. So unless you're ready to climb down from your ivory tower and get your namby-pamby hands dirty, I say it's high time you kept your trap shut."

The air crackles like the prelude to a storm. Jabil lifts his chin and meets Charlie's gaze. "And if *you* can't converse in a civil manner, you can pack up your things and leave."

The veins pulse in Charlie's arms, as if the blood is feeding the muscles contracting his hand, wrapped around the hammer. I'm about to step in, to keep Jabil from getting his head bashed, when Charlie yells and throws that hammer as hard as he can into the field. It flips end over end for yards — the worn metal glinting — before it's swallowed by the grass.

All five of us stare in disbelief at that area of grass. Even Charlie looks shocked.

Tossing my post-hole digger, I pick up my crutches. "Well, think it's time for a water break." I take two steps toward Field to Table and then stop. "By the way, Charlie . . . if pole-vaulting over the perimeter doesn't work out, you might have a career in discus."

LEORA

There's nothing like the demolition of modern society to make me want to clean house. The past two days, under the guise of ascertaining how much food we have, I've organized our cellar and pantry. Under the guise of trying to let in as much natural light as possible, since we're conserving the oil in our lamps, I've used vinegar and newspaper to scour our windows. I have no real excuse to clean baseboards, but it's soothing to get down on my hands and knees and use an old toothbrush to eradicate the grime, which accumulates so quickly because of the firewood brought in twice daily for the cookstove.

The women in our community clean like this once, maybe twice, a year. I do it every month. Sometimes *twice* a month if I'm assaulted with some peculiar angst: Anna having more bad spells than good, Seth talking back to me like a teenager, another birthday celebrated without my parents — all of these disparate events making me feel incompetent until I clean.

The living room is the only room in the house I haven't touched, as I make a habit of avoiding the place where my mother died, as well as avoiding the memory of finding her. Biting the inside of my cheek, I remain standing in front of the cracked living room door, debating about going inside, regardless of whether Melinda from Colorado is up for company or not. She chose this room rather than sharing a bed with *Grossmammi* Eunice, who surprised us all by granting permission for a stranger to stay in her midst. But even though I love my grandmother, I wouldn't sleep a wink if I were forced to sleep in her room.

Though I do want to clean, dust accumulation is not the only thing I'm worried about. Melinda's been wearing the same outfit since the EMP. Despite expensive tailoring, the clothing is beginning to soften with body oil, the pressed creases on the silk short sleeves and linen slacks reducing to a wilt. I offered to heat water on the woodstove to fill the tub for her. I explained to Melinda that she could first bathe in the tub and then use the water to wash her clothes. She didn't say anything, but her expression conveyed that she thought taking a bath in a place where stereotypically "dirty" Old Order Mennonites have been bathing for years would be as barbaric as piercing her lip with a bone. Therefore, for the past three days, she has not washed her clothes or bathed — which I think makes *her* the barbarian, not us.

Decision made, I take a breath, open the door wider, and step into the room. Melinda sits up and finger-combs hair from her eyes. She hasn't moved from the couch except to use the bathroom, and then she had the audacity to complain that the toilet didn't work. She said this although I've told her countless times that the pressurized tank located at Field to Table, which supplied water throughout the community, has also shut down due to the electrical failure. So, if she needs to use the toilet, she must carry a bucket of water in from the hand pump to flush the bowl. Needless to say, she hasn't. I've had to clean up after her every time.

She squints at me. "What time is it?"

"Two o'clock. You hungry?"

"No." Turning, she stares at the window like the curtain's not obstructing the view. "Thanks, though. Maybe in a little while."

There is at least a fifteen-year gap between us, but I feel decades older. Just as Melinda's made no effort to follow my instructions, I've made no effort to conceal my resentment concerning her helplessness. If I can just get her to eat, to bathe, to go for a walk, it will feel like I am stabilizing this Tilt-A-Whirl, if only for a moment.

Melinda takes a sip of water. Her fingers tremble as she sets down the glass. She sees me looking at the prescription bottle magnified behind it and says, "I can't sleep otherwise." She dabs sweat from her lip with her knuckle and reclines on the couch again, careful not to move her upper body, as if it's been injured in a wreck. "I don't have pictures," she says. "They're all on my phone." I glance at her, stunned that she's trying to communicate something other than a complaint, but then look away — her vulnerability as shocking to me as nakedness. Tears are trickling from the woman's eyes, darkening the oily temples of her hair, and yet her expression remains the same. "Nobody carries around pictures of their family anymore. Have you noticed?"

I shake my head while continuing to stare at the curtained window. I have not noticed. No one in our community carries pictures at all, since they're considered graven images, and the *Englisch* customers who used to come to Field to Table never bothered to share their family photos with me, as I was just a quaint, *kapped* anomaly who sometimes bagged up their sandwiches and homemade bread. But Melinda does not care to hear this. She is not speaking to me as much as she is verbally processing the EMP that, for her, brought far more hardships than hauling water and fairly distributing food. For her, the EMP created a vast canyon separating her from her family, a canyon that might never be bridged.

For the first time since Melinda's arrival, compassion overtakes my resentment. I take an afghan from the cedar chest. She murmurs as I spread it over her shoulders, smiling lazily, as if already sedated by the prescription drugs. "Thank you, Leora. Really. You've been so kind." My throat burns with guilt. At a loss for words, I nod and stride out of the living room. I turn before I pull the door behind me and see that her breathing is already deepened by sleep.

Leading Anna over to the kitchen table, I pour a glass of water for her, which she drinks in one long swallow, smacking her lips afterward to show her satisfaction. My sister hasn't learned to speak beyond basic sentences ("Read to you?") and requests — *yes, no, some* for food, *'side* to go outside, and our names, including the ones she's bestowed upon our animals. But now Anna's handicap has turned into a blessing. For *she* is the one who continues through this altered world — unsettled by the changes in her daily routine, yes, but without being hampered by worry concerning the morrow — while I remain disabled by our uncertain future.

I let the kitchen door open to cycle some fresh air through the house, and maybe entice Melinda from her torpor long enough to venture outside; then Anna and I go down the porch steps. Jabil Snyder is in our side yard, digging a hole for the outhouse that we dismantled less than four years ago. I am sure the deacons and bishop now regret their decision to allow the community to have running water in our homes. Since the EMP has rendered indoor plumbing obsolete, we are forced to go in reverse in order to move forward.

Wiping his brow, Jabil sips from his canteen and takes off his straw hat. He pours some water over his head, the excess spattering the ground between his feet. I study him a moment — the liquid trickling down the strong planes of his face and turning his white collared shirt into a translucent skin — and try to see if I can conjure forth that same level of admiration I felt for him a few days ago. But I cannot.

Jabil must feel my gaze, for he puts his hat back on and watches me walk through the uncut grass. Behind me, Anna sings nonsensical lyrics and skips in bare feet across the length of weathered porch before descending another step, an impromptu game of hopscotch. She loves the different textures against her toes, just as she loves the feel of different quilting scraps — velvet, corduroy, satin, silk, lace — that I obtained through a ragbag of *Englischer* castoffs someone left at Field to Table and turned into a quiet book to keep Anna occupied during church.

"How's the roommate working out?" Jabil calls, jutting his chin toward our house.

Embarrassed about how I've been treating Melinda, I say, "Great. How's living with the pilot?"

He drops his gaze and sinks his shovel into the earth. He leans on it, his forearm gleaming with sweat. Jabil looks years older than he is; perhaps that's because, since his father's death, he has had to carry a mantle of responsibility similar to the one I also shoulder alone.

"How's it living with Moses, you mean?" He and I both know full well the person to whom I'm referring.

"Not too many other pilots around here." My joke falls flat, the silence looming between us like the person who altered my world at the instant everything around us crashed. It's not that I long to be with Moses, a stranger, and not with the good-hearted man standing before me — the good-hearted man I've known for years. Jabil may believe that before Moses arrived I would have been open to his courtship; after all, I have been studying him as covertly as he has been studying me. We are two young people of the opposite sex living in an isolated community — and, even better yet, we are not related, which has become something of an issue for the spearheading Snyders. Mt. Hebron families have been intermarrying since the brothers Lowell and Jacob Snyder, Jabil's uncle and father, moved from Lancaster with a few other families and founded the community in Liberty, Montana, in 1988. Thus, this intermarriage has narrowed the scope of finding a mate who is not kin.

But my decision not to let Jabil court me wasn't made by Moses's arrival. It was made by my *vadder*'s disappearance and my *mamm*'s subsequent death. Ever since that time, I've realized I'm not cut out to perform the normal roles of wife and mother, as I am too busy trying to give my orphaned siblings the semblance of a normal home. I wish I *could* be courted by Jabil, because I know he senses that to marry me would be to claim my family as his.

Now that the EMP has revealed an unexplored dimension of life, I'm no longer sure I can remain content with the status quo, even if the status quo is more predictable than the alternative. What if the unpredictable road leads to the only destination worth reaching in the end?

I look over at my sister, feeling as confused and exposed as Moses must have felt when he was bleeding on our kitchen table, gripping my hand and begging me to tell him where he was. I am so disoriented that I cannot understand what I'm doing in this altered world or where — in its daily rotation — I really am.

Jabil turns and cuts the shovel hard into the earth before jumping on top to drive it farther down. He stays quiet as he gathers the dirt and dumps it onto the pyramid beside the widening hole. He always assumes this taciturn state whenever he has nothing to say or is simply too disturbed for words. I am aware that Jabil longs for more than what this communal earth has to offer. I could see it in his sure, quick movements as he extricated the pilot from the wreckage and instructed the men on how to take him inside. I also saw it when he sliced the shirt from the pilot's skin and studied the flesh for abrasions that might reveal a greater internal wound.

"Moses doesn't say a whole lot," Jabil continues, breaking into my thoughts. "But we might have to start halving the community rations just to keep him fed."

I conceal my smile by turning toward the meadow where the yellow plane is out in the elements. I wonder when Moses will come back to sift through whatever survived the crash. It bothers me to think that he's been here already, and I simply missed his arrival. It bothers me that I would like to be here when he comes. Of all the places he could have landed, why did he choose our field? Or did *Gott* choose it for him?

When I glance back at Jabil, he is watching me again, his eyes moving from my eyes and traveling down to my mouth like he's trying to read my lips, although I am not speaking.

Taking off his hat, he wipes the dampness from his hairline and tosses the hat on the ground. Gripping the end of the shovel, he continues pawing the ground and dumping the dirt into a pile. We are the first house to receive outdoor plumbing. I know Jabil has overseen this project for our family, while the rest of the men are working on the perimeter that will encase our community like a fort. Jabil says, "Who knows where Moses comes from." When I glance at him, he will not meet my eyes but keeps staring at the ground. "Last night, he woke up yelling and then rattled downstairs with his crutches. I looked out the window and saw him stumbling up the lane. I'm not even sure he's all there . . . to be honest. I'd be careful if I were you."

"Didn't you tell us this community is supposed to be about peace?" I glower at Jabil until he rises to face me. "Just because you . . . you may not like Moses," I stammer, squinting up into his dark eyes, "doesn't mean you need to turn this into some kind of competition."

Jabil puts the shovel down. We continue staring, our bodies mimicking each other's rapid inhalations. Since when did he become Mt. Hebron's sole judge of character?

A droplet of sweat trails down his jawline and glistens on the protruding cords of his neck. "Leora, I didn't mean to talk . . . badly of him." He extends a hand toward mine.

Anxiety envelops me. I listen to the chickens squawking in their coop, to our windmill's irregular creak, to the women coming back from Field to Table for lunch, their laughter reminding me of bygone days. I move away from Jabil and call for my sister. She ducks out of the miniature greenhouse. The tomcat scampers along behind her, his bottle-brush tail tipped with white. The apron of her cape dress is filled with green tomatoes. But her smile is so satisfied, I haven't the heart to explain why the red tomatoes are the only ones ready to be picked.

" 'Ora! 'Ora!" she cries, running to me. In her haste to show me her treasures, a few of the tomatoes bounce out of her apron and roll across the grass.

"*Kumm,* Anna," I call.

I slide her premature tomatoes into my apron pockets and take her hand. I look back at Jabil and regret my skittish reaction to his kindness and touch. I must not punish every good man simply because one man let me down. But I also do not want to make the same mistake my *mamm* made by leaping headlong into a relationship I might live to regret. So I will continue guarding my heart while relinquishing my viewpoint of every man as guilty until proven otherwise; I will simply view them as I view myself: trying to do the right thing by those I love.

Before I lose my nerve, I turn and call out to Jabil, "Thank you!"

I cannot see him looking because of his hat brim, but I can feel it. He raises his hand briefly in acknowledgment and then sinks his shovel once more into the earth.

The men have decided to use the large pile of logs, originally destined for someone's dream home, to fence in the property — creating the "perimeter" Moses suggested. In four days, how have we, the Gentle People, allowed ourselves to become so debilitated by fear that we've formed an alliance that is based not on what each can give, but on what each can take?

Really, in this way, how are we any different from the locusts we are trying to protect ourselves from? But when it comes right down to it, I am just like everyone else: I do not want marauders pillaging our land, consequently forcing me to watch my little brother and sister starve, so I would have made the same decision if I were in Bishop Lowell's shoes.

Anna, beside me, continues waltzing down the graveled drive. She is blissful, unaware that the world spinning around her spinning body has changed beyond recognition. Shading my eyes, I look at the wall being constructed and see that the bearded *Englischer,* Charlie, has paused in his work to watch. I remind myself not to view every man as guilty, and that I should be accustomed to deflecting the attention Anna garners. Yet my stomach still tightens as I see my sister's cape dress lift and swirl around her strong, tan legs.

"Anna!" I chide and move my body in front of hers, blocking Charlie's view.

She stops spinning, and I bat down her skirt.

Moses must have heard me call out, for he hobbles over on the crutches Myron Beiler's letting him borrow and says, "I want to thank you for the signs. They look great."

I smile stiffly in return and take Anna's hand. Glancing over my shoulder, I see that Charlie has turned back to the wall to continue hammering. But I keep watching him, wondering if he's constructing this perimeter to protect us or to keep us from escaping. The tops are sharpened to pencil points, upended as if to pierce the endless sky.

"Everything all right?" Moses asks.

I do not know Moses well enough to

confide in him my fears. Then again, I do not confide my fears to anyone, so the risk is no greater with him than it would be with Jabil, whom I've known for such a long time. "Know anything about Charlie?"

Moses lifts his shoulders. "He's single. Was living in some underground house before the EMP. Has a temper that boils like a hot pot. He's good at taking initiative."

"Like how?"

"I dunno. He found some construction cones and a sign that says 'Road Out Ahead.' He set them up at the end of Field to Table Road."

"Not sure you can call that initiative."

"At least he's trying. Got any better ideas to keep people from coming back here?"

Moses's voice is thick with frustration. Switching tactics, I ask, "How far did he go?"

"Only to the end of the road. . . . Why?"

"It's about ten miles until you get to the first major town."

"They got any antique car dealerships?"

"Not that I know of. Just used lots. What would you want with an antique car?"

He points over to the lane, where the *Englischer* men have pushed the cars and trucks that were in front of Field to Table into a sentinel-like line, so the useless can be used as part of the blockade. "Anything older wouldn't be fried like the rest of these vehicles with computers."

I say, "Don't know about any old cars, but the museum has some old tractors."

"Now we're talking. I wonder if any of them run."

"Why? What could you do with a tractor?"

"Everything. Drive for supplies . . . scout the area. If we could find implements for it, we could use it to work the ground too."

"You're not serious. You're going to steal a tractor from the museum?"

"Yes, ma'am," he says. "I am. Unless somebody's already beat me to it."

"But you still want to try to go get one?"

His reckless grin is answer enough. I think of Anna and Seth and the supplies a tractor might gather that — a few months from now, when our storehouse is empty — might fill their hungry mouths. I tell him, "I could show you where they are."

Moses tilts his head toward me. "I know it's a small town, but we've no idea how dangerous things have gotten. You sure you're up for something like that?"

A question much like Jabil's before he checked Moses for injuries. "I wouldn't have offered to go if I wasn't sure."

Moses appears taken aback by my

brusqueness, as he should be. "I — I'm sorry," I stammer, face growing hot.

"No harm, no foul. Just want you to know the risks before you're in over your head."

"These days, life itself is a risk."

He smiles. "Won't argue with you there."

MOSES

I hobble down the Snyders' steps without my crutches, though I can tell within a few feet that I still need those things bad. If I squint, I can see Henri up the lane, leaning against a beam holding up the pavilion. He's as recognizable from his hat as from the smoke twisting up from the spark pinched between his fingers. We're not supposed to meet until midnight, a half hour from now, so that means I don't have much time to talk Leora out of coming along on this trip.

I look back at Henri one more time before I continue walking, and it's like looking at an aged version of my father. Boredom doesn't sit well with someone with a mind like a machine and a body used to working sixty-hour weeks, as Henri once did as an experimental wielder for New Holland. I could tell his grease-stained hands were going to be itching for another project as soon as we finished the perimeter. He even talked about continuing the perimeter along the other side of the property, although it already has a six-foot-tall fence where forest land bumps up against the community, making it difficult for someone — to put it in Charlie's terms — to "vault." So two days ago, to keep Henri occupied, I told him about my plan to filch the museum's equipment.

I also flattered him a little by telling him he was probably the only one around here who could figure out how to get the old tractor engines running, if it was possible at all. He eyeballed me a second, sucking his cigarette like it was the straw in a drink.

The greedy old codger knew he could get more from me if he said nothing, so — as always — I couldn't stare right back and wait him out. I caved. I told him if he helped me, in repayment I'd try to find a gas station along the way, which pretty much means we'll have to loot a few places before we can find Henri one pack of cigs. At least his cigarette stash held out until we finished the perimeter today, or else he probably would've taken off without me.

I knock lightly on the Ebersoles' screen door and then open it when no one responds, because I don't want to keep knocking and wake up the family. Leora seems unsettled when I enter the kitchen and see her using a toothpick to administer glue to a wooden dollhouse. By the lamplight, I watch her lips press together, so I know she's heard me come in. She lets go of the dollhouse long enough to turn her face toward the shadows, wiping her eyes with the sleeve of her dress. I remove my shoes and cross the room over to where she's standing.

"It's for my sister," she says, without looking at me. The glued truss falls, hanging from the gable end like an appendage. "It broke a few years ago."

"What made you decide to fix it now?"

"Because it's about the only thing I can."

We're no longer talking about wood glue and dollhouses. I step closer and reach for the toothpick. Leora flinches, and then releases it. I dip the toothpick in the open container and dab more glue along the end of the truss. "You push against that side," I instruct, "and I'll push against this one." Leora presses against the left side of the truss and looks at the space behind my head, so I look too as I press against the right. She's staring at the grandfather clock that stands like a guard in between the kitchen wall and the sitting area, where I've heard the Colorado woman sleeps all day, as if compensating for the rest of us who can't.

Turns out, watching glue dry is about as entertaining as watching paint dry, so my mind wanders, letting me forget how awkward this feels. What would my mother think of Leora if the two of them could meet? No doubt she'd appreciate Leora's individuality and spunk, which caused her — that first day — to stand up and vocalize her thoughts like a woman, and then go outside to swing beside me, a stranger, like she was nothing more than a carefree child.

My mother was once full of individuality and spunk as well. She met my father when he, a graduate assistant, came late to her senior thesis presentation in a political science class at Rutgers University — a calculated move because he wanted to take her out for coffee to make it up to her. She was going to become a human rights lawyer, but his charming gaffe won her heart, and they got married right after graduation instead.

The fumes must be getting to me, because I hear myself speaking these thoughts aloud. "You know, you kind of remind me of my mom." Leora's head remains forward, but she looks at me from the corner of her eye. "What?" I quip. "You didn't think I have one?"

112

"No. Just can't imagine what I could have in common with your *mudder.*"

"Well, her life didn't turn out the way she expected it to, either. She gave up her dreams of law school to stay home with my brother and me since our father was gone all the time." My mother claims that the decades of war have changed him, that he wasn't so abrasive and withdrawn when they fell in love over textbooks and coffee. I can't remember him that way, but I also can't remember our mother being as beautiful as pictures prove she was.

"Your *vadder* was gone a lot?" Leora asks. "Did he abandon you?" I'm not sure if I'm imagining her defensive tone or if she's just curious.

"You could say that." I shake my head, wondering how we ever got onto this topic. But now that I'm this far in, I might as well tell her the rest. "When I was a junior in high school, my brother and I came home from practice and found her sitting in a rocker on our porch, knitting a pink sweater. She told us to sit down. So we sat. Then she told us that our father had a son in Afghanistan, apparently fathered when he was stationed there. Four years old. Just a baby, really. Then she went right on knitting, like she'd told us we were having pork

113

chops for dinner or something. Later, I saw a baby at Mass wearing that pink sweater."

"So your *vadder* left after that?"

"Strangely enough, no. I mean, no more than he ever did, being overseas so much. Maybe that's another way you remind me of her. Her beliefs kept her faithful to my dad when anybody else would've been divorcing him in a minute, kind of the way your beliefs set you apart from the rest of the world."

The front door opens. Jabil steps into the kitchen's dim nimbus of light, holding his straw hat to his chest. He looks at me and Leora, this broken house between us, and his lips press together in a masculine form of Leora's earlier expression. Jabil studies me, trying to get down through my layers to find out who I am. He's going to be looking awhile. Whenever I peer in the mirror of my shaving kit, I can't recognize myself. And it's not just the long hair and beard replacing my military cut; in my pupils, I can see the soul reflection of that little boy in the desert whom I irrationally tried to protect.

Jabil says, "I told Leora the only way I'm letting her go into town with two strangers is if I ride along."

I look at Leora. Her smile appears more like a grimace. I say, "Shouldn't you ask her

114

what she thinks before you start telling her what she can and cannot do?"

The brim of the hat bends in Jabil's hands. "We know nothing about you, Moses."

"And your point is . . . ?"

I know what Jabil's point is, and if I were in his shoes, I'd want to protect Leora from someone like me as well. Regardless, I still bristle at being seen as the bad guy — especially when Jabil considers himself the good. If our lives weren't so messed up, he and I could maybe become friends. But since we're coming at this EMP from opposite sides, so to speak, it's a little hard to meet in the middle. Tension's not only rising between me and Jabil but between the Mennonites and the *Englischers,* exemplified by Charlie's hammer incident. If we can keep up a steady balance of give and take, we might be able to get along. I don't want to have to find this balance, but — as always — it looks like I'm going to be the one who has to compromise. Either this is a side effect of being a little brother, or I'm more into nonresistance than I thought.

Leora murmurs, "Stop, just stop," and lets go of her side of the dollhouse. The truss falls. I watch her face and see that her puffy eyes are looking at nobody but him.

"We'll be taking my wagon," Jabil says.

Moving to the front of the dollhouse, I hold the truss together on my own. Only now, looking at it from this angle, I see that it's a smaller replica of the house I'm standing in — down to the picture window facing the meadow and the long pine table where I woke up to find Leora holding my hand. "Did you ask your uncle if you can ride with me, Jabil?" Try as I might, I can't keep the derision from my voice. "I'd sure hate for you to get in trouble."

Jabil looks like he wants to spit. Instead, he walks over to Leora. "Ready to go?"

She nods and says under her breath, "Don't be rude," before crossing the living room, and I am unable to tell if she's talking to me or to him. Either way, I watch them go and then look back at the dollhouse, which I'm holding together like an idiot. The plastic windows on either side of the door resemble eyes, staring at me, trying to figure out what I'm hoping to accomplish. That's just the thing: I don't know myself.

CHAPTER 5

LEORA

I sit on the buckboard between Jabil and Moses, my spine balanced so the jostling wagon won't knock my body into either of their shoulder blades. Henri sits in the back, quiet to the point that sometimes I forget he's there. Then again, Jabil and Moses are quiet too. The tension between them is as palpable as it was in the kitchen, when they sparred with each other without lifting a hand. Are they attracted to me, or are they attracted to the concept of winning a prize?

Jabil clears his throat in the silence. The rhythmic clomping of the horse's hooves over the asphalt could put me to sleep if my racing mind weren't trying to keep pace with my heart. The stars are brilliant tonight; the moon is full, which is good. We've never seen the city of Liberty as devoid of light as this. It reminds me of a ghost town, though I have only read about such places in books. Cars, trucks, and vans are tilted here and there — reminding me of an ogre's game of Hot Wheels that he cast pell-mell over the two-lane road.

Some drivers thought to push their vehicles to the edge of the embankment and lock the doors, but these are the ones that have been hit hardest by vandalism. Plastic hubcaps, chrome pieces — possibly too heavy for people to carry — and shards of glass from broken windshields glitter in the grass. Perhaps vandals felt the drivers must be locking their doors because they had something valuable enough to protect and, subsequently, to steal.

Flashlight beams slice through the darkness of the hardware store up ahead, fitted with windows that remain intact. The beams appear disembodied, but I know they are not. For what are the people searching? And who are they? I can't imagine the citizens of Liberty, after just one week, would be capable of forced entry and theft. But, then, do any of us know what we're capable of until a situation or a person forces our hands? I am a perfect case study of situational ethics: a trustworthy Mennonite girl riding along with an *Englischer* who's made it clear that he hopes to steal from the museum that survives on insubstantial donations alone.

In the background, high in the crags, I hear the repeated pop of gunfire. Moses's hand goes down and rests on his holster.

"Probably firecrackers," Jabil says, without much conviction, and I wonder: Where is the local police force? The fire company? Perhaps they're taking care of the elderly who cannot forage for water and food, and — I realize with a sinking feeling — perhaps they're also taking care of the patients at the local hospital and nursing home. Both places would be transformed into institutions of terror, since the machines keeping everyone stable have shut off. And what happens when the medicine runs out, and no trucks are running in order to bring new supplies?

I am appalled. I have not considered the severity of other people's plights; I have been wholly consumed with my own.

The mare, responding to Jabil's prodding, shifts into a canter. The wheels click smoothly along Main Street's blacktop, as if we're old pioneers traveling forward in time. I bite back a gasp, perceiving that *this* is where the violent looting took place, and then — I guess — radiated outward, the EMP affecting Liberty like a bomb detonated on the courthouse square. I was not expecting a little town to be affected by such devastation so fast. The quaint line of windows are piebald with holes from rocks being thrown through them or else shattered completely. It looks as if some of the owners have attempted to keep people out by building barricades with pallets, equipment, and furniture they do not care to lose.

But it's obvious the people who initiated this defacement either became bored and moved on or are in the process of making their rounds and will be back. The store owners must know this as well. The proprietor of Liberty's gas station and repair shop is sitting outside the double garage doors with a shotgun resting in his lap. Behind him, the six-by-eight-foot window — which once read *Friendly's* in swirling calligraphy of navy and gold — is nothing but a long, dim rectangle studded around the edges with shards of glass. By the moon's glow, it looks like the owner hasn't been sleeping, eating, or bathing regularly since the EMP. And he certainly doesn't look friendly.

A few of the store owners — maybe believing order will soon be reinstated — have already tried cleaning up the worst of the mess. Rusted oil barrels, filled with refuse, burn brightly. The penny-sized holes drilled through them, to increase the oxygen flow to the fire, cast a crosshatch pattern across the cobblestone sidewalks that were walked by tourists just one week ago. Nobody is huddled around the flames, of course, as even nighttime holds vestiges of summer's warmth. But staring at those barrels, flames lapping toward the sky, I imagine none of this might be fixed by winter. What are people going to do then?

"Looting's worse at night," Moses explains. " 'The light disturbs the wicked and stops the arm that is raised in violence.' "

"A man who quotes Job and knows the behavior of criminals," Jabil says.

"Take it or leave it. That's who I am."

I do not need daylight to see the tension mounting, for I can feel it in the concrete set of their shoulders alone. I long to inquire about Moses's life history, but refrain because I know it would irk Jabil to give Moses extra attention. "Why haven't they come to loot us?" I ask instead.

"They'll come," Henri responds swiftly — the first words he's spoken since we started the trip. I turn around to look at him, sprawled across the pile of empty feed sacks. He nods at me and smiles. The transformation is astonishing, like a storm cloud exposing the sun. But then the wagon jolts to a halt. I face forward and see that a woman's come out onto the street and taken hold of the horse's bridle. Jabil pulls back on the reins. The horse prances inside the harness and tosses her head, as disoriented by this woman's materialization as we are.

"Hate to bother you, but can someone please tell me what's going on?"

The woman's desperate tone reminds me of my mother's voice two years ago, when she had us three children sit at the kitchen table and then paced behind our *vadder*'s chair, trying to explain his disappearance. My compassion stirred, I stand from the buckboard and pull my skirt to the side. Easing past Moses, I prepare to climb from the wagon when his fingers latch onto mine. I look back at him and see his eyes are filled with warning. He releases me, but slowly, our fingertips brushing so that his calluses abrade my skin.

The woman sees me step down and lets go of the bridle. Long skeins of black hair hang on each side of her face. The whites of her eyes glimmer in the moonlight. Though her voice, when she spoke, sounded older, she looks childlike — mainly because of how fine-boned she is, dwarfed by a man's blue parka that billows around her knees.

"We believe it's an EMP," I explain. "An electromagnetic pulse that's wiped technol-

ogy out. Someone might be able to fix it —
but probably not." I pause and scan her,
watching as she hugs her arms to her chest.
"Are you cold? Do you have food . . .
water?"

She shakes her head. "Ran out of food this
morning. Not a crumb left in the place. I
have a baby. How can I nurse him if I'm
not eating?"

I see no baby, unless he is tucked inside
her parka. But she knows — and *I* know —
that I cannot turn a mother and baby away,
even a baby who might not exist. "Come
stay with us," I say, knowing what dissension this will bring to the *Englischers*. I also
know what dissension this will bring to the
group in the wagon. Jabil will agree that it
is Christlike to take this woman in, but I
am not sure how Moses and Henri will
react. I glance behind me. It's impossible to
see Henri due to his position in the wagon
bed, but Moses's censure is clear.

I tell the woman, "You and your baby can
come stay with us," and then add, "if you'd
like," to make sure she's aware she has a
choice.

She looks at me and then looks at the
wagon. "Maybe the government will figure
it out before I have to do anything. Maybe
things will get better."

"And maybe they won't." I reach out and squeeze her hand. "Come if you need help."

The woman nods. I climb back into the wagon, being careful not to brush Moses's legs as I move past him to sit in the middle. Jabil clicks his tongue at the horse without acknowledging me. The mare moves forward. I peer over my shoulder, watching the dark-haired mother standing in the apex of such devastation, the light from the fire flickering across her face.

Outbuildings, salvaged from various historic landmarks around town, surround the Liberty Museum like the ring of a wagon train: a schoolhouse, a pioneer cabin, a replica of a mining shaft. A lean-to, divided with roughly hewn logs, is where the old equipment and tractors are parked. I motion Jabil in that direction; he snaps the reins lightly on the mare's back. Regardless of the town's destruction, no one's thought to dismantle the museum. Even the grainy windows of the schoolhouse are unbroken, which appears abnormal, compared to how drastically everything was demolished just a mile from here.

There is an old fire truck that still gleams red despite the darkness; it actually looks better at night than it does during the day

— the rusted chrome pieces spangled with silver, made new. Two tractors squat like metal skeletons under the shed and resemble pieces from a junkyard rather than the vehicles Moses believes will get us around. But he is overjoyed to see them. If not for his ankle, I could picture him leaping off the wagon like a child eager to examine a new toy.

"What d'ya think?" Moses asks.

Henri leans forward and squints. "Can't think much at this point," he says. "Other than the fact that they're old."

Jabil gets down out of the wagon and ties the horse to the lean-to beam. I watch him stroke the mare's neck, which is damp with sweat. Field to Table enables our community to be more self-sufficient than most, so our horses are unaccustomed to walking to town.

"Do you think she needs water?" I ask.

"Probably," he says, looking worried. "I should've brought some."

Moses calls from inside the lean-to, "You won't be needing that kind of horsepower for long if we can get these beauts running."

The muscles tighten in Jabil's jaw. He is very fond of his horses and has never been around vehicles, other than the two-ton truck Sean used before the EMP to taxi the logging crew to and from jobs. Jabil must feel peculiar to be out of his element — the same man who oversees many aspects of our community with ease.

"C'mon," he says to me. "Let's look in the museum. They're going to be here awhile."

"I don't think we can get inside."

"Sure we can." He continues walking. I follow, curious, and when we're standing in front of the wooden door, he simply withdraws a key from his pocket. "They gave me this when we remodeled part of the museum last year," he explains. "Forgot to return it."

"How convenient for you."

"Convenient for us now."

Side by side, we enter the museum, which is an octagonal log structure with no windows and only one door. Jabil stops briefly to prop it open with a rock. The floor plan is open, except for a few small booths that house artifacts from the days when mining was Liberty's main source of revenue. Then the mines closed, turning the bustling town into an impoverished eyesore that limps along on tourists stopping by for gas and burgers before venturing farther west.

The air is musty, the cement floors clean. We cannot see very far, but weak illumination filters in through the gap where the front door is propped open. This light reveals the taxidermy versions of a cinnamon bear, a wolf, and a mountain lion collecting dust in the museum's loft.

The creatures' elevated position and sightless marble eyes make me feel like they're leering down at us, waiting to pounce. A wooden donation box with a tiny lock sits atop the entrance table. I cannot believe no one's thought to break in and steal from it.

As if in sync with my thoughts, Jabil says, "Probably shouldn't let Moses see that," and gives me a rare grin.

"He said money's no good anyway," I murmur. "Food, medicine, and ammunition are the only things worth taking."

Jabil crosses the gap between us, obstructing the moonbeam directed toward the entrance. "What about heirloom seeds to last us until the next planting season? What about farming implements to work the ground? Don't let him persuade you, Leora. We don't just need ammunition. There are other ways to go about this apocalypse than the use of violence."

"He's not advocating the use of violence. He's advocating the use of common sense." Angry, I turn from Jabil to face the display of buttons from different time periods, many of which are pieces of art in themselves, intricately carved from wood or bone.

He grabs my arm and turns me around. "Are you changing your beliefs?"

"No. But *you* need to compromise, rather than carrying on as if nothing is different."

"Don't you think I know that everything's different?" Jabil says, his tone equally sharp. "Don't you think I wish none of this had happened? That I — I still had time to court you properly, the way you deserve? But I can't. Soon we're going to be busy just trying to stay alive."

Stunned by his declaration, I try to set my anger aside and view him not as someone I should love, but as someone who holds the power to keep my family safe. He lets go of me and steps back, leaning over the booth's protective divider, which cannot impede someone of his height. He runs his fingers through the beads and buttons, letting each one slip through his fingers and clink to the base like hail. I tell him, "Everything else might be different, but my family's problems aren't going to change. Anna needs me. Seth needs me. *Grossmammi* Eunice even needs me, though she acts like she'd prefer to be alone."

Jabil pulls a jar out of the display and sets it on the floor. "Seth *does* need you, but he also needs a man in his life, someone to help guide him during these critical years. I could be that for him, Leora. You all could move into our house, and we could start our own family there." He touches the side of my face with the back of his hand. He leans his head down closer to mine. My spirit feels so numb, I flinch.

Straightening, he removes his hand. "It's because of him. Isn't it?"

"Because of whom?" But I know who he's going to say.

"Moses. Ever since he crashed here, you've been distant from me."

"That's not true. We've just never been close."

He sidesteps my words, knocking over the Mason jar.

"I'm sorry, Jabil. I never meant to hurt you."

"You haven't. Really." He smiles again, the second time in one night, when I don't remember him smiling more than a handful of times in all these years. "The buttons." He gestures to them, strewn across the floor. "Thought you could put them on your clothes if we run out of pins."

"I'm sorry, Jabil."

"Stop apologizing. You've nothing to be sorry for."

Then he strides across the cement flooring and leaves me standing there, alone, marooned in a lake of variegated buttons — a few of which the heels of Jabil's boots have inadvertently ground to powder.

MOSES

Old Man Henri slams the hood. "Engine's cracked," he says.

"And this one's no better?"

He eyes the other tractor, mustached lips twitching. "Least not without the tools to fix it."

I sigh. "Guess that's it, then." I turn to look for Jabil and Leora but see they're coming out of the museum, which irritates me since Jabil never said he had a key. Leora moves across the grounds, holding something to her chest. "We're ready," I say. "Both tractors were a bust."

Neither of them acknowledge me. They just climb up into the wagon, keeping a space between them large enough for a linebacker to sit in. I'm no genius at body language, but even *I* can tell that something's happened. The kind of something that means you could cut the carnal strain with a knife. Ignoring a pang of jealousy, I climb up and sit between Jabil and Leora. Jabil keeps hold of the reins as he steers us out of the museum's lot.

Leora must be so tired that she could sleep anywhere. I take my eyes off the road to glance over at her. Scared she's going to topple right off the bench onto the asphalt, I shake her shoulder. "Leora, hey . . . you could really hurt yourself if you fall from here."

She recrosses her legs and steadies the jar in her lap. "I'm resting my eyes."

"Then maybe try resting one at a time."

She smiles, both eyes still closed. I'm not smiling at all. The sky's lightening to gunmetal, but I can feel us being watched from deep within the shadowed alleyways between the brick buildings. I tell myself, *We're in a wagon being driven down Main Street by a man in a straw hat. Of course we're being watched.* But there's more to it than that. I can perceive danger ahead like I can see the smoke drifting up from the oil drums on the corners. Whatever they're burning — plastic or tires — the black smolder and acrid smell make my pulse race, taking me back to the explosion in the desert. To say I'm lucky to be alive is an understatement; I'm lucky to be alive *twice.* If not for Leora — and yes, Jabil and his loggers, who rescued me from my grandpa's demolished crop duster — a bum ankle would be the least of my problems.

Leora puts a hand on my forearm, and the unexpectedness of it makes me jump. I follow the direction where she's pointing, but I can't tell where the brick building stops and the hard pack of people's bodies begins. I unsnap the top of my holster. My fingers crave the reassuring heft of the weapon in my hands, yet I also don't want to alert Leora to the fact that I think we're being hunted. I should've known it was too quiet on our way through town. For all we know, they could've been waiting for us since we passed in the wagon, thinking we might return with something they'd want to confiscate.

I look at Jabil, trying to communicate the danger we're in. He nods, shifts his attention to the building, and then looks at me, holding my gaze before returning his eyes to the road and snapping the reins on the horse's back. Then he leans forward until his tailbone is hardly on the seat. It takes a second for me to comprehend that he's trying to shield Leora. And for the first time since we met, I have a sense of respect for the man. Though I unsnapped my gun holster for protection, I never thought about using my body to protect her.

Leora's back straightens, her skin a corona

of nervous energy that warms my own. "What do they want?" she whispers, nodding toward the building.

"Probably the horse and wagon."

In addition to whatever is being carried by the horse and wagon. Maybe they also want her. The sweat on my neck goes cold. It was stupid of me to allow Leora to come along for this. What was I thinking? The truth is, I wasn't thinking about keeping her safe. I was thinking more about one upping stuffy Jabil by granting Leora her independence. My muscles tense, retired coils ready to spring into action. The men file from the shadows. They aren't carrying anything that I can see. It's too dark to make out their individual features, and many are wearing baseball hats or ski masks with the brims pulled low.

These men could very well be fathers, husbands, brothers, sons . . . lawyers, doctors, politicians. Not much more than a week ago, this gang could've been upstanding citizens who prided themselves on keeping the neighborhood watch. But now — *now* — they're beginning to panic, to turn rogue out of desperation and fright. Now they realize food might soon become scarce, and their families could starve before their eyes. Therefore they're seeing this mode of transportation as the golden ticket to domination of the food supply, and survival, which means they will do everything they can to steal it from us. Even kill or maim, when before they would've never thought themselves capable of such iniquity.

"Sit close, Leora," I murmur, my eyes fixed on the approaching line of men.

The length of her thigh presses against mine. I take the revolver from the holster and set it on my lap. The tense clack of the horse's shoes sparking over the asphalt can't cover me pulling back on the hammer — that sound of a gun preparing to fire as distinct as a dying breath. The men might be armed themselves, but the sight of my weapon still gives them pause. I squint into the blackness, trying to see the direction of their eyes and anticipate what they're preparing to do. Jabil doesn't say anything, but Henri leans over the wagon to also peer out at the men, as threatening and shriveled as a turkey buzzard.

The shortest of the group appears to be the ringleader, and I wonder if he held this position before the EMP, or if the decimation of the law has placed his shady qualities in a whole new light. He swaggers toward us — potbelly thrust forward, thick shoulders squared — and the men automatically fall back into a V. "How you boys tonight?" he asks in a genteel voice. If he wore a hat, he'd tip it. His hair is cropped close to his head and dyed black to cover up the gray, so that his receding hairline looks smeared against his anemic skin. He has on a biker T-shirt with coppery flames, dress pants, and cowboy boots. Snakeskin boots, I surmise, simply because he looks like the type to wear them.

"Wait — you sure no boy I ever seen." He grins with a mouthful of teeth too white and uniform to be real. The ringleader moves closer. The moon pokes out from behind a cloud and reveals the direction of the man's gaze, as it lingers over the taut angles of Leora's face balanced with curves, which somehow reveal the attractiveness her glasses and shapeless cape dress cannot hide. "Where you come from?" He raises one bushy silver eyebrow. "A time capsule?"

Two of the men laugh and inch closer to the ringleader . . . closer to us.

Beside me, Leora keeps her chin raised. But I can feel how she shakes.

"You all need to keep moving," I say.

The ringleader steps forward. "You're the ones who came into *our* town. So don't think you got the right to tell us which way to head."

"Last I checked," I say, "the town wasn't owned by a group of thugs."

"Well, boy —" his eyes shrink to a glint — "time to check again." He pauses, turns to his group. "What you think they should pay us for passing through? How 'bout they give us this here contraption? I ain't seen too many wagons rolling around tonight."

"It's not worth much," Jabil says, the first he's spoken.

"That right?" the ringleader asks. "Actually, I think it is. And you know what else I think? I think you're trying to pull one over on us." The ringleader moves closer. A henchman follows like an overfed shadow, his eyebrows so bushy and glowering, they almost distract me from the hair missing from his oval-shaped head. One lousy revolver isn't going to be enough to protect us, and I feel sick to my gut, knowing I've exposed Leora to these lowlifes.

I'm trying to figure out how to take the henchman, and then the ringleader, considering I'm not up to par because of my hurt foot. But then, out of the corner of my eye, I see Henri turn in the wagon and reach under the feed sacks. He pulls out a twelve-gauge shotgun as smooth as an assassin and growls, real low, "You got five seconds flat to hightail it from here." He clicks the safety off with one gnarled old thumb, but his face says that he's very capable of pulling the trigger. Twenty pairs of eyes are locked on two barrels. Nobody blinks. "Git," Henri says, waving the shotgun like he could care less if it accidentally goes off. The men nod and begin reversing into the alleyway with their palms raised.

"Hey — you," Henri calls. The ringleader looks over his shoulder. "Yeah, *you.*" He taps the barrel of the shotgun, then smiles. "What's in that there shirt pocket of yours? Cigarettes?" The ringleader rolls his eyes, then fishes in his shirt pocket. He tosses a pack through the air and they land in the back of the wagon, cushioned by the sacks. "Much obliged," Henri says.

The ringleader murmurs, "You'll pay for that," before he slips, like a rat, into the alley between the walls.

CHAPTER 6

LEORA

I take a sip of coffee and watch the peach-colored sun melt the fog that softens the edges of the community like a low-hanging cloud. But I haven't been awake long enough, or slept long enough since our return from town, to appreciate this beauty. The door opens behind me. I turn, expecting to see *Grossmammi,* who's always been an early riser. But Melinda is the one who stumbles like a sleepwalker across the porch and leans against the railing. Her hair is disheveled, her eyes livid red slits peering out of a wan face. As far as my knowledge, this is the first time she's been outside since she moved in.

"Would you like some coffee?" I hesitantly ask. "We have some sugar left."

Melinda's laughter is so laced with bitterness that it's hard to hear. "I need something a little stronger than coffee."

Yesterday, I worked up the nerve to enter the living room and change the sheets on the couch bed. I also worked up the nerve to inspect her prescription bottle while I was there. When Melinda first arrived, the tiny blue pills appeared to be a full month's supply. Now, nine days post-EMP, she has only enough to last her until the end of the week. I have little tolerance for someone who relies on escapism to dull their pain. But whenever I feel frustrated with Melinda, I try to remind myself that being around our family must bring the loss of her own family back, not to mention the loss of being able to come and go as she pleases.

She whispers beside me, "I wish I were dead."

How do you respond when someone makes such an admission? Any uplifting platitudes would sound dull since I have no hope to offer. So I say nothing. I stand beside her in silence and stare down at my coffee, which seems a frivolous indulgence in comparison to her plight. When I risk glancing over at her again, she's looking at the sun without blinking, as if she's willing it to permanently burn memories from her mind's eye. The stark illumination reveals the faint etching of lines around her mouth, the freckles spanning the bridge of her nose, the unruly hair reclaiming her perfectly shaped brows.

The building blocks fortifying Melinda's life — her family, her money, her power — have been demolished, leaving her standing in the center of the devastation, bare and exposed. I cannot claim to possess any of the assets she has in abundance, but I *do* have a family. Despite our brokenness, they bring me security. It hurts me to envisage standing where Melinda's standing right now, knowing that this security is gone, that this is both the beginning of a life . . . and the end. "I'm sorry," I murmur. "I know this hasn't been easy for you."

Melinda finally closes her eyes, the lashes fluttering against the changing light like moths. Tears cling to the individual strands, but she looks upward at the sky's faint tracing of stars and doesn't let them fall. "Thank you," she says, and then turns and walks back into the house, closing the door so quietly that I think, for a moment, I dreamed her standing beside me.

Jabil must've been watching our interaction. Less than five minutes after Melinda goes back inside, he crosses the field with a scythe across his shoulder. His suspenders are straight and his hair is combed. But his eyes — even from this distance — are bloodshot. I wonder if he misled his family, telling them he wanted to get an early start cutting the hay field between our houses, and yet I fear he *really* wants to talk to me again about combining our homesteads.

My mouth goes dry as I watch him tread through the grass, his footprints cutting a darker pattern as they strip away the dew. Forcing a smile, I hold up my cup — diluted coffee, once more the only balm I have to offer — but he shakes his head. He sets the scythe down and climbs the porch steps. He doesn't offer a greeting, just looks at me with his signature austere expression before glancing toward the kitchen window that is backlit by the kerosene lamp.

"Someone reported seeing Moses leaving the community," he says. "My uncle and the deacons came over to our house this morning. To ask where he went."

"There is no crime in leaving. We are not on lockdown."

Mt. Hebron has no enforced curfew. But it's understood that nothing moral happens after midnight. Therefore, the only law we broke last night was illicitly entering the museum — and, discounting the jar of buttons Jabil poached for me, only the *attempted* theft of the tractors. Yet I know

146

there is more to it than that. It took only nine days post-EMP for me not only to violate physical boundaries, but also to violate my ethical parameters. This is why I had such trouble sleeping after our return from Liberty, even as my sister was nestled without fanfare in our bed. I can blather on about my desire to provide for my family, but the truth is that when life becomes hard, I am no different from my *vadder.* I am willing to do almost anything to avoid feeling out of control.

I glance down at my mug, but anything acidic would just combine with the acid climbing up my throat. Leaning over the rail, I dump the rest of the precious coffee on the ground, aware — even as I watch it seep into the earth — that I will soon regret the impulse when we have no coffee left. I ask, "Do they know we were trying to take a tractor?"

"No." He shakes his head. "I mean . . . yes. They know that Moses attempted to steal a vehicle, but he wouldn't say we were along."

Jabil studies me with those somber, dark eyes, but I am unable to decipher them. What do they convey? Sadness, jealousy . . . a fusion of both? He shifts his gaze away. "I overheard that they're thinking about expelling him from the community, allowing him to take only his belongings like the edict says."

My protective instinct rises up, righteous and maternal. "Forget the edict! He can't be expelled. He can barely walk! How's he supposed to survive in a place like we saw last night?"

Jabil shrugs. "He should've thought it through. We *all* should've thought it through. It was an unlawful attempt: trying to get ahead by taking what is not ours. If I could do it over, I wouldn't have gone along, and I wouldn't have let you go."

" 'Let' me go?" I repeat, incredulous. "Moses was right: it's not your place to tell me what I can or cannot do, Jabil Snyder, just as it was not your place to vote on my behalf. You know I'm not interested in courtship, and yet you *still* try to tell me what to do and think."

Jabil folds his arms, his eyebrows raised in shock. I take my glasses off and stare up at him in defiance, forcing him to blink first. He turns from me to stare down the lane, his breath coming out hard and fast. I feel a bittersweet satisfaction, knowing I have the upper hand.

The silence continues. I turn to stare down the lane as well, trying to comprehend how someone could've spied on us when we left so early in the morning, since even dairy farmer Elias Lehman would have been asleep. "Wait. Did *you* tell on Moses? Did *you* turn him in?"

Jabil doesn't say anything, only stares at the pilot's wreckage with his jaw throbbing.

"Are you jealous of him? Is *that* it?" I step closer until I can smell the unwashed tang of his skin. Our breaths rise, the morning sun knifing between our bodies. "You thought that because I turned you down, I must be going after someone else?" I stare at his profile until he looks over at me. Then, guiltily, he looks away. My body trembles with rage at the hypocrisy of this man standing before me, pacifist though he might be, who would wield his power to crush a man he perceives as his foe. It seems I know the real Jabil as little as he knows the real me.

He says, "I'm just trying to protect you."

"I don't need protecting."

Jabil pivots from me, his face stricken. "I hope you're right," he murmurs, so quietly that I have to strain to hear. We don't say anything else, just stare at the field between our two houses, as if joined and separated by the wreckage of Moses's plane.

■ ■ ■ ■

I cannot stay here once Jabil begins cutting hay, but neither can I go back inside to face *Grossmammi*'s inquisitive expression. So I cut across the yard and stride down the lane, not aware where I am headed, just aware that I need to put as much distance between Jabil and me as the community's perimeter will allow. The fog has mostly dissipated, yet the sun struggles to shine through the embellishment of stiff, meringue-white clouds. The workers' hammers ring across the valley like the repetition of a gong bidding us to come and dine on whatever food is to last us until planting season comes again.

The Snyders' chimney is devoid of its spool of smoke, the hitching post lacking the horse and buggy typically waiting in their yard, leaving me to assume that everyone has left. Perhaps Moses has left as well. My heart sinks at the thought, deeper within myself than I would care to admit. I should've never let him close enough to have that kind of power over my emotions.

I walk up the back porch steps, which are laid out identically to ours, and enter the kitchen after knocking on the screen door.

Moses is seated at the table, dust swirling in the natural light filtered through the smudged windowpanes. A plate of food is before him: sunny-side-up eggs with toast, tarnished pepper and salt shakers beside a tin cup of coffee. Other than the eggs, every bit of that fare should be rationed, and I wonder if anyone else in our community has reached that level of comprehension of what is soon going to be lost. But I imagine that Widow Snyder, Jabil's mother, would give Moses her last scoop of coffee grounds and granule of salt because she is as besotted with the pilot as I, regretfully, am.

"Hey, Leora," Moses says.

I don't look at him but focus on the backpack leaning against the wall beside the pile of scuff-toed shoes displaying the age range and sex of everyone living in this house — a backpack with a green bedroll attached to the bottom and a stainless-steel canister with a black, screw-on lid. This must be all Moses could salvage from his plane. I stare at these items, yet remain clinging to the doorframe. When I glance inside, Moses is watching me too.

"Where will you go?" I ask.

"Join the locusts, I suppose." He smirks, but his light eyes are dim.

"We were accomplices." My vison blurs,

voice breaks. "It's only right that if you get punished, we get punished too."

Moses shakes his head. "It was my idea. . . . Let me take the blame."

"I'm not just thinking of you." I point to the line of shoes, as if they are filled by the children who own them. "What will happen when the locusts come? When we only have three men in the whole community who are willing to fight back?" These are contradictory words for a pacifist. But suddenly my genuine convictions are unveiled, even to me: though I would probably never lift a hand in violence, I do not mind if others lift theirs to protect those I love.

"Maybe you should learn how to shoot."

"My *vadder* already taught me how to shoot."

Moses unfolds his hands and leans back in the chair. "Why are you so defensive?"

My eyes burn. I stare through the Snyders' window to our house, which my *vadder* painstakingly built and then abandoned. I look back at him. "Because you're cornering me."

"I'm just asking a question."

His doggedness is infuriating. Having nothing to lose, because he's leaving anyway, I snap, "If I'm defensive, it's because I have to prove my self-worth."

"Prove to whom?"

" 'Prove to whom'?" I laugh. "To myself, the community, strangers on the street. It doesn't matter *who* it is. I feel like someone's always judging me . . . about to take away everything I have left."

"Why would they do that, when you've done nothing wrong?"

"But I *have,* Moses. I was supposed to be watching Anna that day she fell in the barn, and she almost died because of me." I stop, hungry for absolution.

He says nothing. Reaching beneath the table, Moses brings up his revolver. He sets it on the table with a *thunk* that causes me to step back, as if the impact might cause the gunpowder to explode. "You weren't punished or a punisher, Leora. Pain happens. It's a fact of life."

He stands to holster the revolver. Then he stops — still holding the gun — and walks around the kitchen table, actually two tables turned lengthwise and pushed together so that all eight family members can sit in between the kitchen and the dining room during meals. He stands directly before me. A ray from the early morning light falls upon his head, igniting the blond hair with a tongue of fire. He holds the gun out in his cupped palms, an offering of reassurance, but it feels more like the apple Eve offered to Adam before the two of them fell.

"Think how you could protect your family," he says, "when these locusts come, or whoever comes bent on hurting you."

I don't look at him as I take the revolver and readjust my grip to accommodate the odd dimensions and weight. The metal is cool to the touch. I run one finger along the sleek bottom of the barrel until I come upon the trigger. I shudder, envisioning the sleek bullet, the catalyst that would launch from its chamber if I switched off the safety and pressed down. A curve of metal that possesses the power to extinguish a life. I look up at Moses and am unable to tell if he is evil or good. Perhaps he is neither; perhaps — like my *vadder,* like all of us — he is a mixture of both. I say, "God will protect us."

Moses takes the revolver from me, sliding it down into his holster and snapping the top. His impatience is evident as he asks, "What about King David? Wasn't he considered a man after God's own heart, even though there was blood on his hands?"

Once again, I am surprised by Moses's familiarity with the Bible, since that first day we spoke on the playground, he told me he was not a man of faith. Perhaps he has head knowledge, just not heart knowledge. But am *I* not the same? My pacifist viewpoints were solid only because they had never been rocked by real-world events. Now I have desecrated their foundation by taking a revolver in my hands. And yet, my Anabaptist ancestors were driven from their homeland without protest. They were burned alive without protest, some even singing as they walked toward the stake. How were they able to move knowledge from their heads to their hearts? Or did this conviction come only after they saw their companions' devotion and then felt the scorching heat of their own flames?

I stare into the middle distance over Moses's shoulder, envisioning every trial that has yet to take place. Eventually, thwarting the quiet, I reply to his comment about King David. "We're not living in Old Testament times. There's no more need for that kind of violence."

"So tell me," Moses says, leaning closer, his breath evocative of coffee and mint. "What would *you* do if someone came up that lane wanting to murder your family?"

His words, though gentle, hit me like a blow from the hand. I stare at Moses Hughes, again trying to discern whether God sent him here to keep us safe, or whether he is being used by a malevolent force determined to destroy our community from the inside out. And yet . . . how would it feel to be able to protect my family in the way I have always longed to? Just because I harbored a weapon, it wouldn't mean that I would have to inflict violence. . . .

I can feel Moses watching me, searching my face for a sign of what I am about to say. But even *I* do not know what I'm about to say. I just know I cannot imagine taking another's life, even to preserve the lives of my family.

"I don't think I could do it, Moses." I swallow a sudden welling of tears for the second time today. "If someone came up that lane intending to harm my family, I would first invite them into our home and I would prepare a meal for them. We would sit around the table, give thanks, and talk. If, afterward, they wanted to take my life, *our* lives, even after we've been so kind to them, then — I guess — so be it."

Moses peruses me, aghast, and then he looks down at the scarred hardwood floor. "Well — I would say you're a far better person than I am. But I'm not sure whether allowing someone to come into your home and destroy your family is wisdom or foolishness."

Moses picks up his backpack and slips his arms through the straps.

"You are going to leave?" I ask. "Just like that?"

"The Snyders said good-bye this morning, before they left for work at Field to Table." As if I am not worthy of a good-bye at all.

He moves into the foyer and opens the front door. I gaze at him and at his backpack, edged by the frame. For an instant, I contemplate leaving with Moses, knowing my future is insecure whether I go or stay. But I know it would be selfish to leave. My family needs me.

Moses steps onto the porch. I come outside. The screen door taps shut. It is strange to stand on the front porch of the house Jabil would have me occupy, and instead stand by someone I know he does not like, mostly because he perceives Moses as a threat against him. Against *us*.

Moses and I peer out at the community, our thoughts muddled by everything that has — and hasn't — been said. I wonder if his knowledge of the EMP has him envisioning where we will all be in a year: Malnourished? Displaced? Scraping by on the remnants of what we harvested this year? It's hard to foresee where Mt. Hebron will be by then; it's scary to wonder who will compromise their ethics in order to remain.

At the entrance of the community, the Mennonite men are working side by side with the *Englischers* whom we did not know nine days ago. And, honestly, whom we do not know now. From this vantage point, you cannot see any nuances in their appearances, only their joint zeal to fortify the perimeter by nailing coils of old barbed wire along the top — knowing that wire alone cannot stop intruders but will at least slow them down.

The Mennonites are going against the bishop by not leaving the construction project to the *Englisch.* But this is no rebellion. My Mennonite neighbors began working on the perimeter yesterday when, according to Moses's timeline, they realized we are soon going to need protection from the locusts who are rumored to be coming.

Moses adjusts his pack and begins descending the steps. He turns and raises his hand to shield his vision. Through the lattice of his fingers and the shadows they create, I can see the brilliant hue of his eyes. "Thanks for everything."

I nod, powerless to speak. The pilot nods as well and begins walking up the lane. His stride is made uneven by a limp, though his ankle is almost healed, so I surmise it must come from some previous injury. I watch him traverse a few more yards — my own eyes shaded from the sun — and conclude that Moses Hughes is carrying far more baggage than what is visible on his back. In this, our unseen scars, he and I are the same. I look to my right, at my patch of land, where Jabil is cutting down the grass that would've soon withered in the field.

Our eyes meet. The scythe flashes in his hand.

MOSES

Holstering his hammer in his tool belt, Christian strides across the scaffolding. "Hey, Charlie," he calls. "You heard anything about letting the pilot past the perimeter?"

Charlie adjusts his grip on the rusty twist of barbed wire and looks down from the scaffolding, narrowing his eyes. "Haven't heard a thing."

I drawl, "Guess I'll just wait here then, until somebody gives y'all permission to kick me out." I slide down against the base of the logs. It's awkward to sit with a twenty-five-pound, military-issue monstrosity attached to my back. I have to lean forward, my knees almost touching my chest. Looking out at the community, I find it ironic that *I* am the one who thought up this gate, and now it's the very thing keeping me from getting out.

I wait for what feels like forever — and am about to ask one of the workers to boost me to my feet, so I can at least help with the fortification while I'm waiting to be exiled — when Jabil Snyder comes striding up, interlocking his fingers to push his work gloves back on. "Heard you need to talk to me?"

I stare up at him a second, still crunched in that position that's giving me a crick in my neck, trying to figure out what he's trying to pull. I'm not stupid. I know he turned me in to the bishop and deacons and whatever kind of crazy hierarchy they've got going on in this place.

Jabil doesn't blink as I keep looking at him. Then he sighs and offers me one work-gloved hand, pulling me to my feet. "There's been a change," he says. "You can stay."

I stop dusting off the seat of my jeans and look him full in the face, making sure my eyes can confirm what I heard. But Jabil doesn't say anything else, seems to regret what he's said already, so I know it's true. I can feel my temper rising at being led here and there, like I am nothing but a stray dog on a very short leash.

Then it comes together: Jabil watching me and Leora last night as we journeyed through town — his eyes observing everything in the darkness, his big hands holding tight to the reins.

"You never told them, did you?" I ask. "The bishop and the deacons, they don't know. You never even told me you *had* told them. You just implied that they wanted me to go because someone had turned me in — and like a fool, I believed every word you said."

Jabil doesn't confirm or deny any of it. But he doesn't have to. I feel like decking him for being such a punk — and yet, why would an upstanding guy like him lie to get me to leave? I think of Leora's insecure smile, and how she stares at people so hard behind her glasses, as if the clear lenses can somehow hide the direction of her eyes. Jabil looks at me like Leora did, with that same unwavering intensity.

I ask, "You must really love her, huh? If you'd go to all this trouble to get rid of me?"

For a second, I think Jabil's going to attack me. And then all the fight seems to leave him. His hands relax. He stares at his feet and says, "Don't make me regret changing my mind."

"But why'd you change it?"

He looks down the lane, his forehead ridged with furrows as deep as those marking the field. "Because the community needs you more than I need you to stay away from Leora."

Adjusting the strap of my backpack, I reach out and clap my right hand to Jabil's left shoulder. His muscles contract beneath my fingers, the strap of the suspender like a cable about to snap loose. "Brother," I say, staring hard into his eyes, "I am no competition. Just a drifter . . . passing through. As soon as we can figure out this new world of ours, I'm gone."

Jabil nods, but I can tell he doesn't believe me. Which part? I wonder. The part about not being his competition, or the part about just passing through?

I grin at him and clap him once more on the shoulder before letting go. "And I wouldn't give up on Leora just yet, Romeo. Star-crossed lovers are birthed through times like these."

He keeps looking right at me as he says, "I know. That's what I'm afraid of."

I squint against the noonday sun and break another top off a glass bottle with a hammer. I hear Charlie call out, "Here we go."

Curious, I look up at the scaffolding to see that he's stopped embedding glass into the sharpened points of the perimeter and is peering over the other side.

I say, "What is it?"

"Some girl with a baby." Charlie mops his face with a bandanna and looks back at the line of men, who've all stopped working as well. "Y'all think I should let her in, don't ya?"

Jabil blows sawdust from the porthole he's hand-drilling into the perimeter. Looking out through it, he says, "Doesn't matter how much food we hoard. If our community doesn't care for the widows and the fatherless like Scripture instructs, we will not be blessed."

Unmoved, Charlie doesn't open the gate. "This is just the first one," he says. "How many more times am I gonna have to let people in? We agreed that we'd give them water. We never said we'd let them walk right in 'cause they knocked." He makes no effort to lower his voice, which I am sure carries over the gate. This is probably his goal.

"Charlie, shut up," I call. "Open the gate."

He stares down at me, his eyes glittering like the bottle-blue and green shards. Then, to my surprise, he jerks up the giant bolt that works kind of like a sliding lock. With a push, the left half of the tin-covered doors creaks open wide enough for one person to get through. This is smart of him, in case vagrants are hiding on the other side of the road, waiting to breach the gate, but at what point are we really going to start turning people away? Right now, in spite of Charlie's complaining, food is not a problem. We have an abundance of dry goods through Field to Table and canned goods stored in the families' cold cellars. But even abundance has its end.

The men silently watch the woman and child come through the gate, and I'm sure their wielded hammers, handsaws, and drills make a violent first impression. I recognize the woman right away, mostly because she's wearing the same clothing she was wearing when we met her in town. She is smaller than I remember, her spine weighted with a cheap backpack that is so stuffed, the zipper will not fully close. She glances around at the men, hugging the baby tighter, fear in her eyes. I can tell she wonders if she fled town only to find refuge in a place that is no refuge at all.

I break away from the workers in an attempt to assure her we're not as dangerous as we look. "Hey," I say, smiling. "I'm

Moses. The women are all working over at Field to Table." I point to the long log cabin within walking distance of the gate. "You can go up there if you want; they'll help with whatever you need."

The woman is quiet for so long, I would begin to doubt she knows English if I hadn't heard her speak to Leora the other night. Then she says, so abruptly that it catches me off guard, "On my way here, I saw a group making an assembly line down at the river. They were using buckets. But they don't know if the water's clean." She pauses. "Do they?"

"If it *was* clean," Charlie calls, eavesdropping from above, "it's probably not now."

Giving Charlie a look, which he returns with venom, I touch the woman lightly on the sleeve. She flinches, drawing her arm against her body as if it's hurt.

"I was just on my way to Field to Table," I say, acting like her behavior's normal. "Would you like me to introduce you to the women of the community?"

She nods, cupping the child's head to her chest. He's in a sling that looks like it was made from a bedsheet. As we walk past the gate, there is only the sound of construction and our shoes crunching over gravel. "What's your name?" I ask.

"Sal." She adjusts the sling, pulling a knit hat over the child's ears, though it's warm outside.

"What's his name?"

"Colton."

She's sure not one for small talk, so I say nothing else as we draw closer to Field to Table. The bustling women in their somber dresses and filmy, winged *kapps* remind me of worker bees eager to gather every ounce of sustenance before the window of time runs out. The glass doors of the building are propped open with fifty-pound sacks of rice. I wonder how long until rice — the most consumed and plentiful provision in the world — becomes priceless. A few weeks? A few months? Everything's going to get harder, too, as we draw closer to winter, and the land isn't able to compensate for the stores' lack.

"Do people know the community's out here?" I ask.

Sal studies me from the corner of her eye. "Yeah."

"Then why haven't they come, begging for food or trying to steal it?"

"Far as the begging goes," she says, staring down at the sacks of rice, "guess they have more pride than I do. As for the stealing . . . I'd say it's only a matter of time."

Stepping to the side, I let Sal move past me into the dry goods store. So many women are coming in and out that, at first, our entrance doesn't draw any attention. But then I see Leora. She's sitting on an overturned crate next to a large plastic bucket, holding the bucket's foil liner by the edges, while her younger sister, Anna, fills it with rice from a sack. Anna is concentrating on every scoop, her tongue clenched between small white teeth. Colton whimpers in Sal's sling, and Leora lifts her head, scanning the aisles for the child like a mother would. Her eyes land on me. The bag quivers in her hand, spilling irreplaceable pellets of rice across the floor, reminding me of the weddings I have attended where — out of ignorance or apathy — they tossed rice at the bride and groom instead of birdseed. One of the countless wasteful traditions that makes no sense after the EMP.

"What *is* this place?" Sal asks. "A grocery store?"

Breaking our stare, Leora looks down again, her ears bright against her *kapp.* I can't tell if she is pleased or irritated by my reappearance. "Kind of," I tell Sal absently. I glance around. Rows of shelves are faced with canned goods like lima beans, black beans, mixed vegetables, potatoes, diced tomatoes, and condensed milk. Each item is priced with an orange sticker, and some of the cans are dented around the rim. There is even a freezer and refrigerator section, both of which have already been cleared out. There is a produce section, also emptied. A shelf full of colorful glass jars is beside another shelf with nuts, dried fruit, and old-fashioned ribbon and horehound candy wrapped in bags and secured with twist ties.

In the back of the store is a grouping of two-seater tables covered with gingham tablecloths. There is a dispenser of K-Cups of coffee and tea and a blackboard featuring — in different colors of chalk — the menu from ten days ago: a roast beef, horseradish, and cheese sandwich on homemade bread with a baked good, pickle, and a hot or cold drink for $5.99. I imagine commuters stopping by to fill up on fresh-from-the-oven baked goods and mediocre coffee. Will they remember this place? All of the meats, cheeses, produce, and canned goods? Will they try to make it back here and see if anything's left? One thing's for certain: only time will tell.

"Hold on a sec," I tell her. "I've got to speak to someone."

Leora says as I approach, "Thought you'd

be gone by now."

I say, simply, "Me too."

"Is that the woman from town?"

I nod. "Her name's Sal. She and her little boy just came through the gate."

"Charlie let her in?"

"Yeah. But not because he wanted to."

Leora checks that all the grains of rice are tucked inside the foil bag lining the bucket, drops an oxygen-absorber packet on top of them, takes a rubber mallet, and pounds the lid closed. She walks around the canned goods aisle over to where Sal stands.

"Hi there," Leora says. She strokes the sole of the baby's socked foot dangling from the sling. Feeling my gaze, she glances over. I don't know what thoughts are taking place behind those glasses, and she doesn't say anything to reveal them. Someone calls my name. Leora turns from me, and Jabil is standing there, his broad shoulders filling up the doorway and casting a shadow across the floor.

"Moses," he repeats. "We need you at the gate."

Sal says, "Are people coming?"

I turn from Jabil and see her ruddy skin tone has blanched to a flat white.

"It's not your fault," I tell her. "We've been expecting them for days."

Jabil says to me, "You ready?"

I clear my throat. "I am." Which is a lie. I haven't been ready for something like this since our recon mission in the desert, after which they shipped me home with PTSD.

CHAPTER 7

LEORA

Though she is inside the gates, the *Englischers* still consider Sal an outsider — a person who, ironically, is one of their own. Therefore, she is required to go to the *dawdi haus* that has been converted into a hospital, where she will be asked a series of questions by Deacon Good. I don't care for this method of sorting out those who are an asset to the community from those who shouldn't be allowed to stay. I understand we have a limited food supply, and each person should have to work for whatever rations he gets. But I'm unsure which category, in the eyes of the *Englischers,* Sal and her son belong to.

Inside the Beilers' cramped *dawdi haus,* the dark wood and blackout curtains — so patients will be able to rest during the brightest hours of the day — make it appear more like an old-world tavern than my memories of the hospital where Anna spent so many months with occupational therapists.

Sal and I approach Deacon Good's desk. She doesn't flinch when he looks up from his paperwork and begins asking her a series of questions, to all of which she has ready answers.

"Full name?"

"Sally Jean Ramirez."

"How old are you?"

"Eighteen."

"Previous place of residence?"

She just looks at him, eyes sparking. "Montana."

"Yes. Of course." He jots something down. "Any relatives living in the area?"

"My uncle and grandmother. They're the only ones I've got left . . . besides my son."

"Their names, please?"

"Mike and Papina Ramirez."

I can feel Sal watching me, but when I glance over, her eyes are downcast, her teeth worrying a flake of dead skin on her bottom lip.

"And what was your occupation before . . . ?" Deacon Good lets the words hang.

"A . . . healer."

The hesitation is long enough to raise my suspicions. When I look up at Deacon Good

174

— his pen paused, mid-transcription — I can tell that he is studying her face to judge if she is lying as well. "What kind of healer?"

"My grandmother's Kutenai. She taught me which herbs to gather for poultices and tonics and dyes. She was a midwife and told fortunes —"

Deacon Good holds up his hand, but smiles. "We won't be needing that kind of assistance." Despite his gold-rimmed glasses and penchant for learning, his fingers are stained and blistered from where he's been working side by side with the men.

Sal's baby writhes, discontent with being lodged so tightly against her chest. She adjusts him and looks up again, first over at me and then at Deacon Good. "I promise you — my grandmother taught me everything she knew. She *raised* me. I know these woods behind your property like the back of my hand." Sal continues when Deacon Good doesn't respond, her words propelled by her desperation. "I heard people in town talking about coming out here and doing drives to push out the game in your woods to armed standers."

"It hasn't even been two weeks," I interject. "Surely they're not desperate enough to start poaching and killing for food."

Sal shrugs. "Food's running out, and it

doesn't look like Walmart's going to be restocking anytime soon."

"What about that large beef farm over on Willow?" asks Deacon Good.

Sal nods. "Mayor Ramsey tried asking if they'd sell a few head of cattle to the town — had money and everything — but they wouldn't take it. Said money was of no use to anyone. That they needed to come with stuff to barter. But I think they *really* know they'll be sitting pretty if they wait 'til we're desperate enough to give them anything they want." Sal stops, holds her child's dimpled fingers like she's drawing comfort from him rather than supplying it. "Mayor Ramsey finally went and used the money to buy grain off the feed supply; the price was jacked up, but the owners believe that the 'lights' or whatever are gonna come back on and money's still gonna have its use. Ramsey said if things get bad enough, grain is grain . . . even if it was supposed to be used for cattle."

I look at the child, beginning to nod off in Sal's arms. His cheeks are full, his arms and legs plump. Yet I am sure his mother envisions him three months from now — emaciated and too succumbed to perpetual hunger to put up a cry. For his sake, she set her pride aside, accepted my invitation, and came here to us . . . only to find she has to jump through numerous hoops in order to stay. "That's horrific that the beef farmers won't sell," I murmur. "To have the power to help someone and not do it —"

Deacon Good interrupts, "Even here, Leora, in *our* community, we're finding that we're at war with our own flesh. We want to help people by providing good nutrition and medical care. But on the other hand, we also want to preserve ourselves."

"So . . . I can stay?" Sal asks. "Since I can help with medical care?"

"For the time being," Deacon Good says. "But at this point, I can't promise how long."

Our community desperately needs someone who understands the conundrum of the body better than most of us do; therefore Sal's occupation as healer could not be more fitting if she were responding to a Help Wanted advertisement. That being said, I can tell Deacon Good is unsure of what kind of "healing" Sal can provide. Our heritage is all too familiar with the German powwow doctors, whom Mennonites and Amish sometimes called into sick rooms, knowing such dark practices went against their religious beliefs, but when faith and traditional medicine failed them, they were simply too desperate to care. Does Sal's Kutenai heritage rely on the same chants and archaic fallacies in order to bring healing? If so, I know her already-perilous position will not be held in our community for long.

Deacon Good marks one of the small, spiral-bound notebooks I've seen at Field to Table with a check stamper, also from Field to Table: the place where, before *Vadder* left, I used to work in the summers, and after, I used to go with Anna to help break up our days. The notebook and stamp have clearly become the community's passport and seal. When was this decided? And does Jabil know? I understand that unprecedented events are taking place, and so the Mt. Hebron leadership is being forced to make unprecedented decisions. But without our leadership being accountable to the spiritual hierarchy back in Lancaster — for how can they be, without a telephone or the postal service to help them communicate? — I fear that we will be subjected to whatever governing whims the bishop and deacons believe necessary. Even if they're not.

Deacon Good slides the stamped notebook across the desk. "Keep that with you at all times," he instructs Sal. "As our numbers grow, there'll be random checks to make sure every *Englischer* within the community has gone through the screening process."

I stare at him in disbelief, perplexed how — in ten days — fear has driven us from open doors to anyone in need to here: keeping those doors closed unless the *Englischers* can provide something of use. And yet, haven't I *also* feared that there won't be enough supplies to sustain us until the next harvest season? Haven't I *also* considered breaking the rules and hoarding food instead of sharing it equally within the community, so that if it comes right down to it, my family will survive while Jabil Snyder's family — right next door — may starve?

Sal, however, does not seem appalled by our community's lack of charity. "Where will I stay?" she asks, lifting up her parka to slide the notebook into the back pocket of her jeans.

Deacon Good glances at me. I nod, despite our home having reached maximum capacity with Melinda. He says, "Thank you, Leora. You'll receive extra rations to compensate." The immediacy of these rations, I'm ashamed to say, is far greater reward for opening my home to Sal and her child than any heavenly treasure I am bound to receive.

With this news, Sal and I exit the *dawdi haus* and head back up toward Field to Table. Passing the community's entrance, she says, "Those are some impressive-looking guns."

I have heard that *Englischers* sometimes use the term *guns* colloquially in reference to arm muscles. But when I glance over, I see Sal is using the term in the literal sense. Charlie, Henri, and Sean, with their weapons, are tucked behind sandbags lined along the front of the platform.

I ask, "You like guns?"

"No. But I like what they can do. They got ammunition to go with them, or they just for pretty?"

I stop walking and glance over at Sal, wondering why a healer would be so preoccupied with weaponry. She stops walking as well and smiles, revealing a dimple burrowed in her left cheek. "Sorry," she says. "I'm just trying to figure out how secure this place is before I move in."

I consider telling her that guns and ammunition cannot guarantee our protection from the locusts. That God alone is the one in whom we can trust. Then again, I've been spoon-fed pacifist doctrine all my life, and I'm not sure its precepts would be so easily digested by someone who carries a street-wise aura probably acquired through a diet of hard knocks.

I say instead, "I'm not sure how much ammunition they have. If they have any at all. Those guys up there don't really share that kind of information with me."

"Because you're a woman?"

"No. Because I'm a pacifist."

Sal raises one eyebrow. "Like a hippie?"

"I think of *hippie* as a political term. *Pacifist* is more of a religious term. The people who practice it wouldn't take up arms to defend themselves, no matter what."

She snorts. "Trust me, these so-called pacifists will be surprised how fast they'll be singing a different tune when all that's standing between them and death are some standards."

I flinch. Sal doesn't know I'm already singing a different tune. That I am declaring my convictions with a confidence I do not possess, as I prepare to stand between starvation and my family. In addition, a true pacifist would never defend herself, as that undermines the principles of self-sacrifice pacifists try to proclaim through actions instead of words, since the adage is true and the former — actions — speak more loudly. So, what *do* I believe if I would be willing to take up arms to threaten someone's life, even if I would not be willing to take that life into my hands? This is sobering to ponder, especially considering the next few months are going to test my every value — proving, once and for all, whether pacifism is not just a collective belief, but my personal belief as well.

My brother, to put it mildly, isn't too enthused that our new roommate is a girl. "Why can't we ever get a cool *Englischer,* like Moses?" he grumbles.

I knock on the thin wall separating the living room from the laundry room, where we're in the middle of preparing his bed. "What if Melinda hears you?"

He rolls his eyes. "She wouldn't hear a bomb go off."

His snarky comment doesn't translate well in these uncertain days, when we have no idea who's attacked us with the EMP and if we're going to be attacked again, perhaps with a bomb whose devastation will be visible and immediate rather than invisible and growing worse over time. Regardless of the times, I shouldn't let Seth get away with such insolence. But a part of me wants to let it slide because I'm thankful that, though he's old enough to crave a masculine presence, he's too young to like being outnumbered by women.

I tell him, "We're called to serve anyone who crosses our path, not just the ones you think are 'cool.' " I cringe at how superior this sounds. I've never been the kind of fun big sister little brothers like to be around, and lately it seems that Seth isn't only *not* enjoying my company — he is avoiding it. Then again, I think he's been avoiding every person in this house.

Seth is all long bones and joints, like an artist's quick sketch of a body in motion. He collapses this body onto the pallet with graceless ease and mashes the pillow behind his head. "Moses crossed our path first, and he's not staying here."

"He *can't* stay here. That wouldn't be proper."

"Since when's this family been concerned with 'proper'?" His derision seems overblown, considering he only had to give up his closet-sized room to Sal and Colton. But I remember being his age, and how I viewed my room like the calm eye in the center of our household storm. This storm has abated since our *vadder*'s disappearance, which brought me equal measures of relief and guilt, because how could a daughter be happy her *vadder* was gone?

I wonder if Seth's anger and avoidance

183

stem from something more complicated than missing his privacy. Perhaps he is so keenly aware of being outnumbered by women because, like Jabil said, he needs a male presence to compensate for his father's absence. I sigh and kneel beside Seth's pallet, composed of two folded quilts our deceased maternal grandmother made before I was born. I wonder if they were wedding or housewarming gifts. If so, their peacemaking properties must not have worked because my *mamm* never had much of a relationship with her family after she went against their wishes by marrying Luke Ebersole.

I tell Seth, keeping my voice to a whisper, "What if I talk to Jabil about you sleeping at their house? You would have to come over here for meals, to keep the rations the same, but that way you wouldn't feel like you're living in a girls' dorm."

"Whatever, I don't care." Oh, that classic teenage response. I want to shake Seth's ungrateful shoulders until his teeth clack, but — maybe because of this — I reach out and gently touch the soft ducktail at the back of his neck, which never conforms to the community's standard bowl cut. "Stop treating me like a baby," he says, turning toward the cellar door.

Then stop acting like one. The sarcastic response is primed on my lips, probably because I'm a teenager as well. "I'm sorry," I murmur instead. "I know you're not a baby."

Rising to my feet, I leave the laundry, but keep the door open a few inches so the poorly insulated room won't get too cold during the night. I look in on Seth and see, by the moonlight coming through the window, that his narrow shoulders are shaking. My brother is caught somewhere between fear and anger, child and man, and though I know he must find his way out, I don't want him to make that perilous journey alone.

I move closer to the gate in the light morning rain, clutching my small basket of egg sandwiches I made for Jabil as an excuse to talk to him about Seth. Jabil and Moses look up at my appearance. Their gazes are so intense that I halt in my tracks.

But Moses beckons me over. It is then that I hear the hum of human voices, rising and falling in discordant notes. The locusts? My ears ring, as if attempting to drown out the sound. Wordlessly — for who can speak over the clamor? — he hands me a pair of binoculars and points to a porthole in the logs that was apparently drilled for observation. I set the covered basket down in the dirt beside the perimeter and dry the binoculars on my apron before peering through them, sweeping left to right. Raindrops strike the flat stretch of asphalt, transforming the stark reality of people into a less fearsome mirage.

Though early August, many are wearing hats, scarves, and heavy wool or down-filled coats, the buttons and zippers straining to contain a winter's worth of layers. Most are rolling suitcases or carrying backpacks or bundles of blankets and clothes, tied with bungee cords or whatever ropelike material they could find. Others are pushing carts no doubt pilfered from the two grocery stores in town and piled high with the detritus of life, pre-EMP: canned goods, a bag of dog food (the golden retriever happily gamboling alongside), even a set of golf clubs that I think is ridiculous to salvage until I realize the owner might be contemplating using them as weapons. I focus on one toddler boy who kicks his legs, threaded through the seat rungs of the cart. Though his hair and clothing are wet, he smiles and laughs, clapping his hands and banging on the handlebar as the grocery cart wheels rattle over the shining road.

To the child, this new way of life is only a

game, and I wonder how long his parents can keep up the facade. The woman pushing the cart — his mother, I presume — with her stooped back and empty expression, looks world-weary in a way I've never seen before. In eleven days, how can we have become refugees in our own native land?

I step back from the porthole, only having viewed a percentage of the multitude, and yet having seen more than enough. "You think they'll stop here?" I ask.

Jabil says, "They can't. Our resources wouldn't last a month."

"Can some of them stay, at least? Perhaps the ones with small children?"

"Leora." Moses accepts the binoculars and wraps them in a shirt. "Do you want to take these families in, knowing that — because you did — your own family might starve?"

Fury erupts inside my chest. Fury at Moses and fury at myself for having pondered this very question yesterday, but it seems far more brutal hearing my thoughts spoken out loud. "Whatever happened to providing water and soup and medical care to those in need?" I snap.

"Everyone who needs water and medical care will receive it," Jabil says. "But judging by that group out there, we cannot offer food."

I envision that toddler in the grocery cart, happy and plump, even while the woman pushing it looked haggard and thin. And then I understand: she is probably going without food so her child does not. I glance over my shoulder, searching outside Field to Table where Sal is working, and wonder if she did the same for her baby before she found hunger lowering her standards and driving her here. How many mothers are going to die for the sake of their children? I know if I were in their shoes, I would encourage Seth and Anna to eat while I remained hungry. There is honor in sacrifice, but where is the honor in turning people away?

I crouch and pick up the basket. Pulling back the damp tea towel, I show the men the warm squares of egg nestled between homemade bread. "We have eggs in abundance, and we still have wheat. We could at least give them one meal before we send them on their way."

Moses and Jabil look at each other without speaking, and then Moses says, "Leora, forgive me, but there's no nice way to put it: These people are either going to starve or

not; one meal's not going to make a difference."

"Yes, it *will*!" I cry, pressing a fist to my
chest. I recall the women in our community
coming to our house one at a time, one day
at a time, for a week after our *vadder*'s
disappearance — and then again after
Mamm was buried on Mt. Hebron land.
They would take tentative steps up our front
porch, their arms laden with cooking trays
bearing hot casseroles and pies. I'd seen
them do the same for Mt. Hebron families
recuperating from a birth or a death. We
had experienced neither with my *vadder,*
but we were as exhausted as if we'd experienced both. Tears sting my eyes. I dash them
angrily away. "What if that one meal provides a young mother with the strength to
walk one more mile, and because she can
walk one more mile, she is able to reach a
place of safety for her family? A place where
medical care and food are not dispensed
only to those deemed 'worthy' by the few
holding the power to give?"

Jabil and Moses glance at each other
again. "Leora," Jabil says, "you know as well
as I that no such place exists like that for
miles on the road where they're heading. . . .
But let me talk to Bishop Lowell." He sighs.
"I'll see what he can do."

Below, between the gaps of the three two-by-sixes we use to walk the scaffolding, I watch Jabil escort another group of fifty through the gate. The families look exhausted, but it is no wonder, considering that most of them aren't used to walking *one* mile, to say nothing of the ten they just walked to get here from town. One heavyset man mops sweat from his reddened face and collapses at the table, like we're nothing but an American café where he can order and be served his food. But he's a rarity. The rest of the refugees stand in a neat line in front of the table, where the women are serving egg sandwiches and bowls of soup. If I hadn't witnessed hardships like this before, just not in my homeland, I would weep as I watch one young boy devour a piece of bread and then wipe tear-dampened crumbs from his cheeks.

"Looks like we got trouble," Charlie calls from the other set of scaffolding.

Since Henri's off answering nature's call, I take hold of his rifle and peer down the scope. An old, beat-up blue Suburban is bouncing down the right-hand side of the embankment to avoid hitting the pedestrians who are waiting to enter the community and therefore clotting up the main road. None of it would seem too threatening except for the hawkish brute who's leaning out of the passenger side with a rifle of his own pointed up to the sky. Most of the people don't see him waving his weapon because the vehicle is driving right next to the wooded hillside that encloses the valley. But the few who are far enough in front of him — so that when they look back, they see the barrel of his gun — scatter like chickens having spotted a fox in the coop.

"Who's to say he's coming here for trouble?" I call over to Charlie. "I wouldn't be driving a vehicle down the road unless it was guarded too." Even as I say this, the tension inside of me mounts. I can see the driver now — this beefy-looking guy with sunglasses pushed on top of his head. The lenses glint as he turns to survey the perimeter. Our eyes meet, only for a second. Yet in that second, I know they're not just out for a joyride, but that they want what we have. They're young too. If I peer past the driver's attitude, and the passenger's gun, I can see that the two of them might be in high school.

I shift the scope to the left to follow the Suburban as it whips around in the road — making the people disperse in every direction.

Charlie yells down to Jabil, "Shut the gates!"

I peer at the soup tables and lane below and see Jabil and his brother Malachi frantically trying to usher the last of the fifty people inside the community before they have to close the gate. But the mass begins to panic. Grocery carts and backpacks are transformed into battering rams as people shove against each other, trying to force their way through. The Snyder brothers give up and press against them with the gate, but it's like trying to hold back a tsunami. I maneuver across the scaffolding boards, which bend beneath my weight, and look over the perimeter again. The Suburban is barreling right across the highway and up to our gate. The two boys probably started up their family's junker — old enough not to be affected by the EMP — much like we had in mind with the tractors at the museum in town. Bored and scared, they decided to pillage the countryside, hurting other citizens because they want to increase the odds of their own survival. Exactly the way gangs are born.

The passenger begins yelling and waving his gun. The sun makes it difficult to tell if other people are in the backseats of the vehicle. The crowd shoves harder against the gate. I hear something crack. The whole entrance might give way if someone doesn't divert their path soon.

I hear a gunshot from the Suburban. A whole swarm of people scream, fuel thrown onto the fire of pandemonium and terror. I reach again for Henri's rifle, but — across from me — I see that Charlie has his rifle in his hands. The gun recoils against his shoulder as he pulls the trigger.

When I glance over the perimeter, bracing myself for blood, I see that he's only shot out the left front tire of the vehicle, bringing it to a standstill. But the people are trapped between it and the closed gate. Nobody appears injured, so I guess the guy in the Suburban must have shot up into the air just to make a statement. One guy, around my age, moves to the edge of the riotous crowd. It is clear that he is trying to protect his young family behind him, and he doesn't budge, even when the raging jocks spill out of the vehicle. I watch his face lift in defiance as the driver with the sunglasses pulls a pistol and cracks the butt of it across the guy's temple.

I don't believe the jocks know that their tire burst because it was shot out, or that they are in the crosshairs of weapons resting steadily on the perimeter. If they did, there is no way they would be so ruthless and bold. I watch the father's body crumple to the lane. A woman, who must be his wife, tries to soothe their young daughter even as her own eyes are alarmed with fright. To my shock, the driver raises the pistol and aims it at the prostrate father, but we'll never know if he intended to kill him right where he lay. For Charlie pulls his trigger before the other trigger can be pulled, hitting the driver center mass and dropping him.

The guy from the passenger side jumps for cover behind the Suburban and aims his weapon toward the source of the gunshot. But he doesn't get a chance to shoot back. I watch the second guy's body collapse from behind his cover — which obviously did not cover enough — at the sound of another shot from Charlie. The crowd really starts to panic, probably envisioning their own bloodied bodies sprawled across the gravel leading up to the gate of a community known for its nonresistance. Well, it's not so nonresistant anymore.

"It's all right," I call over the perimeter. "Please . . . everyone remain calm as we take care of the wounded."

It's like shouting into the void. People are splitting off: some running back toward town, others moving around the idling

Suburban and the two bodies so they can keep pressing on to a larger city, where there is surely even greater violence taking place than the blood that's been shed here today.

"Keep watch over the gate," I call to Charlie, because I don't think he's the type who can pacify a crowd on the verge of stampeding. I scale down the scaffolding, having purposefully left Henri's rifle propped against the perimeter. I feel vulnerable without it, since I don't know who else is armed and may try to break through the gate just like those jocks did, but the sight of it would only serve to increase the crowd's anxiety.

Jabil is on the inside of the gate, and a few of the Mennonite men are with him. I see their fear and gather from it that they have no idea who's been shot or what just happened since the observation porthole is blocked by the bodies of the crowd.

"I think everything's okay," I tell them. "Charlie was forced to shoot two guys who were about to shoot a helpless father." I consider pointing out that they shot first, *not* Charlie, but this seems trivial in light of death. "I need through the gate," I say to Jabil. "I have to calm them."

He nods and instructs Malachi to help him lift the sliding bolt and heavy metal bar.

They open the gate just wide enough for me to squeeze through, and then I hear the bar slide back into place. Being on the other side of that gate fills me with a sense of defenselessness that I know the other people here must also be experiencing.

The two thugs are sprawled across the lane. Their blood is the first of much, I am sure, to taint this hallowed property. The driver is facedown; the passenger is on his back — the latter appearing asleep except for the neat bullet wound bored into his head. As I had guessed, both of them are wearing high school rings on the same fingers where wedding bands will now never be: one gaudy red stone, one blue. Leaning closer, I see the football and baseball insignias, and the year they expected to graduate, which will now never happen.

Once I compose myself and raise my gaze, I see the young wife cradling her husband's head in her lap. He is still bleeding from where he was pistol-whipped, but I know he will be okay. I stand to address the people. They're in such a frenzy, I have to whistle between my teeth to make them take notice of me. When they *do* turn their heads in my direction — many faces bearing traces of dirt and tears — I can't remember what I want to say.

Clearing my throat, I begin, "I'm here on behalf of Mt. Hebron Old Order Mennonite Community. If you'll please just calmly move back from the gate, we will work at allowing the elderly and those with young children to come in for soup and bread. I'm sorry, but none of you may lodge or camp here. If you would like, you can stay over there." I gesture to the field that used to be part of one big valley until the highway came through and cut it in half.

Charlie slips out of the gate behind me, and I watch the crowd's unease ripple outward, like a pebble tossed in a shallow pond. If I didn't know him, I'd be uneasy too. Then again, do I know him, really? With his dirty flannel shirt, unwashed hair, and gun slung over his broad shoulder, he looks like a mountain-man Rambo. Although the community is decently equipped to deal with the EMP, this place has certainly been no four-star suite. I know the stink of my construction sweat is almost as bad as Charlie's, but his body odor still forces me to move.

"You heard the man," Charlie says. The entire group immediately takes one step back. He turns to me. "Jabil says we gotta bring the bodies in and give them a proper burial." And I can tell he's just repeating orders he doesn't want to fulfill.

I turn my back to the crowd and lower my voice. "How're we going to bring them in?"

Before Charlie can answer, the left gate opens and Jabil comes out through it, carrying two stacked stretchers made from canvas and wood. When Jabil sees the bodies of the young men, his face goes white. He shakes his head, nostrils flaring. I think, *I know, I know.* For all the death I've seen, there's something downright appalling about having to bury some kids who were barely old enough to die for their country — and yet died one week after its collapse.

"Can you help me?" Jabil asks.

I nod and crouch, rolling the limp body of the driver onto the first stretcher and trying to straighten the limbs. The body is warm, but the eyes are glazed. I close the lids, as I have closed the eyes of many of my comrades. And of my brother. But this does not feel the same. Not at all.

Malachi slips through the gate, holding two bundled sheets against his chest. He snaps the blank sheet out over the body, calling to mind a surrendering flag, though I doubt such a flag would hold an ounce of weight in this new war. Charlie and Malachi grip the ends of the stretcher, and Charlie backs up until they fit the driver's body through the gate.

Meanwhile, Jabil kneels over the boy who was the passenger in the Suburban. He stares down at him a second and then strides across the stretch of pavement, where he retches in the grass with his hands on his knees. He stays like that for so long, I'm not sure — judging by his convulsing back — if he's crying or still throwing up. Perhaps both.

Then he turns and wipes his mouth with the sleeve of his shirt. He walks back over to me, his jaw set. His eyes are almost as lifeless as the boys'. "I remember him," Jabil rasps. "He used to come into Field to Table with his mom. That was . . . a long time ago."

Jabil doesn't need to hear that, over time, people can change, lose their innocence. He just needed to speak, to recognize a spirit that's passed on, so I don't say anything. I pick up the booted feet of the passenger's body and Jabil takes the shoulders. We carefully maneuver him on top of the stretcher before Jabil covers him with a sheet. The two of us bear the boy through the gate and set him down next to the other body. Jabil goes back outside and returns, escorting the young husband who was knocked unconscious, along with his child and wife.

I watch Charlie give Jabil a look, but he doesn't say anything, as he must know he's skating on thin ice as it is. Yes, he probably protected lives by extinguishing two; however, that's not always how you perceive it when you see dead boys lying beneath white sheets.

Leora comes over from the soup table, the ladle dripping in her hand. "Who got shot?" She looks around the group, and I can tell she's trying to make sure everyone's accounted for. Her eyes land on Jabil, and then they land on me. She lowers them and cups her hand beneath the ladle, catching every drop of broth like it's liquid gold. I know our supplies are diminishing. I wonder if Leora regrets her decision to provide nourishment for the first batch of strangers who came through the gate. But I am starting to learn that she's not the type to keep the last bowl of grain for herself if it means another person going hungry. I wonder if Leora's character being so different from mine is what draws me to her, like a magnet unable to resist the opposite charge.

Jabil says to Leora, "These men drove up to the gate with guns. They tried to intimidate the crowd by shooting, and they assaulted that man over there." He points to the guy whose head wound is now cinched with a strip of cloth. "Charlie shot them both. They died instantly."

By filling in the gaps of the story and calling the deceased *men* instead of *boys,* I can tell Jabil's trying to make this first foray into warfare not seem as ghastly as it actually is.

"I never knew it would come to this," Leora whispers. "At least not this soon."

In the distance, I hear Leora's sister calling for her with her unique cry of " 'Ora! 'Ora!" Leora wipes beneath her eyes and walks away. I watch her go, her shoulders slumped with defeat, and I find myself hoping warfare doesn't strip her innocence like it's stripped mine.

CHAPTER 8

LEORA

The boys who were shot yesterday were buried last night. The men placed their bodies in homemade caskets and lowered them into holes dug at the edge of the property, where the fence separates us from national forest land. I decided to come out here this afternoon while Anna takes her standard Sunday nap — a picture book tented on top of the covers and her arms outstretched, as if everything is the same as it has always been. I didn't realize, until crossing the lane away from our house, that this is the first time I've been alone since the EMP. For a moment I battle guilt, wondering if Anna will be all right without me. But I cannot watch her every second, protecting her from the outsiders and from my own people, whom — considering what happened right outside our gates — I am also not sure I can trust.

The small gravestone is marked only with my *mudder*'s name, Dorothy Ebersole, and not with the dates of her birth and death. Myron Beiler crafted the simple marker out of kindness, since there was nothing, not even a wooden cross, that we could afford. A few weeds have sprouted since I last tended the area. I pull them and leave in their place a fistful of Indian paintbrush — one of the wildflowers she always loved. I glance at the sunken mound, where her own pine box has settled, and try to picture the transformation that has taken place in heaven rather than the one beneath the earth.

I walk over to the new, unmarked graves, convex with soil. I am sure they are deep, just as I am sure the caskets were as sturdy as they could be, considering the necessary haste of burying the men within twenty-four hours after their deaths. Jabil never does anything halfheartedly, and I know from the guilt I saw lingering around his mouth last evening — when the men hitched up the wagon to carry the bodies across the field — that these burial rites were a kind of penance for such a careless extinguishing of two lives. I don't blame him for not stopping the shooting; I don't blame anyone. I merely think there must be another way to approach this end of our world.

I stand by the graves for some time, until the sun begins to descend behind the snow-covered mountain range and, like a parting gift, wraps the valley with a ribbon of fire. Then I look beyond the graves into the forest, thick with feathered pines and spruce, the ground adorned with leftover ferns and cones. I step closer to the fence, gripping the cold wire squares, and see — down the row — an intricate spiderweb waiting to ensnare the creator's prey. I understand that we could set traps. We could hunt and fish. We could gather roots and nuts and herbs. If what Sal claimed about herself is true — and not a scheme to remain on this property while everyone else is turned away — she should be the best person to help me discover what we need to survive.

Hope rouses in my chest as I stare deep into the forest. Then, next to a towering pine, I see a contrasting flash of white. I blink hard, wiping the crust of old tears from my eyes. The deer is exquisite, an albino more phantom than whitetail buck, and so unlike anything I've seen, I almost think the horrors of yesterday have distorted my mind. Its rack is symmetrical, the tines curling forward into lengthened points. The soft folds of its nostrils look darker compared to the blanched color of its fur. We stare at each other in the fading light, his hide rippling with the primal urge to run, even as his strange pink eyes remain affixed on me.

I know this deer is the one hunters have been seeking for years: the exotic creature left behind when the former fenced-in hunting reserve became national forest. Yet somehow he has remained — adapted and survived — despite the odd color of his own hide setting the odds against him. If he can survive, maybe our community can survive too, through compromise and adaptation. And thus, we must embrace this alliance with the *Englischers,* even if doing so means compromising everything about the sanctity of life that we've been taught.

I glance behind me — wondering, suddenly, if anyone else has contemplated coming to pay their respects to those who may or may not have intended to snuff out our lives, like a hand clamped over a candle flame. Not wanting the whitetail's survival uncovered, I clap loudly, my palms stinging with the impact. The buck snorts. His tail stands up, the white tip as elongated as a spear. He bounds into the woods without looking back. This is when I comprehend the buck has remained, adapted, and survived not despite having a community, but because he has none.

I walk up the porch steps and sit on the bench to remove my shoes, since the soles are clotted with mud from my graveyard vigil. I set them aside to dry and look up at my house. Illumined by the kerosene lamp, the picture window appears like a shadow box, framing my family as they sit up for a meal my *mudder,* of course, has not prepared. Sal, her son in her lap, has assumed my usual place at the head of the table. Anna and Seth are sitting across from each other. *Grossmammi* Eunice is sitting up as well. Watching the scene, I feel both pleased and heartsick. My family is capable of living without me; therefore, I can no longer hide behind them rather than embracing a future and a plan.

Sal says, when I enter the house, "Hope it's okay I made my way around your kitchen."

"Please —" I hold up my hand — "you're more than welcome to make yourself at home."

And she *is* welcome, though I typically abhor someone invading my territory — even someone who isn't a stranger. And food isn't the only way Sal has helped. She has been staying with us for less than forty-eight hours, and she has swept the house, beaten dust from the rugs, and organized the dried goods and meats and cheeses, which have been brought in from Field to Table, according to product and color, so I have to fight no compulsion to redo her work. Sal believes she must do these things to compensate for her stay. I would console her by saying this is not the case, yet I know it's true. Melinda — who must be sleeping — has not pulled her share of the weight, and so she should technically be ousted from the community. But the guilt I battle, because of how I first treated her, won't let me turn her in.

"Has Melinda been up yet?" I point to the living room door that is, once again, closed. Sal shakes her head and fills Seth's mug with coffee. I never let him drink coffee in case the myth is true and the caffeine stunts his growth — not to mention that it's right before bed. But Seth just watches me, his eyes crackling with defiance, and takes a sip. Some things aren't worth arguing over, especially since he seems to be purposely antagonizing me, and I don't want to give him the reaction he seeks. If he's being forced to face the responsibilities of adulthood, I guess he should be able to drink coffee like a man.

My *grossmammi* says, gumming around a spoonful of food, "They talked about the Four Horsemen when I was a girl, but I never thought I'd last long enough to see the end of times." Her words are muddled by mashed potato and by her native Pennsylvania Dutch accent, which hasn't lost its potency over the years, despite the different places she's lived. I'm sure this combination makes it next to impossible for Sal to understand her, and I am grateful. Nothing like mentioning the Four Horsemen of the Apocalypse to top off the night.

I leave my family to finish their meal in peace, as my stomach is too unsettled to join them, passing through the kitchen and opening the door to the living room. The space is fetid with the scent of trapped air and unwashed clothes, but it does not hold the same dark power it used to. Perhaps that's because there are too many current issues to remain debilitated by past events. I stride across the room and yank back the curtains. I have been patient with Melinda, but there's a point when I have to stop letting myself be treated like the proprietor of a hotel. I glance at the couch where she sleeps and see the pillow and crocheted afghan, which we lent to her, stacked on the left-hand side. The end table beside the couch is cluttered with a still life of breakfast remnants, the whole of which I brought to her this morning: apple peelings, a piece of jelly toast nibbled along the crust, a white ceramic mug whose interior is ringed with a tea stain, the bag withered on the saucer beside it. I turn and survey the entire room, searching for her or for something I may have missed.

Looking at the pillow again, I see a small white square stamping out the embroidered background. I walk over to the couch and peer down at the pillow, finding a note written on a piece of stationery Melinda must have found in the desk. I pick the note up and study the erratic penmanship, for a moment unable to form the letters into words: *Thanks for everything,* it reads, *but just waiting here is killing me.*

There is a lump in my throat I would've never thought Melinda could summon — despite our moment on the porch, when I viewed her unshed tears. It's not only because she's left; it's because I don't know what's going to happen to her now that she's reentered our disjointed society. We could've figured something out if she had spoken with us. I regret not telling her those hollow platitudes, for offering someone false hope is better than offering them no hope at all. But maybe it wasn't my silence that drove her away; maybe she just couldn't handle the strain of separation from her family and decided it would be better to risk everything instead of moldering in a stranger's house, marking the infinite hours of her life with pills.

I close the door behind me, strangely calm in the wake of Melinda's departure. Sal, *Grossmammi* Eunice, and Seth look up. Baby Colton and Anna — who is stabbing her carrot with a fork — are the only ones who remain oblivious to my face, which must give my news away before I've had the chance to speak. "It seems . . ." I pause to breathe shallowly through my mouth. "It seems Melinda left sometime while we were at church."

Seth sets his coffee mug down at once and rises from the table. He pulls his hat over his shaggy brown hair. I move toward him and hold on to his arm, partially to show my affection and partially to emphasize the severity of the request I'm about to make. He stiffens under my touch but doesn't move away. How have I not noticed how tall he's grown? How handsome he's become? But I have to admit that he has been overlooked since long before the EMP.

Anna's special needs require so much attention that Seth has often been treated more like a cherished neighbor boy than a brother or a son.

"Find Jabil and ask if someone let Melinda through the gate," I intone. "If they haven't, she might still be around." My brother nods at my instructions and leaves, his purposeful stride such a mirroring of my *vadder*'s that I have to turn from the sight.

Sal meets my eyes, and I can tell she understands the severity of what has happened all on her own. If Melinda — as weak and dehydrated as she was — has already gotten past our gates, she is as close to death as if she had accidentally overdosed — her death the tragic end I had been preparing myself for whenever I entered that same dank room where I found my *mudder*.

I beckon Sal toward me, and she rises with Colton on her hip. I pull the living room door closed behind us and ask quietly, "Does Melinda stand a chance?"

Though I am at least three inches taller than Sal, I feel young and naive standing next to her. I find myself pondering — looking down into her black, bottomless gaze — what those eyes must've seen to possess such knowledge. "No single woman stands much of a chance these days," she says.

"That's why I had to leave town." Sal turns from me and switches her son to her other hip. "You mind if me and Colton move in here?"

I am so taken aback, I don't know what to say. Her request seems not only premature, but coldhearted, since we don't know if Melinda is truly gone. On the other hand, I got so distracted by the arrival of the refugees and the shooting that followed, I never got around to speaking to Jabil about Seth staying at their house. So for the past two nights, my brother has grumbled each time he's had to make his bed on the laundry room floor. If he were my son, I would teach him a lesson by making him sleep there even when his room opens back up.

But I am not his mother; I am his sister. I don't want to squander these uncertain days teaching him lessons I am barely old enough to learn. I want the kind of fun relationship with him I've never made the effort to have with anyone.

"I . . . suppose," I tell Sal. "You can sleep in the living room. But —"

"Great," she interrupts, smiling. "You think your grandma can watch Colton while I run to get some things from the apartment?"

Again her request surprises me. No one has ventured past the perimeter since the young men's deaths have set the community on edge. And yet here an eighteen-year-old single mother wants to get some things from her apartment like traversing the ten hazardous miles to Liberty is as easy as walking down to Field to Table for bread.

I say, "Let me ask. I'm sure she wouldn't care."

Indeed, the question has hardly left my mouth when *Grossmammi* Eunice reaches for the child. Her cataract-filmed eyes gleam with happiness as he's placed in her arms, and those eyes are about the only feature that reveal she's not tapped into some long-buried fountain of youth. You would never guess an eighty-nine-year-old Mennonite grandmother — who is legally blind, no less — would be vain about her appearance, but she is. Two days ago, I informed *Grossmammi* Eunice that our coconut oil can no longer be used as a daily tonic for her skin and hair. But judging from her glistening face, so far she hasn't listened. I guess she figures it is more important to remain wrinkle-free than to cook our food.

When I come back from the outhouse, Sal has left to return to her apartment, and Anna is sitting at the table with baby Colton on her lap. *Grossmammi* Eunice is sitting beside her in case Anna makes any sudden movements, which could put the child at risk. But my sister does nothing untoward, just continues nuzzling that eight-month-old like he is from her own flesh. My heart seizes as I close the door behind me and remain clinging to the cool, round knob.

Shortly after our *vadder* left, Anna led me into the bathroom and showed me proof that her cycle had begun. I hugged her tight and cried into her braided hair, mourning her physical transition into womanhood far more than I had my own — possibly because I knew my sister's mental transition might never match it. But here she is, loving on a child with a maternal instinct that does not always come naturally to me due to my impatience.

"Come, Anna," I call. More firmly, I repeat her name. She looks up from the child, her cheeks flushed pink. "Let's go to our room." She shakes her head, holding the baby closer to her chest. "You can bring Colton." Only after this suggestion does my sister comply and rise to her feet. She smiles as she walks by me, her spine straight as a dancer's as she supports the baby's head with her hand. I follow her into our bedroom. She sits on our bed with Colton on her lap, and I stretch out beside her. With one hand, she strokes the hair not pinned beneath my *kapp.*

The band across my chest begins to loosen only once I force myself to submit to the fact that Melinda might be gone, or she might not want to come back if we're able to find her. I am aware the level of my grief overtakes my level of affection for this woman. Is it the sad familiarity of her dependence on the prescription bottle, or the fact that when she was under the influence of its contents, she never liked for me to see her eyes? But somehow, someway, Melinda's disappearance has enlarged the pain generated by the disappearance of my *vadder.*

Anna continues stroking my hair and murmuring her nonsensical lullaby. Tears drip onto the spinning star quilt on our bed — tears that I have pent up inside me since the night we knew he wasn't coming home, after which so much changed so fast that I didn't have time to process it. I turn toward her and curl up like the babe in her arms. This is the first time in two years I can remember receiving comfort from a member of my family, rather than doling out what I don't have to give. I wonder if my sister possessed this nurturing ability all along, and I have been too focused on trying to be her guardian to see it.

MOSES

The volunteers gather beside the gates at dusk. Most carry lamps or flashlights — the necessary use of oil and batteries making me wish we could've searched earlier, by the renewable source of the sun. I spot Leora on the fringes of a larger group, which — looking closer — I see is only composed of the twelve-member Risser family: a massive search party by themselves.

When Leora moves past me, I reach out, and she steps back — the lamp swinging, throwing blades of light across the lane. I steady her on impulse, my hand still extended. She flinches at my touch and meets my eyes. I can tell, despite the dim light, that she's been crying. "You okay?" She doesn't answer but focuses on the space over my shoulder.

I pivot and look to see, of course, Jabil — the man who seems determined to keep his fingers in every administrative pie — climbing the scaffolding. Like a town crier he bellows out the information I've already learned: Every nook and cranny, field and dell of the community has been searched, so we know Melinda is not on the premises.

But no one remembers opening the gates for her, either, so she must've been desperate enough to climb over the national forest fence while we were at church. I have to wonder if the sound of yesterday's gunshots was what made her understand the perilousness of our situation so she decided to take her chances and run.

"For safety purposes," Jabil continues, "I think a man should accompany each group. We need people to go to the Mendenhalls, the McCords, and the Slocums and ask if they've seen a female who fits Melinda's description."

"I'd like to see how the McCords are doing anyway," says Myron Beiler, the man who loaned me the crutches. "Our family will go there."

"Thanks." Jabil scratches something down on his list. "How about the Mendenhalls?"

Eugene Risser says, "We can go there."

"You mind swinging by the Brooks' place on your way out? Brian McCord said they were out of town when the EMP hit, but we should check their grounds too, just in case."

Eugene nods, and I watch Jabil's thick brows furrow as he holds a flashlight above his paper and makes another note on his list.

"Now," Jabil says, "Leora?" I watch Leora nod in response. "I was wondering if you'd like to check on the Slocums. Since they're the farthest away, I'll take you in my wagon."

Concealed by the darkness, I roll my eyes. *A man needs to go with each family for safety purposes;* yeah right, Jabil just wants an excuse to cozy up to Leora.

"And you, Moses —"

I give Jabil a look that I hope conveys how enthralled I am by his convenient administrative tactics.

"You can stay here with Charlie and guard the gates."

"Gee, thanks," I drawl. "I'm sure you sweated hard over where to put me on your list."

Jabil's busy scratching away on that stupid list, but I can see the grin fighting to overtake his mouth. He knows exactly what he's doing. Straightening his back, Jabil tucks the flashlight under his arm. "All right, everybody, if you come across Melinda or hear any news of her whereabouts, come to the front gate and ring the triangle. I'm not sure we'll be able to hear you at the Slocums' place, but everyone else

221

should. . . . And be safe!"

The three families begin to disperse, their flashlight beams and lamps signaling like Morse code into the darkness. Someone claps me on the back. I glance over my shoulder and see Jabil, no longer attempting to hide his smarmy grin. "Keep a watch out for us. Will ya?"

"I'll keep a watch, all right," I retort, trying not to pay attention as he gives Leora a hand into his wagon and then climbs up beside her. Snapping the reins on the horse's back, he drives out through the gates. I pull the gates closed and slide the massive dead bolts — which Henri soldered after the shooting — into place. Sighing, I clamber up the scaffolding that Jabil just climbed down and sit on my usual perch next to Charlie, who's wearing a headlamp and sipping some of our dwindling coffee rations from a teacup, the image incongruous with the .22 balanced across his knees. The outline of Jabil and Leora vanishes down the road: his suspendered back and wide-brimmed hat, her rigid posture and *kapped* hair making them look like they are decked out for a historical reenactment.

Halfway to the Slocums' residence, our wagon overtakes a small, solitary figure. My blood pounds in my ears. I turn in the seat and struggle to peer at the person's features concealed beneath a hood. I know the odds that it's Melinda aren't in my favor, since she wouldn't be caught dead in a gray sweatshirt, but I still reach across Jabil's lap and pull back on the reins.

He looks over at me, startled, and I jump down out of the wagon before he has the chance to stop me. I feel more helpless walking down that highway than I have ever felt in my life. Bonfires glimmer in the meadows where the refugees are camping. The pungent scent of wood smoke used to fill me with anticipation of fall: hunting season when the men would return from the mountains in their bright-orange garb, their mules packed down with the field-dressed game; applesauce day at our neighbor's stove with a bubbling apple crumble waiting to be eaten as our reward; hymn sings around a bonfire, sitting on scratchy straw bales with our hands warmed by mugs of hot chocolate or coffee. Now, though, the wood smoke fills me only with dread, since we have no idea if the refugees in those meadows are families just trying to survive, or if they are mendicants plotting to over-take people like us, traveling the road.

The staccato pop of gunfire causes my nails to dig into my palms. I glance over my shoulder to see Jabil turned around on the bench seat, watching me as well. But the road is eerily deserted, considering the deluge of people who were standing in line for our soup kitchen when those two high school boys were killed. I wonder if their violent deaths caused the refugees to fear us: a community which preaches nonresistance at any cost and yet, at the first test, does not live up to its claims. Or perhaps there is something patrolling this road that we should also fear, and it's keeping everyone but this small, solitary figure away. Perhaps I should fear her too. More gunfire makes me cry out and duck.

The person walking toward me laughs. "You ain't been on the road for long, I take it?"

The voice is too harsh to be Melinda's.

"No, I haven't. Have you?"

She shrugs. "Lost track o' time."

We meet in the center of the highway: her well-worn sneakers on the right yellow line, my muddy black shoes on the left. Her stench is unbearable, but not wanting to appear rude, I remain where I am. The woman folds her arms. Moonlight dapples her features, overtaking the shadow cast by the hood. She is older than I thought. The skin of her face is pitted and raw from having been exposed to the elements. Her eyes, pinched between crinkled folds, are pale.

I have such difficulty distinguishing the irises from the whites that I assume the woman is blind until she reaches out and grapples my wrist in one birdlike claw. I leap back — another scream scaling my throat — but she just says, "Have you seen my dog? Griffin?" She releases me and squats on the road with the agility of a child, demonstrating that her pet is less than half a foot tall. "He's straight-up Heinz 57. Skinny and black with a white chest and tail. He disappeared two days ago, when I was in town."

"I'm so sorry. Haven't seen him."

The woman stands and glowers over my shoulder. "Didn't expect you would. . . . That is, unless you seen him on a spit." I am compelled to look at the meadow of bonfires too. "I think them people ate him." Her smile — showing off more gums than teeth — is a bit deranged, and I wonder if she was homeless long before the EMP.

"You haven't seen my friend, have you?" I ask, though it seems odd to swap inquiries with a woman searching for her dog. "Name's Melinda? About thirty-five with short blonde hair? Rather pretty." *Or at least she was.*

The woman shakes her head; then clarity comes to her pale eyes, like she can see right through me. "I've passed so many people all trying to find somebody they lost, makes me wonder if they cared that much about losing them before they was gone."

I thank the woman and head back to the wagon, knowing that what she said is true. Before Melinda left, I would've never guessed how hard I would try to find her.

"Should I take you home?" Jabil asks as the wagon pulls back into Mt. Hebron.

"It's past midnight." I glance over. "Where else is there to go but home?"

He doesn't respond. Moses latches the gate behind us. I turn on the bench seat and see him standing between the gate and the wagon, staring to the left, though nothing is there but the outline of Field to Table in the dark. For the second time tonight, I leap from the wagon. Jabil says to the horse, "Whoa, whoa." The wooden wheels roll to a stop. He calls after me, "Thought you were going home." When I don't respond, he continues, "You shouldn't be out this late."

I keep walking away from him but call behind me, "Wasn't I just out this late with you?"

Moses has climbed on top of the scaffolding again. I feel the draw of his eyes as I approach, but he says nothing. I mentally berate myself for jumping from Jabil's wagon when I'm obviously wanted more there than here. I turn back to trail its tracks, which have gouged parallel grooves in the crusher-run gravel. The wagon is still close enough that I hope Jabil doesn't turn around and see me, slighted and trying to catch up. I take two steps in his direction when Moses says, "Need something, Leora?"

Rattled, I about-face. I look up at him and shade my eyes, as if that gesture will help me see better in the night. I lower my hand. "Have you heard anything about Melinda?"

Moses gets up and walks to the scaffolding's edge. He smiles down at me. "Sorry, no. No one's seen anything." He pauses. "You and Jabil were the last ones back."

"We were also the farthest from the community."

"No doubt that was planned."

"Well. Not by me."

Coughing a laugh, Moses shakes his head.

"No, not by you." He thumbs the air over his shoulder. "Charlie's making rounds. Wanna come up? It'll be a little while before he gets back."

I bite my lip to keep from smiling; I'm never brazen enough to ask for what I want. I grip the rungs, and scales of paint slough off like dead matter. Moses doesn't offer me a hand, but directs a flashlight at my hands so I can make the climb on my own.

"How 'bout you?" he asks, once I've reached the top. "See anything?"

I shake my head and sit on the scaffolding edge beside him — our feet dangling, the heels of our boots tapping lightly on the rungs. "A window was broken and a lamp turned over. But nobody was there. Looked like the Slocums just packed up their stuff and left."

"They have people nearby?"

"Doubt it. They moved here from Chicago to homestead." I experience a bout of sadness, recalling the Slocums' framed paintings, depicting peaceful scenes juxtaposed by the dwelling's abandoned state. "Why didn't they come here?" I ask. "We could've helped them."

"Would we have, Leora? Sounds good in theory, but if it came down to our families or theirs, would we *still* have shared our rations equally, or kept some for ourselves?"

"I think, if it came down to that, we'd have to pray and ask God to provide."

"Then you'd better start praying."

I peer across at him. "What do you mean by that?"

Moses doesn't say, just shuts off the flashlight and lies back on the scaffolding's boards. He props his hands behind his head. "Today I counted the sacks of rice at Field to Table. I thought at first they'd been distributed to the community, but Jabil said that wasn't the case."

"So . . . we don't have as much food as you thought?" Moses confirms this with a nod. My voice breaks. "How am I going to take care of my family?"

"Maybe it's not your responsibility to take care of them."

"If it's not mine, whose is it? My *vadder*'s?" Moses appears stunned by the anger in my voice. I try to explain. "My *mamm* . . . she never got her footing back after our *vadder* disappeared. So overnight the yoke of that responsibility fell across my shoulders. I could tell she felt bad that I had to work so hard; life was hard on all of us, but it was especially challenging for her and for me. I guess that's why she was eager to get me married — believing life would be easier if I just gave in and shared Jabil's last name, along with his social and financial standing in our community. But I never gave in. I always wondered if she wanted me to be with Jabil because she had my best interest at heart, or because she saw in him the man *she* should've ended up with — if she'd only used her head."

Moses sits up and leans back on his arms. He looks over at me and then looks ahead. "I won't tell you what I think you should or shouldn't feel, or what you should or shouldn't do, 'cause I don't know you well enough and it's not my place. But I *will* say that I think you've been really brave, Leora. Nobody should have to go through what you've gone through." Our fingertips brush. It might be an accident of proximity or on purpose. But neither of us pulls away.

I lift my shoulders. "I wouldn't say your own life's been a walk in the park."

"No, it hasn't." Each word is measured and poured out when he continues. "But it's been nice, lately . . . having somebody like you to walk beside me."

Our hands remain close. I stare up at the sky in silence — my heart pulsing like the stars.

■ ■ ■ ■

CHAPTER 9

■ ■ ■ ■

LEORA

I change into my nightgown without lighting a lamp, so Anna won't awaken, and climb beneath the covers while still fastening the last few buttons. The sheets are cool and undisturbed, the mattress bowed beneath my weight only. I sit up and touch the space where my sister should be, her body like a warm parenthesis curved against the wall. She's not here.

Throwing back the covers, I swing my bare feet to the floor. The hooked rug can barely quell the cold and damp that's beginning to seep up through the floor joists — a prelude to the seasonal change. I pull the curtain back from the window and see the ground is soft with fog that swirls beneath the sickle moon's light.

I thought I had eradicated my sister's periodic insomnia with the natural remedies of calcium, magnesia, lavender oil, and chamomile tea. But because I didn't see Anna in the kitchen or bathroom when I came in from talking with Moses — and the living room is occupied by Sal and her baby — I suspect that she's somewhere outside, sleepwalking. It would not be the first time she's escaped my watch, especially as I've been distracted since the EMP.

I pad down the hall, carrying my shoes, and slip them on by the door. Anna's are here, distinct from the rest of ours because they have Velcro straps instead of laces, making it easier for her to put them on. I touch a match to a lamp wick, lower the globe over the flame, and open the door quietly so the noise won't disturb Sal and Colton. My rapid thoughts ease as I stand on the back porch and see my sister's nightgown shining, like a beacon in the dark.

Setting the lamp on top of the porch post, I walk down the steps. The hem of my own nightgown dampens as I cross the grass. Anna continues walking away as I follow her, causing the distance between us to remain constant.

I don't let myself imagine how far she would go if I were not here to draw her back. Anna is not only impervious to pain, she is also impervious to fear — an innate characteristic the two of us certainly do not share and which was no doubt intensified by her accident.

After some time, I am finally able to close the distance between us. Afraid to startle my sister awake, I move toward her slowly. I search her face, her pale skin turned opalescent by the moonlight. "Anna," I whisper. "Anna . . . I'm going to take you up to the house." I touch her elbow and turn her body toward mine. As I do, I see an ink-like splatter on the front of her gown. I reach out and touch it. Wet. I look down the length of cotton and see more stains. I smell the dark substance now staining my fingertips, and my heartbeat recaptures its panicked rhythm from ten years ago, as one can never forget the scent of blood.

My sister allows me to lead her to the porch, and I am no longer sure if she is sleepwalking or suffering from shock. Did she get caught in the barbed wire twining the fence? Was she attacked by an animal — or, I shudder to even contemplate it, a man?

Retrieving the lamp with one hand, I take Anna's in the other, and together we walk up the porch into our house. Someone is standing in front of the kitchen sink.

"Leora . . . Leora," Sal soothes, seeing my

reaction. "It's me."

My throat tightens. I cross the kitchen and set down the lamp. I pour water into a quart jar from the bucket we reserve for drinking water and lead Anna to the sink. Using a cloth, I wipe the dirt from her face, hands, and feet. Sal hands me a fresh cloth to wipe down Anna's legs, which are scratched and smeared with blood.

"What happened?" Sal asks.

I swallow hard, trying to stave off tears so my display of emotion won't further disturb Anna. Sal pours a glass of water for me and holds it out. I take a small sip and manage, "I think she was attacked."

"Attacked by what? An animal?"

"I . . . I'm not sure. Hundreds of strangers have been in and out of here since yesterday. I hate to even think like that, but —"

Sal interrupts. "My grandmother used to say, before she gave up talking, 'Never trouble trouble until trouble troubles you.' You can't let yourself get so worked up like that, Leora. We know nothing for sure yet. Maybe she stumbled on a dead animal. Maybe she cut her foot."

"I can't help troubling trouble. Not when the worst usually turns out to be true."

"What's been the worst?" Sal reaches into

the drawer for another dishcloth and begins dabbing at the bloodstains on my sister's nightgown like she's dabbing off mud.

Her nonchalance makes me want to prove her wrong. "Like how Anna fell, and it was my fault. Like how my *vadder* disappeared, and my *mamm* died. How my sister's been attacked, and I have no idea how to find out who it was." Sal continues dabbing. The grandfather clock ticks. I hate how she trapped me into displaying and defending the saga of my life, when it's pretty clear it doesn't match up to hers. Jerking the rag from her hand, I snap, "It's not *going* to come out."

The abrupt gesture and tone appear to awaken Anna. She begins to cry, dispassionately, like tears trailing down a wax mannequin face. I glare at Sal's back and then catch myself. I cannot treat Sal the way I treated Melinda, not if I'm going to learn from my mistakes.

Closing my eyes, I breathe deep. "I'm going to get her changed. Mind giving me a hand?"

I have been dressing and undressing my sister since I learned to dress myself. That is not the part I need help with. The part I need help with is what removing those clothes might reveal. Sal doesn't say anything. She just follows us, carrying the lamp. My hand trembles as I reach into a drawer for one of my nightgowns. I turn and see that Anna's stopped crying, which unsettles me more than if she continued. Sal sets the lamp on the bureau, and together we lift the stained gown over my sister's head. I trace a hand over Anna's vertebrae, seeing no bruises or cuts. Why is there so much blood on her legs if the rest of her body looks fine?

"Should we check if she's bleeding?" I ask, glancing up at Sal, hoping she knows what I'm asking without having to spell it out.

Sal places a hand on my arm. "I'll do it. Stay here so Anna's not scared."

As I guide my sister into bed, she seems blessedly clueless to anything but the fact that I'm tucking her in the same as I do every night. Pulling back the hem of her nightgown, I hold the lamp aloft but avert my gaze. Sal tugs the hem down seconds later. "I can't tell."

I lower the lamp, weak. "What are you saying?"

"Nothing. But that doesn't mean nothing's happened and that doesn't mean it did."

"How do I find out if —"

"An exam," Sal interrupts, mercifully.

"But nobody's doing those right now."

"I wouldn't want to put her through that anyway."

"Then I suppose you got to wait and see what happens."

It takes me a moment to understand. "My handicapped sister could have been raped tonight, and you *still* act like this isn't the worst thing that could've happened!"

"I never said anything like that. But the worst *didn't* happen. Your sister's not dead."

"Stop acting so superior! Like you've got the monopoly on suffering or something!"

Sal looks at me. I turn away, desperate for relief from her gaze. "If you'll just stop and listen," she says, "I don't think you'll hear *me* complaining about how life's done me wrong."

She backs soundlessly from the room. Trembling with emotion, yet oddly numb, I straighten my sister's legs and pull the quilt up around her shoulders. I climb in beside her and pull her close, stroking her hair the same as she stroked mine a few hours ago. Only after her breathing has evened do I press my face into the pillow and let myself cry. But I soon will myself to stop. Like coffee, tea, sugar, and coconut oil, tears are a luxury that must be conserved.

MOSES

People are already singing when I cross the lane over to the pavilion. The church services are being held here since there are too many of us to cram inside the schoolhouse, where the community would normally meet.

This is my third Sunday in Mt. Hebron, so it should be starting to feel familiar, but I'm not sure it ever will. Like a bunch of troublemakers, Charlie, Henri, and Sean have taken their usual seats in the back row on chairs with hand-painted — rather gaudy, in my opinion — flowers and decorative scrollwork: the mishmash hauled in from kitchens around the community. I take the seat next to Henri. His leg keeps jigging. When I look at him from the corner of my eye, I see he's gnawing on a piece of straw — for all intents and purposes, making him resemble one buck-wild Nebuchadnezzar. So I take it Henri's out of cigarettes. I'm surprised they lasted this long. He must have had quite the stash.

Somehow, I never picked up smoking, but I have to admit I'm as addicted to caffeine as Henri is to nicotine. The fact that I haven't had my coffee this morning (I'm saving my rations for when I need to stay awake on guard) combined with all this noise makes my head feel like it's trapped in a vise. The singing stops, and the jarring silence seems to echo across the cement floor. Henri and Sean sigh in relief. I smile to myself.

Closer to the front, the deacons read from the Bible. I can pick up bits and pieces of the German language because my family was stationed in Karlsruhe for the first four years of my life. One of the deacons makes a motion, and all the Mennonites turn and kneel to face the back, but it feels like they're really facing *us* — the line of insubordinate *Englischer* guards who are protecting their synchronized hides.

The deacon starts praying up a storm, and it's not in German or in English, but maybe somewhere in between. Next, Bishop Lowell gets up from the bench and strides, on his misshapen legs, to the front of the pavilion's floor. I squint to take a closer look at the fearsome gnome of a bishop. It might be my imagination, but his hair appears whiter than it did nineteen days ago. His suspenders appear to have more than an ornamental purpose, since his waist has been whittled down to nothing. It hits me that he probably hasn't been eating much since the EMP. Is it because of nerves, or because he's trying to make sure everyone else remains fed, even if he's not consuming his daily rations? Bishop Lowell and I haven't gotten off on the right foot, but you have to admire a man who puts his people's needs before his own.

"My community," he begins, straightening his back with some effort, "I am sure you can tell we are at a crossroads. Yesterday, Jabil and Malachi calculated our assets again, and either we misjudged them the first time, some of us are consuming far more than our daily share, or we have fed many more refugees than we had originally planned. It seems —" Bishop Lowell's voice catches. He looks down, and I understand that his eyes are not watering from fatigue alone, but he is trying not to cry. "It seems we will only be able to feed the refugees and ourselves for another month or two before we run out of supplies. Our rations are reduced to the point we will not have enough to survive the winter."

There is not one intake of breath, but I can feel the gray weight of this revelation settling over everything like a pall. Even the air, as the wind shifts, wafts the odor of something dead, and I wonder what undiscovered thing is putrefying in the woods or field.

Charlie calls out, "Then stop feeding every moocher that comes by hungry."

I wince, though my reaction is hypocritical. I had that exact thought the second I stepped under the pavilion and saw the neighbors were here. When the community dispersed to search for Melinda last week, they extended an invitation to the substantial McCord and Mendenhall families to attend Mt. Hebron's weekly Lord's Day celebration — or whatever they call it. To my annoyance, they accepted, giving us another fifteen mouths to feed, in addition to the family of Liberty civilians whose father received a head wound during the shoot-out. But I reckon, this being the Lord's Day and all, I shouldn't be so stingy.

Someone bolts to their feet, and when I glance up from my hands, I see that it's Leora. She's standing in front of a bench located across the aisle with the rest of the women from the community. Her profile, bleached of color, is emphasized by her dark cape dress that resembles funeral attire. She is shivering, her arms folded across her chest, though it's hot enough under the pavilion to stick my shirt to my sweaty lower back.

"In this," she says, her voice shaking, "in this alone, I would have to agree with Charlie. Not only are we depleting our storehouse by feeding the refugees; we are putting our own families at risk by opening our gates."

This does not sound like Leora at all. Thinking she's setting aside her own charitable efforts to keep her family fed, I say, "We have the Suburban. We could use it to go out and find or barter for supplies around town, so we can —"

"You mean *steal* supplies. You're the one who said that whatever food grocery stores used to carry is long gone by now." I know Jabil's the one speaking. I turn and our eyes lock over the heads of the people, and I can feel that fierce tug in this: our battle of wills. And I have to wonder — looking over at Leora, whose eyes shift between the two of us — if we are not only battling wills, but battling over her.

"Look —" I spread my hands — "we've got a family of refugees right here from Liberty. Why don't we ask them what it's like in town?"

The man rises to his feet, then reaches down for his seated wife's hand. Their toddler-age little girl is on her lap with a cotton dress and messy pigtails, sucking her thumb as hard as Henri, beside me, is chewing on his piece of straw. The couple's around my age, but their regular features — brown hair, brown eyes, slim, runner builds gravitating toward gaunt — are lined with exhaustion that makes them appear older than their years.

Since the riot a week ago, this family has been recuperating in the *dawdi haus,* where some cots have been set up and curtained off for privacy. Other than Charlie, I don't think any of us are going to have the nerve to send them out into the streets even though the father is mostly recovered. Our first discussion sounded good to our ears: giving the refugees food and water and then booting them out the door. But it's so easy to forget that discussion when you come face to face with those who are hungry — whose lives might be sustained, if not saved, with a bowl of soup and a piece of bread.

I call out to the father, because it's clear he's at a loss for where to start, "How bad was it? Did you have to leave things behind?"

The man drags his free hand across his face. "Had to." He sighs. "Didn't have time to do anything else. About two weeks after everything crashed, it seemed that law and order fell apart. Violence was growing so that people were getting robbed over a simple can of beans or — or a pair of shoes. That's when Tammy, my wife, and I decided to leave, figuring we'd be better off on the move rather than waiting around to see what was going to happen. We packed everything we could in two bags and tied them on our backs. We tried going around the edge of town, thinking that'd be the less populated route. But by the time we got to Burt's, the shelves were empty . . . carts gone, and we saw a bunch of people exiting town just like we were doing."

He looks at his wife and daughter. "The gangs were flushing us out of our homes. It was down to join them or run. There's no doubt there's a lot of food and valuable items still left in town. But it's all being controlled by the gangs."

I thank the man, and he takes his seat. I let his words sink in, and then I stand and look at the group. "Is it really stealing to reclaim what's been taken by criminals and use it to help the needy — most likely some of the very ones who it was stolen from in the first place? If we are careful, I'm sure a few of us could go into town and make it back with supplies of some sort. And from what he's just said, I think we need ammunition as much as food. If we're well armed, we won't be as vulnerable when these gangs finish cleaning everything out in town and come knocking on our gates, trying to steal whatever we have left."

"I take it you'd like to lead this operation?" Jabil asks, a bite to his voice.

I jam my fists in my pockets. "I sure wouldn't have to, but I think I could."

"Where do you suppose you're going to find this food and ammunition?"

Charlie replies to Jabil, "I don't know about food, but there's an armory in town . . . over near the old T-shirt factory."

Jabil continues, speaking to both Charlie and me. "And how are we supposed to know you all will keep your end of the agreement and won't use unnecessary force or violence?"

I make no effort to hide my irritation. "If you're so concerned, Jabil, why don't *you* go with us and see? You could keep a gun trained on me at all times and shoot me dead if I start using force you deem 'unnecessary.' "

To my surprise, Jabil says, "All right, I'll go."

Then he seems to think twice because he glances over at Bishop Lowell for permission, who nods his head with the air of a king. "But make sure any houses are visibly abandoned before you enter," Bishop Lowell instructs. "And abide by our community rules, even if you are beyond our border. Don't shoot at anyone, Moses, unless they shoot at you first."

I nod, of course, and Jabil does as well — though he would literally rather die than shoot someone. Needless to say, I do not feel as compelled.

Because it's the Sabbath, we are not supposed to work but have a day of rest. How are we supposed to rest, I wonder, when we know a gang is devouring the town only ten miles up the road? How long until they pick the town's carcass clean and then scuttle over here to discover what else they can find? The idea is especially disturbing, considering we do not have enough manpower or firepower to hold back a large crowd. But I can tell the bishop is trying to establish a sense of harmony by encouraging the community to do the types of activities they did every Sabbath before the EMP. So we rearrange benches and chairs around tables carted over to the pavilion from the soup kitchen. Bishop Lowell leads us in the silent prayer, and we begin to eat. The soup is more watered down than it was yesterday, each slice of bread not as thick.

I'm using crust to soak up my broth when Leora comes and sits down across from me. "You should come to the singing tonight," she says. "The distraction would be good for you."

Her warmth and invitation catch me off guard, since she's not said more than three words to me all week. "Maybe," I say, giving my best noncommittal shrug. "But I've got to change the tire on the Suburban for tomorrow and go over some tactical stuff with Charlie."

She looks down, tracing the table's wood grain. "About that supply run to town you're planning. . . . If you find some ammunition . . . I might need some."

"Ammunition? For a pacifist?" My smile disappears when I see her face. "Sorry, that was a bad joke. But all the ammunition in the world isn't going to bring Melinda back."

Leora sits on the bench with her hands knotted. "This is not about Melinda."

"Well, I'm sorry —" I toss my spoon into the empty bowl — "but I can't help you unless you tell me what this *is* about."

Red blotches mottle Leora's neck, revealing her discomfort even more than her clenched hands. "I need you to help me find ammunition because this — this is about revenge."

Any shocked expression I had before was just a warm-up to what must be registering in this instant. I glance around the pavilion and see that no one's paying attention as they are too busy consuming their meals. I lean across the table and lower my voice, just in case. "When I first came here, you told me your nonresistance was founded on stories of martyrs who died for their beliefs. That, no matter what, they never took up arms to defend themselves or their families. And now you're telling me you want to take revenge?"

Leora smiles — as if she knows full well how preposterous she is sounding — but tears pool in the corners of her eyes. She says, "I guess you could say I'm having a crisis of belief." She pauses, reaches for my hand. "Will you help me, Moses? You know about guns and ammunition; surely you must know about revenge."

"Revenge," I murmur. "Yes, I'd say I know it well."

In the distance, at the edge of the pavilion, I see Jabil standing in half sun, half shadow, watching us with eyes like two cups of ink. I push back my chair and rise with my bowl. I set it down on the tray and walk up the lane. But when I pass the *dawdi haus,* I turn and look back, seeing that Jabil is now sitting on the bench . . . sitting beside Leora.

Unknowingly absorbing the darkness in her that I have just left.

■ ■ ■ ■

CHAPTER 10

■ ■ ■ ■

LEORA

The August air holds the first hint of autumn's chill, causing me to hunker lower in my cotton wrap that my own fingers have spun. Yet I cannot enjoy this shift of the seasons as I wonder — skirting the firelight and scanning the faces of those I've known for years — if someone in the community molested my sister last week. Or if someone, deep in the shadows, is biding his time until he can strike again. I am not sure which thought fills me with more rage.

It may be imprudent, but imprudent or not, I have asked Sal not to tell anyone about the attack because I do not wish to evoke more fear in our community, which has been on tenterhooks since the shooting. But my main motivation is not selfless. I simply do not wish for my sister to be treated like an untouchable more than she already is. If it's discovered that I took a life to avenge my sister's, I will be untouchable. Yet Anna will continue to be ensconced inside the community, where, I pray — devoid of her attacker — she will remain safe.

I walk toward the refreshment table, heaped with a bounty of apples in every color our orchard provides. Olga Beiler has made apple pies, apple dumplings, and wassail. The spices waft on the air like a promise that life will be unsullied again. Though in the aftermath of last week, that can never be the case. I fill a heavy stone mug with the beverage, simmering in a cast-iron pot suspended over the fire. Olga smiles at me and asks how I am doing. I reply that I am fine. All the while, my heart is a drum beating high inside my ribs.

I glance around the bonfire, searching for the face of an *Englischer* I know I wouldn't be pursuing if he didn't possess the knowledge of corporeal retribution that I need to learn. But I am not pursuing him for his knowledge alone. No, I remember sitting across from him beneath the pavilion and feeling such a connection to his brokenness that I wondered if the two of us, together, could become one perfect whole. Is this, then, what draws people to each other? Not the combination of perfect selves, but the mirrored fragments we see reflected?

Olga studies me as she leans over the fire and stirs the wassail to keep the spices circulating. Bishop Lowell has encouraged this singing, accompanied with refreshments, because he wants to keep his people's spirits up, especially since they know the truth regarding our supplies. But how much longer can we indulge in extravagances such as this?

Olga strikes the spoon against the top of the pot. Her fleshy arm wobbles as she points to the outskirts of the gathering. "Jabil's over there," she says in Pennsylvania Dutch.

"Danke," I murmur without looking in his direction. I move away from her with my cup. Square straw bales have been circled around the fire. The hex symbol on the Snyders' barn behind us is composed of jewel-toned triangles, as intricately patterned as an auction quilt. Above the barn's roofline — almost obscured by the weather vane — the moon is so thin, it's outshone by the firmament's plethora of stars.

I do not take a seat on a bale, as I am afraid Jabil will claim his place beside me as he has done at every other singing for the past three months. Instead, I stand near the fire, sipping the too-hot wassail, just grateful for something to occupy my hands.

I don't admit to myself who I am waiting for until Moses appears on the other side of the fire. There must be fifty members of the community gathered here, but they fade into the background until all I can see is him. The two of us continue to stare — the fire moving like a sentient being between us — until Jabil breaks the spell and comes to stand so close to me, the fabric of his pants brushes against my dress.

"Can we talk?" he asks.

I nod stiffly and pull my wrap up to cover my head. Jabil draws me away from the fire and over to the barn, his hand burning his possession into the small of my back. A hymn that I have heard since infancy begins, the lyrics acquired more through osmosis than effort. But listening to *Ausbund* 112 now — "The one who lives in God's love is a disciple of Christ and knows the truth. Love is kind and friendly and does no one harm" — the meaning resounds in my spirit more than ever before.

Am I truly going to walk away from everything I've been taught?

My Anabaptist forebears suffered far worse than anything my sister might have suffered last week, and hymns like this germinated from that bitter seed of hardship. Yet they persevered; they turned the other cheek and prayed for those who persecuted them. And here, at the first test, I am planning to take revenge.

Jabil turns me toward him, maneuvering my body as if a prop on a stage. We are shielded between the slats of the barn and the boughs of a heavy pine that was probably planted back when this community was founded in 1988. Cracked corn, left over from where the Dutch bantam chickens have feasted, crunches beneath our shoes. Somewhere in the woods, a lone wolf howls as if trying to harmonize with the community. Jabil's fingers seek mine. I am surprised how cold and callused they feel. My head pounds.

"I would wait for you forever, Leora," he murmurs, voice quaking, "if I just knew I weren't clinging to false hope."

I should cut him loose once and for all; I know this. I remain silent. Truth is, I do not want him to stop waiting because I fear this would make me want him. Like my *vadder* at his worst, I am only attracted to what I should not have.

"Leora?" The three syllables of my name are fraught with a thousand questions.

I look up at Jabil. Those benevolent dark eyes, the waved dark hair lapping over his collar, the sharp angles of his shoulders, cheekbones, and nose. His steadfastness without my giving him anything in return is a testament to his faithful heart. Jabil Snyder would be a good husband to me and father to our children. This has never been in question. What *has* been in question is if there is more to this life than steadfastness.

I peer over Jabil's shoulder and see Moses, the almost-feminine sweep of his pale lashes contrasted with that unkempt beard as he stares unseeingly into the flames. The community members are singing all around him — their faces joyous despite the looming tribulations — but his own countenance remains somber. Is he thinking about his broken places? Is he, I dare ponder, thinking about me, wishing he could be here in Jabil's stead?

"I'm sorry," I tell Jabil. "Everything in me wants to tell you that you are not clinging to false hope . . . but I can't say that. Not yet."

Withdrawing his hand from mine, Jabil flexes his fingers as if he is going to reach out to me again, but then he folds his arms, squares his shoulders, and I can almost perceive some tender place within him hardening against me. "Not yet?" he says. "Is it because of what we are facing as a community, or because of the person who's now inside it?"

I long to tell him I have no idea what he's talking about, but we would both know I was being dishonest. Jabil no doubt sensed my attraction to Moses from the time he withdrew the pilot's body from the plane's wreckage and brought it up to the house, and — despite my misgivings at seeing a partially undressed man — I felt compelled to never leave Moses's side. If this is true, the fact that Jabil continued checking Moses for injuries proves what kind of man he is. Any woman would be honored to have him as her husband. That is, at this point, any woman but me.

"Maybe I just need time," I murmur. "We don't know what's going to happen tomorrow. We don't even know what we're going to feed our community in a month. How could we embark on any kind of relationship when faced with such uncertainty?"

Jabil glances away from me, his eyes glittering with suppressed anger or regret. "Love has always prospered in times like these. Don't blame your uncertainty on the state of things around us."

Struck mute by his words, I watch his departing silhouette become absorbed by the darkness. I remain sheltered by the pine

259

boughs until the heat once produced by his proximity is replaced with an arctic wind. Yet even now, I have no desire to return to the warmth of the fire.

Lamplight glows through our picture window as I follow the lane. It must be Sal, but it reminds me of *Mamm* and how she used to wait up for me after every hymn sing, doing a pile of mending or laundry until I came in the kitchen and told her about my night. Only once did she speak to me about marriage, but even before that night I inferred that, deep down, she yearned for me to join my life with someone who would be as steadfast as her husband was inconstant. It is touching, the sort of life she envisioned for me. But I am not sure if such a life is even possible. Or if that is the sort of life I want.

Four years ago, when Jabil first asked if he could walk me home from Mt. Hebron School, where I was attempting to teach students almost the same age as me, *Mamm* seemed certain that our future together was simply a matter of time.

The image of him then — such boyishness in his expressive brown eyes, such a stoop in his shoulders, as if, as an adolescent, he feared the great man he would become — makes me want to weep. I am not the only one the responsibilities of life have changed.

Entering the kitchen, I see no sign of *Mamm* or mending, of course, but my eyes and heart still yearn for one more glance. The only sign of Sal's being here is that the supper dishes, which were previously cluttering up the sink, have all been washed and dried. Shrugging off my cloak and bonnet, I set them on the chair and trace the craftsmanship I religiously condition with linseed oil, as if trying to conjure forth the *vadder* who was an artist of inanimate things.

For a month after he left us, I waited, listening for my *mamm*'s nocturnal migration to the couch and the mourning that ensued. I could not sleep until I heard her, and I could not sleep afterward for the anguish evoked by her stifled wails. One particular night, when I feared my *mamm*'s crying would awaken Seth and Anna, I rose from the bed I shared with my sister and padded across the cool hardwood to the living room. *Mamm*'s body was coiled in a fetal position — not a blanket covering her, her slim calves and bare feet pale in the dark.

I could see her mental undoing as if a hidden door had opened and the cogs and wheels of her mind were suddenly made visible. I covered her with the afghan and pulled it up so the braided tassels brushed against her chin. Her swollen eyes opened. I knelt beside the couch and took her hand, though I didn't want to bring comfort to her as much as I wanted *her* to bring comfort to me. But she didn't. She couldn't. She was too consumed with her own sorrow to see that she and I were mourning the same man.

She looked up at me with a nearly tangible imploring. "Just learn from my experience, Leora," she said, tears coating her voice. "It is better to open your heart to someone dependable than to someone exciting who, in the end, will only make you cry."

The night I knelt, providing comfort to the woman who had previously done everything in her power to comfort me, I glimpsed beneath the layers and could see that she was not unshakable. Instead of loving her through her vulnerability, I judged her for it. My heart aches with the memory and with the wish that I could turn back time. But I cannot go back. Regardless of what the future holds, I must go forward.

MOSES

Charlie and I sat up at the Snyders' kitchen table late last night — our eyes straining against the muted glow of a kerosene light hanging overhead — and pored over a map of the city, trying to gauge which areas to explore and which areas we'd be better off to avoid. It would've made sense to have Sal in on our planning, since she knows this area better than either of us. But the community made a rule that *Englischers* aren't allowed to interact with the opposite sex after dark. But I remember Leora with Jabil at the hymn sing, their shadowed bodies slanted toward each other and their hands clutched tight. My gut constricts at the memory, and not for the first time I understand that the Mennonites aren't being held to the same standard as the rest of us.

"Why you so distracted?" Charlie asks. "You thinking about that skinny four-eyed gal?"

I've known guys like Charlie before, and it's better to lie low and ignore them. Otherwise they'll know they're getting to you, which only makes it more fun for them. So I just keep looking down at the map that's spread across the hood of Charlie's truck, circling the area where he remembers seeing the armory on a side road branching off Main Street. The same street where we intersected with the gang; therefore, we're hoping we'll have better luck avoiding them by going into town during the day versus at night.

The Silverado — now part of the blockade — is parked next to the Colorado woman's Mercedes SUV, which looks as abandoned as it is, with its tinted windows and black paint job glazed with dust. The sight of it makes me depressed, thinking of her family that will forever be haunted by her loss while I'm already struggling to remember her name.

"We going to do this thing or not?" I ask, shouldering my backpack.

Charlie tightens the straps of his matching backpack and stands behind me, zipping open compartments and counting everything before zipping them shut again — making me feel like he's an overbearing father making sure his kindergartner is prepared for his first day of school. But I figure I might as well let him, since he's the one who got me set up in the first place. He was even so generous as to give me an MRE — Meal, Ready-to-Eat — that has enough calories to put blubber on a whale. Who cares that the food's expiration date is '06, or that the cheese squished from the tube is a strange nuclear orange? Charlie swears that expiration dates don't matter on MREs, as long as everything's sealed tight.

"Where's my pipe bomb launcher?" he asks, like he's asking for a stick of gum.

"In the back of the Suburban."

"Good boy." Charlie hooks a camo hat backward over my head, which I take off and stack on the pile by our feet. For years, Charlie's been lugging around this arsenal of stuff that he picked up at different Salvation Army stores, so that the covered bed of his truck looks like some life-size GI Joes went skinny-dipping over yonder and left their clothes behind. Charlie makes excuses for what we guys call his "play clothes" because he says he knew things were going to turn sour, so he wanted to make sure he was prepared whenever they did. I bet he never thought he'd be stuck in a pacifist Mennonite community when they did go sour, though.

It's about the biggest contradiction you can imagine: this redneck Rambo, who's bent on blasting anything that moves, confined to the rules of a community that doesn't want us to hurt a fly. But I know why Charlie stays, and it's not only because he thinks he's the ringleader of our rough-and-ready militia. It's because he has no one else around here, not even a dog, and surviving can be a lonely business when you're doing it by yourself. I know because after I came home from the desert and cut myself off from the rest of society, that's exactly what I tried.

"Jabil gonna meet us at the Suburban?" Charlie asks. The same question he's asked and I've answered about a thousand times. I'm starting to think it's a nervous tic — a way to fill up the stagnant air until we get moving again. Over at Field to Table, I hear Henri slam the Suburban's hood. He crosses over to us, wiping grease from his stained hands. I notice a gold wedding band gleaming against the grime, but he's never mentioned a wife. I guess some people might be grateful for the separating effects of the EMP.

"Everything looks good," he says. "But it's been hot-wired, so the ignition's ripped —"

Charlie interrupts, "I know about hot-wiring." I look over at him and raise an eyebrow. Despite his bandolier of bullets, shining like the pirate caps on his back teeth, and camo bandanna, Charlie reminds me of an overeager Boy Scout, not someone who skulks around town, hot-wiring vehicles. He acknowledges my look and shrugs. "I read about it somewhere."

It wouldn't surprise me a lick if Charlie's one of those eccentric geniuses who has the social skills of a hermit but who could've invented the lightbulb if Thomas Edison hadn't gotten to it first. I'm grateful he's taken a good look at the map. If we lose it, maybe his photographic memory can recall where we're supposed to go — and more importantly, where we're *not.*

About halfway up the lane, I spot two people walking. I shade my eyes against the sun and see that it's Leora and Sal. A ring of turkey vultures rises above the field behind them, like Gothic versions of Icarus, trying to reach the sun. With timing so perfect it must be calculated, Jabil comes out of the *dawdi haus* right when they're passing by and nods stiffly as their paths overlap. Leora nods too. Even from here, I can see the tension swaying between them like a massive heat wave. I'm not going to waste my energy trying to figure them out. It's none of my business what they do.

"Hey, Jabil," I say as he mournfully watches Leora enter Field to Table with Sal.

"Hey, yourself." Jabil gives me a look that reminds me of his uncle.

"Well —" Charlie claps his hands and smiles — "everybody's here. Good. I'll drive, Moses can ride shotgun with me. Jabil?" He nods at Jabil, who appears annoyed by Charlie's enthusiasm. "I want *you* to guard the back."

The skin pulls tight across Jabil's cheek-bones. "I can't 'guard' anything. You know that. And besides, I'm not going along because I want to; I'm going along to ensure that you all honor the community while you're out there."

Charlie snorts. "Somebody got his suspenders in a knot." But I cut him a glance and he looks ashamed, or as ashamed as someone socially impaired like Charlie can. Switching tactics, he says, "I guess — uh, you can ride shotgun with me, and Moses can guard the back. I mean, *really* guard it. We gotta be smart here, guys. No doubt the town's got plenty of weapons in the wrong hands, and I bet even decent people are getting desperate enough to do things they normally wouldn't." But his flashing pirate's grin contradicts his warning.

Charlie gets into the Suburban and cranks the engine. Jabil takes off his hat and ducks down low before maneuvering his lanky body into the passenger side. I open the back hatch and climb in, place my revolver crosswise on my lap, and see that an AR-15 is already propped in the corner within reaching distance. The interior smells of sweat and gore. The sagging ceiling's tacked with a constellation of pushpins. But the Suburban runs like a top, and not only does she run, the tank's almost full of gas, which is a priceless break.

Charlie shifts into reverse and then drive, directing the Suburban's dinosaurian body out past Field to Table and toward the gates that are being guarded by Henri and Sean.

Nobody in the community is coming out to wave good-bye or wish us luck — not even Leora, which surprises me somewhat, considering how eager she was for us to obtain ammunition. Part of this might be because it's still so early and — besides the few women who have been up since before dawn, packing supplies at Field to Table — nearly everyone's in their kitchens cleaning up breakfast or out in their barns doing chores. But I have to wonder if the other reason they're not saying good-bye is because we're not the good guys going off to war and we're not the bad. Our survival instincts have mixed black and white until our consciences are color-blind to anything but the indefinite shade of gray.

I am about to turn around to peer through the windshield when Sal comes out of Field to Table and stands in the center of the lane where the weeds need cut, watching us with her legs firmly planted and her left hand making the sign of the cross. It's a gesture I saw my devout mom do all her life, but it seems out of place on Sal, and not only because she's using the wrong hand. She doesn't seem the type to rely on anything other than herself, and she sure doesn't seem the type to pray for others. Yet I shouldn't judge. Over the years, I've seen self-proclaimed agnostics hit their knees and pray with the fluency of longtime disciples when faced with a life-and-death situation. Maybe Sal's trying to comfort herself the best way she knows. Or maybe she somehow knows about my Catholic background and is trying to comfort me.

Before my first deployment — back before I witnessed such carnage and began to believe we're all just an accident of physics — I too tried to imagine something greater than all of us, and I prayed with a zeal my mom would've been proud of . . . if she'd known. I went so far as to get a cross tattooed on my chest, hoping that when God saw my broken body sprawled on the parched mosaic of the desert floor — struggling to take its next breath — he would notice that symbol of consecration, more than the blood on my hands, and draw me close to himself.

But then, I wasn't the one who died. Regardless of the number of my deployments, and no matter how many close calls

I had, I was *never* the one who died. Aaron was the same. It got to where our comrades started treating us like talismans and felt invincible if we were around. *"Moses and Aaron gonna lead us out of captivity and into the Promised Land,"* they joked, slapping our Lightweight Helmets before climbing out of the Humvee, like we basketball players used to slap the locker room beam before running out for the big game.

The point is, I couldn't protect them. *We* couldn't protect them. Instead, too many times they were felled while we remained standing and walked away unscathed — men who had wives and children at home and, some, newborn infants they'd only seen through Skype — which seemed unfair, since we had nobody back home to mourn us but our parents and grandpa.

Then that changed. A black cat crossed the road. A mirror broke. Salt spilled. A rosary bead slipped through my mom's fingers. Something. And the protective membrane rent. My brother was felled, and I remained, disoriented and bloody, but — miraculously, *cruelly* — alive.

I can feel my lungs compressing, and when I look down, my fingers are wrapped around the gun, knuckles ridged and white. I've carried a gun since I've been home, something tangible in place of my intangible faith, but I haven't used one in a year. The thought makes me sick.

I consciously relax my hold and look away from the lane and out through the windshield. Henri, up on the scaffolding, jerks back on the bolts and pulls the counterweight to open the gates. Sean leans down and smacks the roof, the unexpected jolt making memories rise like bile in my throat. I turn around to face the smudged glass of the hatch, trying to breathe through my nose without making it obvious and to focus on anything but my panic.

Refugees are camping in the field across the road, probably waiting until the soup line starts up again, so they are going to be disappointed when it doesn't. Still, there are not as many as there were two days ago, and I wonder if the blood marking the gravel outside the community has made everyone pass over us like the death angel passed over the Israelites' hyssop-swiped doorposts in Egypt. Who knows what kind of rumors have been circulating about what happened that day the boys were shot from our gate. I hate to admit it, but if the refugees fear us, it may be a good thing since we will soon be unable to feed ourselves — not to mention the strangers who expect to take from us and then continue on their journey.

The groups of people cluttering the main road now part around the Suburban like two halves of the Red Sea. It's clear from how little attention they pay to our vehicle that it's not the first working one they've seen since the newer ones shut down. Their soiled clothes blur into the surrounding landscape as Charlie presses the gas and we pick up speed. It's impossible to count the magnitude of their numbers, but I know they can't all be Liberty citizens trying to escape.

They must be making their way from the various smaller towns that dot the countryside, hoping to find some help and safety in the larger county seat. But having reached their destination, it is obvious that they can see the best thing is to keep moving. This may also be true for the Mt. Hebron community, despite its pretense of self-sufficiency and the fortified wall, which could be breached far more easily than any of us are willing to admit.

Along the road are suitcases of all styles, shapes, and hues. Most have been ransacked and are yawning open — the unwanted contents spilled across the grass. I see a guitar case covered in concert decals and a jogging stroller, the wheels intact, which causes me to pause and wonder what happened to the child. I see Jabil looking at the stroller as well — his profile ashen. He presses his thumbs against his temples as if to ward off a headache. Having been sheltered inside the community, he must find it horrific to imagine what choices other people have faced.

I call up to him, "It's harsh, isn't it?"

Jabil nods. He puts his hat back on and folds his arms, as if embarrassed I saw how that empty stroller affected him. But he should know I am being affected too. Adrenaline surges through my veins at a faster rate the closer to our destination we draw, as I anticipate someone attempting to hijack our vehicle around every turn. But Liberty, which was teeming with life three days post-EMP, is a ghost of its former self. The buildings have been gutted of every usable resource. The road is strewn with a confetti of refuse. The Dairy Shack has been burned to the ground, smoke wafting into the air from the center of the blackened pile of ash.

Jabil spreads the map across the dashboard and traces his fingers down the blue and red veins of the city. "Where do you want to go first?" he asks.

Charlie says, "Armory," and meets my

274

eyes before rolling his in the rearview mirror, as if saying that was a stupid question.

Jabil looks over at Charlie looking at me, and though I know he must feel slighted, he makes no comment. He simply measures the space and says, "It should be a few blocks from here."

Charlie turns the wheel, navigating down the streets. The leaden sky presses down on us like a weight, the gray swatch tapering out to the gray asphalt, as if we've been decimated by nuclear fallout rather than an EMP. Up ahead, we see someone — more of a ghost clad in rags than a man — dart around a large building resembling a civic center and then enter through an emergency exit. Charlie maneuvers his rifle and awkwardly angles it out the window. Jabil takes a small Bible from the pocket of his pants. The image of them sitting side by side would be comical if our situation weren't so grim.

I listen to the sound of the tires rolling over asphalt, the inhalation through everyone's nostrils with no audible exhalation, making it seem that the air itself lacks the ability to sustain life. My hair stands up on end, and I wonder if it's because we are in immediate danger or if it's because I am expecting, at any moment, to be fired upon.

Charlie motions to the building. "There must be something good in there."

"You're kidding me, right?"

He shrugs, already making his way up the sloping drive, the structure's corrugated roof glinting. "I could take 'im," he says.

I keep my mouth shut, since he's the one driving and wouldn't listen to me anyway, but it seems pretty stupid to enter a building we know is occupied simply because it might have something we want. This thought process reminds me of those two high school boys who tried penetrating our gate, which doesn't bode well for our reconnaissance mission. A small black-and-white dog comes trotting down the center of the street, still wearing its collar. I can tell by the way it's reacting to the sight of our vehicle that it's been abandoned. In a few weeks, maybe less, that dog will starve to death or, worse, become a starving person's next meal.

"Anything back there?" Charlie calls to me.

"Nope. Nothing but a hungry-looking mutt."

"Good. Who's staying with the truck?"

Jabil says, "I will."

I look at him, wondering how he's going to protect himself and the vehicle without a weapon. "Take this." Jabil eyes my gun that I'm trying to pass over the seats. "Just take it," I say. "You don't have to shoot it, but the sight alone might give you an edge."

Jabil takes my gun, holding it by the barrel as if it can shoot by itself. Charlie drives around a landscaped stand of trees and parks next to a storage shed behind the center, where the Suburban will hopefully remain out of sight of anyone patrolling the street. He switches off the engine, but neither he nor I make an effort to get out. "Well." Charlie clears his throat and fidgets with the keys. "I reckon we're not gonna find out what's in there just sitting in the truck."

The two of us exit the vehicle and walk in silence up to the building, which is elevated above town, providing a rather unsightly widescreen vista of the destruction and desolation of what was once, no doubt, the beautiful town of Liberty. My chest tightens as I pause in front of the national and state flags, flapping in the same gusts of air twirling the litter in the streets below, and I see that someone had the forethought to lower them to half-mast. I am surprised the flags haven't been stolen for cover, or for spite, since our government has failed its citizens — or at least the citizens of Montana, since we don't know how far the tentacles of the EMP have reached. But perhaps even mendicants have their looting limitations.

I continue walking, keeping the AR-15 ready and my head down low. Charlie is ahead of me by about ten steps. We move around the side of the building, searching for the emergency exit the man used. I glance over my shoulder at the Suburban. Jabil is sitting on the passenger side. His straw hat blocks the upper part of his face so that I can only see the firm set of his jaw and mouth. In front of me, Charlie's boots clang on the metal steps as he goes up to the door, propped open with a tennis shoe. An invitation or a lure. Either way, not a good sign.

Before opening the door, Charlie pauses just long enough for me to know that most of his machismo is for show. Without thinking, I pad up the steps as quietly as possible and slide in front of him. I can tell he's scared. I'm scared too, but I've been trained to master fear and use it to focus instead of letting *it* master me.

I ease in through the propped door and hold it open for Charlie with the side of my shoe. I shoulder my weapon, my eye taking everything in across the iron frame of the sights. The hallway's white tiles are illumined by the sunlight streaming in through the sparsely placed windows. The space itself is musty and rank. If someone's living in here, I imagine they feel safer with the windows shut. Humans tend to revert to their basest — almost childlike — instincts when faced with insurmountable fear. I've also noticed that those who most fear losing their lives usually do. Maybe this is why I have lived through so many deployments: I don't fear dying, so death does not come for me.

Seeing nothing of alarm or interest, I turn and start making my way down the hall. I hear Charlie trudging along behind, as light-footed as a gamboling bear. There is no use telling him to be quiet, so I just keep moving. A row of rooms, apparently offices, are on our left. To our right, on the wall, numerous iconic national images hang, set off by heavy gold frames: the Empire State Building, the White House, the Statue of Liberty, Mount Rushmore, and the three New York firefighters raising the flag in front of the remnants of the World Trade Center . . . all such symbols of national pride. The irony of it does not pass me by, for who knows what has befallen these symbols now.

I stare for a second and then shift my eyes to the left again, peering down through the row of offices. Most are locked when I try the doors, and then I see that the fourth has been jimmied with a crowbar. I push the door with the barrel of my gun, scanning behind it and the desk before stepping inside. The desk drawers have been dumped onto the floor, documents and papers crumpled and stamped with shoeprints. On the desk are three framed photographs. The first is a picture of a family on vacation, all lined up against a backdrop of snow in thick winter coats and clutching skis. Next is a picture of them at the beach: same people, same blond hair, but now all tanned and lined up against a backdrop of water. The last picture — a 4×6, like the rest — is just of the parents twenty or so years ago. They're holding each other close and smiling, like they can never imagine anything going wrong in their picture-perfect world.

"See anything?" Charlie asks, poking his nose around the door.

"Not much. I'll be right there." For some reason, I can't leave without turning all three pictures facedown, as if I'm closing the eyelids of someone who's died. Then I pull the door behind me, and we continue walking down the hall. I peer through the rectangular window on the left side of two huge wooden doors. Basketball nets and the polished gleam of the court make it easy to discern that the space is a gymnasium. I take a breath and push the right door open.

Immediately, I know the bathrooms along the back wall are the source of the horrible stench that hit us as soon as we stepped into the building. The trash, sleeping bags, suitcases, and clothing strewn in front of the bleachers reveal that many people were using the civic center for shelter and therefore were probably also using the toilets as if they still flushed.

If so many people were staying here, where are they now? And why did they leave their sleeping bags and clothes behind — if that is what they've done — since they are going to be wishing for every layer come winter? Moving closer, I spy children's toys among the tangled detritus — including an unmoving figure that makes my pulse skip until I reach down and touch the synthetic blond hair of a life-size doll. There are plastic bags, cooking pots, plates, a broken flashlight, and numerous candleholders, the wax burned down to the bases' metal disks.

Charlie crouches beside me to examine the goods. I didn't hear him come up, which is annoying. But I know that my audible range, after such proximity to the bomb's explosion in the desert, is not what it once was. I used to take comfort in my hearing loss after I received my father's phone call, trying to get me to reenlist. I figured it was bad enough that — even if he somehow talked me into it — my failed physical would exempt me from another deployment. Yet now I take no comfort in my minor handicap; I know it's liable to get me killed.

The gymnasium door opens, and Charlie and I both whirl to face it. But it's only Jabil, his straw hat haloed by the sun filtering weakly through the skylight above.

"Why aren't you watching the vehicle?" I ask.

Pocketing his Bible, Jabil makes his way over to us while examining the pile of refuse. "Thought I saw somebody else come in the building. I worried that you guys were trapped." Stepping over a sleeping bag, he stops and opens it with his foot. Inside is the emaciated figure of a man, his face so lifeless that I know he's already dead.

"Be careful," I warn as Jabil rests his hand against the man's forehead — checking, I guess, for the warmth he's not going to find.

"He — he's dead." From his horrified expression, I deduce that Jabil's not seen many bodies. Charlie has no such qualms. He strides over and peers down, focusing the lens of his headlamp on the corpse. The man's condition tells me he's been living this kind of lifestyle for far longer than the three weeks since the EMP. He was possibly homeless — a drifter who ambled around the streets and then took advantage of the abandoned center and the items that the citizens of Liberty left behind.

"Well," Charlie says, "this is most likely how he died." I think he's referring to the quart jar next to the body, which is filled with a clear liquid resembling homemade moonshine. But then he leans down and plucks a prescription bottle from the sleeping bag's zippered mouth. He holds it a few inches from his face and reads, "Boulder Drugs, Melinda A. Clarke, eszopiclone."

"Melinda?" I snatch the prescription from Charlie and glance at Jabil. "Isn't that the name of the woman who was in the community?"

He nods, paler than when he first touched the corpse. Rising to his feet, he takes off his hat and reaches for the brown bottle in my hands. He holds it at different angles in the muted light, as if he thinks that will somehow change the words printed on the side. Clearing his throat, he says, "Boulder's in Colorado. It's her. She must've come here first."

"You think?" I say. "Of *course* she came here first. What I want to know is where she is *now.* And how this dead guy got her stuff."

Jabil crouches again and squints at the corpse. Charlie obliges by angling his head-lamp and switching on the high beams that he turned low to conserve the battery. Even Charlie keeps quiet as Jabil continues staring. Finally, Jabil puts the prescription bottle in the sleeping bag where we found it and stands. He puts his hat back on. "Who knows how he got it," he whispers, as if at a wake. "I just hope she's okay."

"Maybe he killed her."

"Charlie!" Jabil and I cry in unison, though he's speaking our own thoughts.

Charlie grins to himself, pleased by our reaction, and I feel like smacking his head-lamp against the wall while it's still on his head. Then Jabil and I look at each other, and Jabil's expression morphs from shock at Charlie's callous remark to contempt aimed, I believe, at me.

Out of habit, Jabil clears his throat. "We can't let Leora know what we found here." He glances at Charlie, who's busy adjusting the strap of his headlamp. "You listening to me, Charlie?" Charlie lets go of his head-lamp, abashed, and nods. "She's been under a great deal of stress. She doesn't need to think her old roommate's dead on top of it."

"But doesn't she have the right to know what we found?" I ask.

"Maybe. But I don't want to tell her until we know more." He pauses. "What're we going to do with the body in the meantime?"

Charlie says, "Who says we need to do anything? He could be a murderer."

"He still has a soul."

I sigh. "We'll have to bury him later, guys. We don't even have a shovel."

Charlie shakes his head and strides toward the gymnasium doors. Jabil follows. I lean down and retrieve the prescription bottle from the sleeping bag and slide it into my pocket. But before I pass through the emergency exit, I remind myself that what Jabil said is true, and I decide not to show Leora the bottle. It's better not to put unnecessary stress on her at this time. We are dealing with her heart, and Jabil's not the only one who wants to protect it at all costs.

CHAPTER 11

LEORA

My basket is half-filled with a cornucopia of root vegetables — the richly fertilized soil caking to the tapered ends — when the Suburban crackles down the lane and deposits Moses and Jabil in front of the Snyders' house. I rest my palms on the edge of the raised bed and watch both men turn to watch the vehicle pull away, a tail of low-lying dust trailing behind.

From the back, they appear oddly similar despite their differences in height, coloring, and dress. Perhaps this is because their appearance is overshadowed by the characteristics of their inward man, which matters to me most: integrity, work ethic, and a desire to protect the weak.

Wanting to find out if they had any success at the armory, I wipe my hands on my apron and rise from the garden, crossing the stretch of lawn between the Snyders' house and ours. Moses and Jabil stop speaking when they see me coming. They look at each other, their expressions pained in a way that makes me want to turn back.

Overcome with shyness — and more than a little confusion — I ask, "Find anything?"

Jabil woodenly replies, "A pack of toothbrushes, fire starters, some blankets, and a case of refried beans probably looted from Burt's Grocery."

"No ammunition?" I look at Moses.

He shakes his head. "Finding stuff like that was just wishful thinking. You wouldn't even recognize Liberty, Leora. Two and a half weeks of scavenging has totally destroyed the buildings — some still standing, most burnt to the ground. But the flip side is that I was also expecting to be faced with more danger than we were."

Jabil adds, "Yeah, we barely saw anything." This unnecessary echo confounds me less than his flexed jaw and hands that make his entire body appear constricted in warning. However, I came over not only to find out if they had any success, but also to show my appreciation for everything they've done for Mt. Hebron. So with considerable effort I soften my features and ask if they'd be interested in joining my family for lunch.

I watch them visibly brace before accept-

290

ing my invitation. I feel a moment of anxiety, picturing Jabil bonding with Moses during their foray into town. And if they do, what might such bonding mean for me? I collect my basket of vegetables and go up the back porch steps.

Inside, I slide a tray of cooked butternut squash onto the countertop and place a fresh loaf of sourdough bread on the table. Jabil and Moses enter.

Moses takes off his shoes and washes his hands at the sink. "Need help with anything?"

The men in our community consider the kitchen a woman's domain, just as we consider the logging pavilion a man's. Recovering from surprise, I respond, "Guess you can help me peel the squash." In silence, Moses and I stand side by side as the steam rises between us, redolent of our treasured hoard of nutmeg and cloves. I take off my spectacles, clean the fogged lenses on my apron, and slip them into my pocket. The kitchen brightens. Over my shoulder, I watch Jabil light the kerosene lamp hanging above the table. The use of fuel seems an extravagance, considering the sun is shining outside. Then Jabil looks at me, and I can tell he has lit the lamp not for illumination as much as to thwart the intimacy fostered by the dimness.

Taking the hand beater, I puree the goldenrod-colored vegetables into soup. Somehow, Moses anticipates my every need — mashing the roasted onion and garlic, adding a pinch of cayenne and sage, the two of us moving in a culinary dance whose steps are improvised yet sure. I lift my gaze to his, and we stare at each other in the vivid light. I am painfully conscious of his warmth and of his breathing, which is as hitched and uneven as mine. For the first time, I am grateful I am not hiding behind my lenses or behind my unnecessary desire to be the stand-in patriarch of my orphaned family, so that I can never allow myself to be just what I am: a young woman with the desire to be desired and loved.

When the soup is prepared, the table spread with a cloth my *mamm* once kept in her hope chest for special occasions, along with a crystal relish tray of pickled baby corn, okra, and cheese, I find that I am shaking from the revelation of my hunger. Not wanting to reveal my unsettled state, I wait a moment to let my flushed cheeks subside and then return to the table to see that Jabil has already claimed my seat. Over the years, he has attended enough meals to know that this was my *vadder*'s old chair, so I am sure this is a hated move.

I sit down and fold my hands on the table. Moses, also having attended enough meals to anticipate our actions, bows his head. Then, feeling a gaze upon me, I open my eyes. But Moses is still praying. I glance over and see that Jabil is perusing my features as I had seen Moses earlier perusing the map of Liberty that was spread across the hood of the truck, as if searching for dangers not readily foreseen. Our gazes remain locked as the silent prayer continues and the grandfather clock marks the seconds pouring through the accelerated hourglass of our world.

Contrite for keeping my eyes open during prayer, I reach down into my apron, withdraw my spectacles, and put them on. Truth be told, they are not needed. My minor astigmatism improved more than three years ago. But by that point, my *vadder*'s unstable presence in our home left me longing for something behind which I could hide, even if it was made from a medium as unstable as glass.

The prayer time ends. Young Colton opens his mouth like a little bird as he waits for *Grossmammi* Eunice to fill it with a spoonful of soup. Sal, his mother, has disappeared again. The third time this week. Anna dips a torn portion of sourdough into the soup and munches happily, wiping her mouth with the back of her hand. I pass a napkin to her. She smiles and cleans the corners of her stained lips. Tears sting my eyes as I realize that my sister probably does not comprehend what happened to her that night in the field.

Anna hasn't allowed me to examine her, and I'm not sure I would have the stomach even if I could. It is hard enough to see the scratch on her face and recall the blood marring her gown. Later, I checked that Anna was sleeping and got up from our bed. I carried her nightgown out to the woodstove, stoked the fire, and tucked it down into the box. Watching the flames devour the soft cotton, I viewed the action as a portent of my future revenge.

I hear Seth asking, as if from far away, "How'd you learn to fly?"

I glance over at Moses, to whom, no doubt, the question was addressed. "My grandpa." Jabbing his spoon in Seth's direction, he smiles. "Actually, I was about your age when he took me and my brother up for the first time."

"Did you ever fly a fighter plane?" Seth's eyes gleam with interest. I watch Jabil shift in his seat, uncomfortable with the direction of conversation. Or maybe he's uncomfortable that the conversation is not being directed by him.

"No, but my grandpa did. He was in Vietnam."

"Did he — ?"

I break in. "Seth, that's enough."

My brother glances at me. "Don't treat me like a kid."

I am taken aback by his resentment and am preparing to defend myself when Jabil says, "Thank you for the delicious meal, Leora, but we should be hitting the road."

"Again?" I ask. "You just got back."

"We had to come get some things for Charlie."

Seth looks at Moses. "Can I come too?" His voice fissures on the last syllable, and his face grows red. Moses, with his airplane and his gun, is every boy's childhood hero brought to life. But I fear the adult awakening Seth would experience if he ventured into Liberty with him.

"I'm sorry," Jabil answers before I can tell Seth no. "It's not safe."

Jabil's caution brings sorrow to my eyes. My sister was attacked by something — or someone — because I wasn't cautious enough. Maybe if I'd married him like *Mamm* wished, it wouldn't have happened.

295

Setting my napkin beside my plate, I murmur good-bye to the men and leave the room. Even with our bedroom door closed, I can hear the restrained hum of voices in the kitchen, the clinking of cutlery against plates, followed by the shuffle of boots crossing the hardwood floor. The front door closes as Jabil and Moses leave to scavenge for supplies.

Enough time passes for me to drift into a restless sleep. I awaken to a hand touching my shoulder. I lift my face from the quilt — my vision blurred — and see that Sal's returned and is staring down at me with Colton on her hip, his mouth still bearing traces of butternut soup.

"You okay?" she asks. "Upset about Anna?"

I nod and glance over her shoulder toward the door, wincing as I see she's left it cracked. Wiping my eyes, I get down off the bed and close the door with one hand. I turn back and say, "I've come to my own conclusions about who attacked her. But that doesn't mean a whole lot."

"Your own conclusions?"

"That night, after I found Anna, I saw a light on the lane. Charlie'd been wearing a headlamp when he was guarding the gate." I shrug. "It's not much, but it makes me wonder if he was returning to his post after what he did."

Sal moves to sit down on our bed but then keeps standing. "Have you talked to him?"

"You can't just come out and accuse someone of something like that. Can you?"

"No," she murmurs. I look at Sal's downcast face and am shocked to see that the same person who usually never displays any emotion appears about to cry.

I place a hand on her shoulder. "It's not your fault. There's nothing you could've done."

Sal glances up and meets my eyes, her own potent with anger. "I was here," she says. "I should've heard something. I should've *known.*"

"And I *wasn't* here. Don't you think that haunts me, too?"

She reaches up to clasp my hand that's resting on her shoulder. Her nails are ragged and filled with dirt. When she sees me looking down at them, it's as if an unseen portal between the two of us slams closed. Her face resumes its unmalleable veneer, and she leaves without another word, the soil left by the treads of her boots the only proof that she was in our room.

As planned, we return to the civic center to bury the dead man. Jabil remains outside, standing like a defenseless sentinel halfway between the vehicle and the emergency exit. Charlie trails me down the hall, covering my back more thoroughly than he did before. At first, everything appears the same as it did this morning: the smell, the hodge-podge of possessions, the shining expanse of parquet floor marked for a basketball game no one might ever play again.

But then I come to the section where the body used to be. The sleeping bag and the mostly empty jar of moonshine are gone. I glance over my shoulder and spot a bearded man curled up on the bottom row of the left-hand bleachers. As I draw closer, the man stands and holds up his hands, fingers spread, like he's expecting a fight. He appears younger than the dead man, though just as weather-beaten and thin.

Charlie must see him too. He opens the gym door. "You all right in there, Moses?"

The bearded man looks from me to Charlie and then down at my hands.

I lower my gun. "Everything's fine."

The door closes. The man blinks at me. I'm not here to cause trouble, but I'm not sure the same can be said for him. I take a step closer, and the man takes a step back, his calves pressed against the bleacher's varnished wood. He looks to the right and then to the left — trying to decide, I guess, which would be the best route of escape if the need should arise.

"We came earlier," I explain. "That's when we found the body. What'd you do with it?"

"Buried him. Waited 'til you left. Thought you were the gang."

"The gang?"

"They were here last week. Didn't give people time to pack —" he motions to the items scattered around the edges of the court — "just drove them out the doors with guns. Then they went through the building, picking out what they wanted and leaving the rest behind. Once Victor and I knew they were gone, we came here to stay, figuring they wouldn't be back."

"Victor? Was he . . . ?"

"The dead guy?"

I nod.

"Yeah. He was."

"Were the two of you homeless?"

He smirks. "Let's just say I haven't had a roof of my own in the past two years."

On a whim, I pull the prescription bottle from my pocket. I toss it to him, the pills

299

clinking. He catches it in one hand. "We found this on the body. Mean anything to you?"

He turns the bottle over. "Victor musta stole it from me."

"You're the first man I ever met who's named Melinda."

The man looks up and squints. "I got this stuff fair and square."

"Guess that depends on your definition of *fair.*"

"Look, all I know's some woman came here about a week or so ago, telling me she'd do just about anything to get home. I have some connections, so I directed her to a friend of a friend, and she gave me some pills as repayment."

I quip, "How generous of you to help her. You've not seen her since?"

He shakes his head. "I didn't take advantage. I swear. I'm not that kind of guy."

Anger deepens my voice. "No. You just turned her over to those who are."

"You know nothing about me, man. I got a wife and kids."

I begin studying the man's features. Something about him looked familiar, and now I start to suspect why. Same prominent cheekbones, dark hair, and eyes.

"How many kids?" He looks at me like

I'm crazy. I lift the gun. "Answer the question!"

"What's wrong with you? *Three* kids. Two girls and a boy."

Taking a breath, I say, "About three weeks ago, my plane crashed in a field in the Mt. Hebron community. The family who took me in told me that two years ago their father disappeared." The man's astonishment confirms my hunch. "*You're* Luke Ebersole — the man who disappeared — aren't you?"

He hesitates, looking down at the bottle, and then nods.

"Why don't you go to your family? Let them know you're alive?"

Luke pockets the bottle and plucks at his threadbare shirt. Wrists protrude like branches from the sleeves. "Believe me, nobody wants me showing up like this."

"Maybe not. But I think it's worse not showing up at all."

He kicks at a Coke can lying near his feet, sending it rolling across the floor. "Why you think I'm sticking round while everybody else's left? It's not simple, getting clean. I've tried."

I think of his eldest daughter, perpetually waiting for a man with no intentions of ever coming home. I think of myself, waiting for my own father to come back, and whenever he did, trying to be his little soldier so he would want to stay. "Then you gotta try harder."

He folds his arms. "I got no time to try. Word has it another gang's coming this way that's going to —"

"Which way?" I cut him short.

"Supposedly from the north. That's why town's so deserted. Nobody's stopping here anymore because they know what's on their heels."

Now I understand why the number of people walking past our perimeter has increased over the past few days. Everyone's trying to get out while they can. I recall the items spread along the sides of the highway, like a mutant Hansel and Gretel trail leading out of Liberty. These were not people merely weary of their burdens; these were people running for their lives.

"Will you tell my wife and kids about what's coming?" he asks.

This backhanded consideration makes me sick. "Your wife's dead, Luke."

"You're kidding me."

" 'Fraid not." I don't care if I rip his heart out. He deserves it.

Luke's knees buckle like an easel. One second, they're propping his body; the next second, he's down. Peering up at me through his scum of hair, he rasps, "When?"

"I don't know for sure, but I think it was around a year after you left. Your oldest daughter's been taking care of Anna and Seth on her own."

He pauses, processing. "And my *mudder*?"

"Leora's been taking care of her too." I stare down at him, his arms dangling over his legs, the bald patch on his crown shining in the light. "You should be ashamed," I spit.

He lowers his head and sobs. "I am. I am."

My courage falters when I see Leora and her sister sitting on the front porch steps. Anna's making a necklace by stringing the buttons pooled in her lap; Leora's mending one of the dresses that I recognize as hers because she was wearing it the day I crashed, when everything both ended and began.

Overhead, the rising crescent moon winks like one of the buttons glittering in Anna's lap. Anna passes another button to Leora, and she sews it onto the dress, which seems odd since I've never noticed buttons on any of the Mennonite women's dresses before. Leora glances up as I approach. "Hello," she says.

"Hey," I respond, yet my thoughts are

consumed by the man I met in the center, an abstract sketch of the fully fleshed father and husband he had been. And I wonder if news of his proximity would be a burden or a gift.

Anna's pale eyes dart between me and her sister. An intelligence is there I haven't noticed due to the impediment of her speech . . . if she ever speaks at all.

I straighten my back. "Okay to talk in front of your sister?"

"Depends." Leora doesn't look up. "What do you have to say?"

"It's about something I heard in town."

"Go ahead. I'm not letting Anna out of my sight."

Leora's curtness makes me realize I came here with information I have no clue how to give. I decide not to tell her about her father but about the drifter I met in town. For now, just like I told Jabil, she doesn't need to know they're one and the same.

"Is it true?" she asks, once I'm finished conveying Luke's news.

"The person who said it seemed to know what he was talking about."

She sets the dress down and looks up, gripping a button in her palm. "So what are you going to do about it? Use the Suburban to scout the area?"

"Believe me, if a massive gang saw a vehicle coming up the road toward them, they'd kill the driver and hijack it without a second thought. No, I'm wondering if there's somewhere I can go that's up high and offers a long-range view down the main road? I am talking like way out of *their* long-range view. If there's something like that, maybe I could take Charlie's spotting scope and see what's coming miles before it gets here."

She pauses, fingering the button. "If any large group is coming from the north, they'd be coming down Highway 87. And if I'm remembering right, you can see up that road for miles from the fire tower. I wouldn't completely trust it, though. It hasn't been maintained in ages. It's been years since I've been up there myself."

"And it *might* be occupied."

"A fire tower occupied?" she asks. "By whom?"

"By any random person looking to take advantage of a remote structure. Especially one with a vantage point like that. But it's worth checking out. Could you show me on a map?"

She shakes her head and picks up the needle again. "I've only been there a hand-ful of times. It's the same trail that takes you down by Glacier Falls."

"Where's that?"

Leora sighs. "I guess I should take you."

"No way. I want you safe."

Face half-concealed in shadow, her thoughts are hard to read. She glances over at her sister. "I don't think there's any safe place anymore. I'm in as much danger walking in my own yard," she says, spearing the fabric of the dress, "as I would be walking in the woods with you."

■ ■ ■ ■

CHAPTER 12

■ ■ ■ ■

LEORA

I return to the community cemetery at two in the morning, alone. The lamp swings from my hand, revealing the bouquet of Indian paintbrush on my *mamm*'s grave that has lost its vibrancy and on the new graves, still bare. Soon enough, though, grass will begin pushing up through the mounded dirt, to remind us that those boys are not dead, for life does not end with death. Our souls are merely indwelling our bodies until our bodies are returned to dust and life awakens anew.

I walk past the graves, and my lamp reveals Moses leaning against the fencerow where I stood to watch the albino buck, the day after the two boys' temporal deaths. With a magician's flourish, he pulls a tea towel from the water bottle pocket of his backpack. "I imagine it's a long walk," he explains, "and we're going to get hungry. I packed breakfast."

"Jabil's *mudder* didn't mind you in her kitchen?"

"She didn't even know I was there."

"She *will* know once she sees some of her food is gone." The mention of Jabil dissolves the flirtation building between us. "You ready to go?" I ask, my tone guarded.

Moses nods. I set my lamp on the fence post and scale the wire squares before hoisting my body over the fence and jumping down. Moses stands on the other side, shaking his head, before climbing the fence and jumping as well. "You could put a GI to shame," he says while I gather the lamp.

"What's that?"

He grins. "Never mind." His headlong stride retains traces of a limp, though he attempts to conceal it whenever he notices anyone watching him.

"I saw an albino buck when I was out here visiting the graves the other day," I murmur, to cover up the fact that I'm watching him now. "He was the most exquisite animal I've ever seen. After the game reserve was turned into national forest, a few of the animals that were brought to this area — like the albino buck — were never rounded up because they belonged here." I stop walking. "He doesn't stand much of a chance, though, does he?"

Moses stops walking too. The swishing sound our footsteps were making in the fallen pine needles ceases. "People are getting desperate, Leora. If somebody spots your buck, they won't see a rare albino; they'll see meat that can feed their family."

I nod, for of course I understand and cannot blame the person who will eventually slay the white deer. Yet somehow, in this world where so much is becoming ugly, I want to preserve the one thing that appears just as beautiful as it was before any of this happened.

I tuck myself deeper into my shawl and look up at the conifers soaring high above our heads. The absence of Liberty's peach-colored light pollution has become almost normal to me since the EMP reverted night-time to its original dark. We continue traveling in a stillness that feels as natural as the movement of our feet. I contemplate asking Moses to tell me more about his life before he crashed in our field, but I sense that, like me, he is glad to leave behind some aspects of his past.

Something suddenly bursts forth. Pulse thudding, I hold out my lamp in an attempt to see farther than its ten-foot radius of illumination. Moses, beside me, grabs the flashlight from the side pocket of the back-pack and directs the beam toward the underbrush. We see the silver haunches and tail of an animal loping off into the trees. Then it stops as abruptly as it appeared and turns toward us, eyes gleaming like candles from the reflection of the light.

"A coyote?" he asks.

"Looks more like a wolf," I whisper. "There are a few around here."

If it *is* a wolf, I know it is more scared of us than we are of it. But I find myself sidestepping closer to Moses as we continue up the trail. My legs begin to burn against the strain of the incline, and — rubbed raw by my boots — the skin scrapes away from the backs of my heels. If Moses's ankle is bothering him, he doesn't mention it. But I doubt he would mention it even if it was. After another half mile, when my tights are glued to my heels with blood, I detect the sound of water breaking over rocks.

Moses lifts his head. "Those the falls?"

"*Jah.* You should see them in the light."

We keep trudging on, making our way toward the thunderous roar in the darkness. I extend the lamp again, and the weak beam reveals the slick facades of the boulders that have been worn away by the water's contin-uous motion. Despite my sore feet, I maneuver around the rocks effortlessly, placing my boots at angles so they are not trapped and then picking my way through the thick tree roots that have wormed through crevices.

"You said you haven't been here in a while?" Moses asks.

"That's right," I reply, keeping my voice neutral. "Not in years."

I remember our picnics here and how my *vadder* and I tried once, for hours, to teach Anna to swim in the falls' shallow end: spray clinging to his black beard, her floral chore apron floating in the froth as we held her body between us, and the *Englischer* tourists gaping at us from the hanging bridge, like we were on display the same as the mountainous terrain.

"Would you like to see him again, if you could?"

Startled, I glance at Moses. "Who?"

"Your dad. Was he the one who brought you here?"

I exhale hard. "I've given up on a reunion. I've all but given up hope that he's alive."

"But what if he *is*?"

"I'm not sure I'd have the strength to welcome someone back who abandoned us."

"Can you at least tell me a little bit about what happened?"

This question comes across forced, purposefully attentive, as if — in Moses's mind — he is jotting everything down. I don't respond right away, trying to decide if there's any harm in relating our family's saga to this man, who is no longer a stranger and yet not quite a friend. "Two years ago, a driver picked my *vadder* up for his daily commute to Sandpoint. He had a booth there, displaying handcrafted furniture — tables, cradles, rocking chairs, clocks. But that night, the driver did not bring him home. *Mamm* used Field to Table's phone to call the driver, but he said my *vadder* gave no clue as to where he was going or why he was going there."

He simply cleared out his booth and left.

We'd been relying on my *vadder*'s furniture profits for years. But, subtracting expenses, there had never been enough income left over to place into savings. After his disappearance, the community tried taking care of us by finding him. When that proved futile, they brought wagonloads of split wood, venison jerky, and produce from their gardens. But my *mamm* soon became embarrassed by these gifts, which — from her biased perspective — seemed to confirm her parents' belief that erratic Luke Ebersole would never be able to provide for her. So kindly, yet firmly, she started refusing these gifts and working with my brother at Field to Table.

Moses takes a seat on a boulder, his expression grave. "We found a body the first time we went to the civic center. When we returned to bury him, your dad had already done it for us. *He's* the drifter who warned me about the gang. He's why we're here."

I struggle to comprehend Moses's words. Gripping the lamp, I pivot away from him and face the trees. "What makes you think it was my *vadder*?"

"Leora." I hear him stand. I flinch as he touches my back. "Look. It was him. I'm sorry for not telling you earlier. I wasn't sure you'd want to know."

Tears blister my eyes. How has my *vadder* been this close the entire time? How has he become a drifter? And yet, don't I know the answers to these questions before they're even asked? Didn't I hear the arguments between my parents when they thought my sister and I were sleeping? Didn't I, upon waking, so often notice my *vadder*'s mottled eyes and shaking hands?

Toward the end, before his disappearance, work seemed to overtake his life. But my *vadder* remained frantic about conjuring up more business and more money. My *mamm* would often be sitting at the kitchen table

315

beside him, begging him to stop. To stop working so hard, to spend more time with our family . . . to get the help he needed and we deserved. I thought she meant help running his business. But it is clear now. *Everything* is clear now.

I close my eyes, letting my rapid thoughts be swept under by the falls behind us. I know I am not ready to face the man whose abandonment decimated my *mudder*'s will to live and therefore rendered us orphans in experience, if not in fact. It does not matter that our world has changed and everything is at risk. He thought of no risks when he left us. So I will not give him the courtesy of my love, which turns out to be as conditional as his.

"I'm going to need time," I whisper, not sure if I'm heard over the water and thankful if I'm not. Swallowing hard, I say, "Please don't tell my brother about this . . . not yet, anyway."

"Of course," Moses replies. "Whatever you need."

The two of us are quiet for some time. Then I hear the tinny clang of metal. I turn and am astonished to see him dumping items from his jeans onto a cradle in the rock, more than likely carved by the Kutenai, who came here eons before we did. He has a pocketknife, a watch with a broken band, and a few quarters, nickels, and dimes that are obsolete since the EMP. I set my lamp on the boulder and watch him take his holster off, pull his belt out through the loops, coil the leather, and set the gun and holster beside it.

"You're going swimming?" I ask, but of course he is.

"With all this water, can't resist the chance."

"Couldn't you just stick your feet in? We've got a long climb ahead."

His laughter is muffled as he pulls off his shirt. "If you've been sweating like me, you'd know that I need to stick in a little more than my feet. But I'll be quick. Promise."

I avert my eyes and sit on the rock beside his last worldly possessions. I am more than a little irritated that he would reveal such life-altering information and then go for a casual swim, as if every day daughters discover that their estranged fathers are alive. Angling my head, I watch the pale, inverted triangle of Moses's torso as he picks his way down to the shoreline and submerges his legs and waist. He stands motionless for a second before diving in, fully embracing the water's cold.

When he resurfaces, whipping back his hair, he grins and waves. "Come on! It's great!"

I shake my head and sit on the rock with my knees drawn up to my chest and my arms wrapped around them. All the while, I can see myself as I was three . . . four years ago, before adulthood prematurely descended and my future prospects changed. I recall feeling weightless as my arms pulled my body through the water, despite my sodden cape dress's vain attempt to weigh me down. Oftentimes, just our family came to Glacier Falls with a picnic basket and an old quilt my *mamm* didn't mind spreading across the ground. But if other members from Mt. Hebron came to enjoy the sun and water, they were taken aback that my *vadder* allowed me — even *encouraged* me — to swim. Yet I think perhaps watching me, his eldest daughter, gliding through the shallows with the ease of a fish gave him hope that he too could fight against the current of his addictions that were slowly pulling him under, and us right along with him.

I unspool my shawl and unlace my boots — not in celebration of my *vadder*'s survival, but perhaps in memory of that bearded man who used to toss me, laughing, into the pond in Millersburg, Ohio, believing in me enough to let me rise on my own and swim. I take off my chore apron, fold it, and place it on top of my boots with the solemnity of a ritual. I wasn't wearing my *kapp* three or four years ago when I would come here so unfettered by life's cares and woes; therefore I never had to worry about the water ruining the delicate fabric. But to take it off now — in the presence of a man who is not my husband, no less — would be drawing close to a precipice whence I can never return. However, have I not already leapt over a precipice, as I abandoned my pacifist ideals for the sake of revenge?

I pull the bobby pins from my *kapp* and drop them, plinking, into my shoes. I let my taut bun loosen and cascade down my back. I take off my glasses and tuck them into my apron pocket. Then I take mincing steps down to the water. The wind whips my hair into a damp cloud. I take hold of the thousand errant pieces and fold my arms behind me, out of guilt and out of habit, preparing to wrap them into a single plait.

Moses calls to me over the roar of the falls. I glance up and see him bobbing in the current. He cups hands around his mouth and repeats, "Let it down." I watch him and my face burns. But I keep my arms bowed behind my neck — my hair held in place — like the last parapet of my inhibitions. I have no idea how long he has observed my transformation from obedient Mennonite girl to . . . what, exactly? Someone who sheds her prayer covering at the slightest provocation? Was Moses Hughes sent here to tempt me in every weakened area of my life, as Christ was tempted in the desert? Or is he simply an impetuous man who wants a self-conscious former schoolteacher to have a good time? I am not sure if I will ever know the truth; I am not sure I will ever know who he is . . . or even who I really am.

I divert my gaze from Moses's. Then I release my fingers, letting the strands of my hair fall where they will. I begin to laugh as they cavort around me, and I feel such a mixture of sadness and relief, I know I've needed to let go of my death grip on life for quite some time.

"You a good swimmer?" Moses asks.

Rather than give him a response, I stretch out my crossed arms and dive under, sliding through the water with ease. I don't rise to the surface, but allow the surface to close over me — swimming with my hair streaking out behind until I can hear the pounding falls above. I allow myself to come up inside the pocket of turbulence, effervescent with bubbles created as the cascade plunges into the pool. Moses swims over and continues treading the current, inches away. I can almost feel the warmth of him radiating through the water. His feet touch mine.

"How come you came into my life at the moment our world fell apart?" My words are distorted by my body's trembling.

"Maybe I came to show you there's more to this world than your community."

"Maybe you came here to lead me astray."

At this, Moses's playful smile evaporates. He tucks a wet hank of hair away from my face. "Or maybe," he murmurs, 'the God of your fathers hath sent me unto you.' "

I jerk back, alarmed by the intimacy of his hand touching my cheek, of his bare feet touching mine. I don't know if these gestures — these quoted words — are confirmation of my theory or denial. Either way, they are more intimate than the first kiss that I have imagined all my life and yet, at nineteen years old, have never actually known. The twilight magic turns to mist, and the preternatural warmth insulating my body grows cold. I stare at Moses, memorizing his water-colored eyes, before allowing my cape dress to pull me back down into the current, until the carefree woman I have allowed to come to the surface also disappears.

MOSES

Leora's breathing quickens as she leads me up the side of the mountain to the neglected fire tower. Most of the wooden steps are rotted and needed replaced years ago. I take care to place my weight toward the edge of each step and not in the middle, keeping a firm hold on the metal railing that follows the steps as they switchback toward the top. Although Leora is taking the same precautions as I, the height and safety of the tower does not seem to bother her, so I am not about to let her know how much it bothers me.

By the time we reach the tower's pinnacle, we are both out of breath. The sun has made its way over the distant skyline, filling the valleys and fields below with its welcomed light and warmth. We stop and stand at the very last row of steps, just below the small — maybe 8'×8' — boxlike structure that is perched on the very top. It is a sight to behold. The black asphalt road is clearly the main highway coming from the north. Wisps of smoke periodically dot the grass alongside it, which I am guessing are campfires built by the refugees — the smoke rising a hundred feet or so, and then going in horizontal lines, streaking across the valleys below us.

"How far is it out there?" I ask, pointing to the highway disappearing around a bend and then reappearing up ahead as an even thinner black line.

"Not sure," Leora replies. "Probably farther than it looks."

A wooden trapdoor is at the top of the steps above us. I lean around Leora to jiggle the padlock, making sure not to brush against her. I can see her start shivering as the wind picks up. Her cape dress looks mostly dry by now, but her hair — more than likely never cut — tapers to a steady drip down her lower back.

"You warming up?" I ask.

Leora nods, her mouth sealed like that padlocked door. Having nothing to offer her but my shirt, which I know she wouldn't take, I turn and peek through the door's cracks. I see a small desk, a folding chair, a potbelly stove with a pile of logs beside it. I guess this is where rangers once sat for hours on end, scouting the forest for signs of smoke.

Taking the pack off my shoulders, I set it in front of me, open the top zipper, and dig for the spotting scope that I swiped from Charlie. I use the clamp on the bottom of the scope to secure it to the metal framework of the tower. Leaning down, I peer through the lens, which makes the highway's yellow lines miles away seem close enough to touch. I study the area, but there's not a whole lot to see other than the expected abandoned vehicles and junk that was also scattered along the road by travelers. I can easily make out random small groups of people, but most of these seem to be camped. I direct the spotting scope to the farthest point, where the highway goes out of sight, and try to bring it into focus. Finally, getting it just right, I sweep the area again.

"Wow." I glance at Leora standing beside me, squinting against the light, her glasses back in place, along with that endless storehouse of her reserve. "You wanna look?" I ask. She nods, and I step back, giving her room to kneel in front of the scope. "Can you see that?"

"See what?"

Reaching over, I adjust the scope for her, trying to align it with the group that I saw in the distance.

"Wait," she says. "I see them." She studies the people for what seems like minutes before looking up at me, concern etched across her features. "Do you think they're more refugees on the move, or that they're the gang my — my *vadder* was talking about?"

I bring my own eye back to the scope. "Hard to tell," I say. "One thing's for sure, though: there's a large group coming this way."

"Even if that's not a gang, it's only a matter of time until one *does* come. And we wouldn't stand much of a chance, would we?" Leora's voice shakes.

Unable to give her an honest answer, I reach out and put my arm around her narrow shoulders, feeling the goose bumps rise on her flesh. My breath is warm against her damp hair. Leora raises her head, and I see a level of fear in her eyes that was not there before.

"Sometimes . . . sometimes I feel I'm living in a dream. Or a nightmare. No matter what I do," she whispers, "no matter how hard I try, everything still keeps falling apart."

"Maybe it's not your job to keep it together."

"You keep saying that. But if I don't, who will?"

"Why don't you trust God to do it for you?"

"Because I have a hard time trusting

anyone. Even him."

That day we met, Leora spoke with such conviction about her faith, I believed it wasn't like everyone else's: a talisman clutched to ward off inconvenience or pain. I assumed her faith was *real* and have since used it as a template by which I can look back and judge the journey of my own. Now I know she struggles the same as I do, the same as everyone does. The reality is harsh, reminding me of the time I went into the garage to find my father sobbing.

I recall how he lifted his gaze and saw me standing there, the keys to my Ford Ranger dangling from my hand. I was sixteen years old and so eager for an excuse to drive that I was going to travel fifteen miles to the grocery store to buy my mom half-and-half for her morning coffee. My father's face was so twisted with sorrow, so red with embarrassment, I stepped back into the laundry room — knocking over the cat's water bowl — and pulled the door between us, relieved to block that image of him staring at the picture of our family, tacked to the corkboard with a finishing nail, from my mind. But he showed up for supper that night, more cheerful than he'd been since he came home. He never explained to me why he'd been crying, and I never asked. Two months later, after he left, Aaron and I learned about our father's illegitimate son.

I didn't want to hear it, to accept that my war-hero father was fallible, human; and now I know that Leora is human as well. Am I drawn to her because she fulfills my idea of perfection, or am I drawn to her *despite* the reality that she is as human as I?

"Is it because you don't trust God?" I ask. "Or because you don't trust yourself?"

Leora frowns. "Neither . . . both. I don't know, Moses. I let someone down. I let someone get hurt. I promised myself I would never let her get hurt again."

Then, so slowly I almost believe I'm imagining it, Leora turns and rests her head against me. I don't look at her, in case that would make her feel self-conscious and pull away, but reach out and trace a set of initials and dates gouged in the fire tower: *DT loves JH 4-ever, 11/21/12.* Looking at those initials, I wonder if any of us left on this planet have time to leave such a meaningless mark behind. But unlike the wise Solomon once declared, nothing is meaningless. I bet even *he* would have started to see the meaning of life if he could see the end of time.

I tell her, "You asked me once if I knew about revenge. Well, Leora, I know far more about guilt. I wake up with it. Go to sleep with it."

She says against my chest, "What happened?"

"My brother died. In the war."

"It can't have been your fault. Why do you feel guilty?"

It sounds like such a simple question, but I'm not sure I can explain it. "We were in Afghanistan. There was this kid . . ." I remember the boy's blameless guise, which lured us to him, giving way to anger as he yelled in Pashto and opened his hand, revealing wires and a trigger mechanism.

"He was all wired up, so we knew he had a bomb strapped to his body under his jacket. My brother had no choice but to shoot the kid before he could detonate the bomb. But it went off anyway. My men — and my brother — were all killed."

"I'm so sorry," Leora says. "But I don't see why you think it's your fault."

"It's my fault because *I* should have been the one to pull the trigger. I had a better angle, and I probably could have disarmed him without setting off the bomb. All those men died because I couldn't do my duty."

"I don't blame you for not wanting to shoot a little boy, even if he was trying to kill you."

"It wasn't that," I say, wishing my motives

were as much like hers as she would like to believe. "Somehow, in that instant, I imagined my father's Afghan son. He would have been about that age. I wanted to save him from himself. But all I did was kill everyone there, while I was forced to watch it all in what seemed like — and seems like — slow motion."

Honorable discharge for what amounts to killing my flesh and blood: there has never been such a contradiction of terms.

"It wasn't your fault," Leora stubbornly insists.

"Maybe it wasn't and maybe it was. Either way, I know my brother wouldn't want me wasting my life feeling guilty, wishing he was here instead."

Without disturbing Leora, I reach into my pocket for my knife. I flip the blade open and carve her initials into the tower, then my own. "What's the date?" I ask.

"August 27," she says. I scratch a circle around our two names, not a heart and certainly no mention of love. But I can feel a shift taking place on that tower as I stare at our initials, *LE* and *MH*. I know Leora feels it too. Have I been brought here to save her and myself from the bondage of our culpability, as we struggle to understand the one who is without fault?

As in anything taking place right now, only time will tell the future. But I can't resist wrapping my arms around Leora — anchoring her physical form against me — before the two of us descend the fire tower to, once again, stand on the unsteady touchstone of the earth.

LEORA

The two of us are in midstride when Moses reaches out and seizes my hand. I follow the direction of his eyes and see the community's nondescript headstones shielded inside the fence. But I can tell these are not what has captured his attention.

"Come over here," he says, the words more mouthed than spoken. I move closer to him, and he jumps in place. "Hear that?"

I do. There is a hollowness beneath our feet incompatible with the rest of the surroundings. Having asked a rhetorical question, he does not wait for my answer. Just kneels and begins scraping away the soil. Soon, I can see blond plywood patches showing through the thin potpourri of pine needles and leaves.

I kneel beside him, and together we push up the board, which is heavier than it appears. Moses shoves it back, and the board collapses, spraying dirt. Someone has chipped a crude cellar out of the earth that's about three feet deep and four feet wide. Inside it, a grocery sack is filled with cans of corn, carrots, and beans, each bearing the orange price stickers from Field to Table. Beside the grocery sack, packets of powdered milk and dehydrated eggs, along with sealed clear bags of what appears to be loose flour, are stored in two snap-lid plastic containers.

"Recognize anything?" Moses says, his tone rife with sarcasm.

I cannot reply. I am struck dumb by shock. Our supplies have been dwindling fast enough through normal use, and now to think someone has been stealing our rations. My mind's eye scrolls through the faces of the community, trying to recall a cunning expression that would make the Judas obvious: the person outwardly agreeing to the community's edict while inwardly making other plans; maybe the same heartless person who attacked my sister and left her to wander alone in the field.

"Who would do this?" I hiss. "Charlie? Sean?"

"Don't know about Sean. But Charlie would know better than to store food like this. Those containers aren't watertight. All of it —" Moses gestures in frustration —

"would be ruined in no time."

"They had to have access to Field to Table."

"Which eliminates no one in the community."

We look at each other, each of us drawing our own conclusions, and none of them are good. I am thinking of the *Englischers* as our main suspects. Moses, no doubt, is thinking of my own people as well as his.

"Let's go," he sighs, putting the board back in place and scraping the leaves and dirt over it. "We don't want anybody seeing we've been here."

"We can't just leave everything. That food could feed a family for a week!"

Moses pivots, jabbing a finger toward the camouflaged cellar. "We have to find the culprit, Leora. Whoever's done this is going to come back. It's only a matter of time."

"How do I know *you* won't just come back?" I say, only half kidding, for I'm once again trying to deflect my attraction. To protect myself, and him.

"And do what, exactly? Take the food and run?" His hand falls to his side. He shakes his head. "Don't you know me better than that?"

"That's just the thing," I murmur. "I don't know you well at all."

Looking at each other, both shivering in our damp clothes, I feel a sense of loss for reasons I cannot explain. Moses nods — whether acknowledging what I said or acknowledging that it's time to continue, I don't know. So we walk in silence back up to the fence separating the national forest from the community. Moses climbs over first and turns, opening his palms to me. Paralyzed, I continue to stand there, peering through the wire barrier separating us and seeing it as a reminder of how guarded I've been with my heart.

Climbing to the top of the fence, I reach down and put my hand in his. Part of me wishes to withdraw it as quickly as I held it out for him to hold. But I can't draw myself away. Instead, he and I remain melded together for an instant that seems suspended above the constraints of time: me looking down at him — this earthbound pilot of whom I still know almost nothing — and him looking up at me with a kindness and patience I do not deserve. His hand is smaller than Jabil's — only slightly larger than my own — but rippled with calluses, as if he's worked in the fields all his life.

Moses is the first to lower his gaze, and I can see he is trying to guard himself just as much as I have been trying — and failing

— to guard myself from him. Regardless, he helps me over the top of the fence and slips his hands around my waist before lowering my body gently to the ground. As my feet touch Mt. Hebron soil, I find myself yearning to remain in the arms of this man rather than return to the familiarity of my community and home.

CHAPTER 13

MOSES

For security purposes, Charlie boarded up the two glass entry doors to Field to Table like we were bracing ourselves for a hurricane, which — in a way — I guess we were. But it evidently didn't work, since the thief has been pilfering supplies from the inside out rather than the outside in. I use my flashlight to scan the aisles of empty shelving, searching for some sign of a burglary. But of course, there's nothing. Not even a footprint marking the painted cement floor. Eventually, I give up my amateur sleuthing, close and lock the doors behind me with the key Jabil keeps beneath the welcome mat, like he's just begging for somebody to find it.

I don't know who would have the gall to steal canned goods and flour, desiring to survive while the rest of the community starves. Everyone I know seems to have too much pride to reduce themselves to that. Or if not pride, then too much morality. Although we've all pretty much concluded that electricity and the normal life it provided — even for the Mennonites, who lived mostly without it — are not returning anytime soon, there is still this unspoken hope that, at some point, the current will suddenly flow again and the lights in the town of Liberty will shine.

But the longer it goes since the EMP, the more I can see panic eating away at the community, swallowing all their determination and hope. I suppose I can't judge someone for attempting to preserve their own hide when watching that mass of people coming down the highway from miles off made me want to do everything I could to preserve my own.

I leave Field to Table and walk over to the perimeter that appears as fortified as those boarded-up glass doors. Sean and Old Man Henri are the only ones on duty, and for a second I wonder if I should bother telling them what Leora and I saw. All of us are sick and tired of rumors, which are in overabundance as if to make up for our storehouse's lack. But these aren't just rumors.

So I recount my morning to Old Man

Henri and Sean. No surprise that Henri narrows his eyes at me, grizzled mouth puckering as if sucking on a lemon drop. I can't tell if he's trying to absorb all the information I'm giving or trying to convey that he doesn't believe a word I've said.

"But you couldn't tell if they was friend or foe?" he asks, once I'm done. I shake my head. "How you know, then," he continues, "they wasn't another group of families trying to find someplace safer than where they left?"

I shrug. "Could be. That's just not the feeling I got when I saw them."

Sean leans back against the scaffolding and crosses his arms. "I'm with Henri on this one, Moses. We can't make decisions based on what some drugged-up homeless person says."

"So you want to just sit here and take the chance he's wrong?"

Sean shakes his head. Old Man Henri sighs. We're at a standstill, and nothing I say is going to budge them in my direction. Not sure who else to talk to, I walk up the lane to the Snyders' house. The door's locked — the first time it's been locked since I came. At first, there's no response. Then the youngest Snyder girl, Priscilla, opens it and peers up at me.

"Your *bruder* Jabil home?" I ask, using one of the only Pennsylvania Dutch nouns I've picked up, since Priscilla, age five, hasn't completely grasped the English language. She nods, chaff-colored braids brushing her heart-shaped face.

"May I speak with him, please?" Priscilla must understand more than I think, and be feistier than she appears, because she tears off into the house, yelling for her eldest brother.

Jabil comes to the door so fast, I get the feeling he locked me out on purpose and has been waiting for my return. Hands fisted at his sides, he leans against the frame, glowering with the same expression my father used to give whenever I would come home after curfew my senior year of high school, reeking of anger and Brut cologne.

"Seth Ebersole came over around two this morning," he says. "Seems Anna woke up and saw Leora was missing. The funny thing is, *you* were missing as well. I told Seth not to worry, that you two were probably out for some —" he throws one hand in the air, a bitter sneer on his face — "stroll."

I say nothing, hoping he'll move on to another subject. But it soon becomes clear he has no intention of moving on until he's understood what I've been up to with the girl he thinks belongs to him, even if he's got no right — that I can see — to claim her as his.

My silence must tick him off because he steps out on the porch while leaving the door ajar. He emphasizes our height difference by leering down at me. I know from personal experience that the only reason he's posturing is because he feels threatened, so I don't do or say anything — just stand here, slouched, and place knuckles against the side of my jaw to pop my neck. Really, I do everything but yawn.

My casual behavior drives him over the edge, which was my intention. "You need to get something straight," he says, all but poking a finger in my chest. "You're not good for Leora. You'll *never* be good for Leora. She simply likes you because you are the antithesis of me."

I almost ask him what *antithesis* means, to act like I'm some dumb Devil Dog, chockfull of hormones, with no conscience or heart. But though I want to keep toying with Jabil, we've got no time to lose. So I straighten up and look him in the eye. I tell him that Leora's father is alive and, though not well, was the homeless man I spoke with. The one who warned me about the gang.

"Who this gang is," I finish, "or what they've been up to, I can't say, but what I *can* say is this: we'd better figure out what we're going to do about it."

"That's easy. We'll find protection in the shadow of his wings."

"I'd rather find protection in the shadow of my semiautomatic."

Jabil barks, "Don't be sacrilegious!"

"And don't be ignorant! God gave us minds for a good reason!"

"He also gave us hearts to trust."

Riled, I look away from him, at the warped cookie tray of butternut squash seeds drying in the sun. At the rusted chains holding up the front-porch swing. At the gutter hanging slightly off the roofline, more than likely pulled down under the weight of last winter's snow. All the while, I'm envisioning the community's nightmarish screams as they run down the highway, clutching their children and leaving all material possessions behind. And Jabil wants me to do nothing to prepare for the gang? To not put my body in action, but to use my heart to trust?

"You really believe, don't you?" I ask.

He nods. "Like I believe I can see you standing before me."

"I respect you for that; I do. I wish I had more of whatever you got. But it's not going to be good if this gang gets here, Jabil. We're not talking about some washed-up gang leader like that one we met in town. We're talking about ex-cons and drug addicts, made desperate without their fix. We're talking the lowest of the low. These aren't the kind that just steal; they're the kind that murder and rape and pillage, leaving nothing but destruction in their wake."

He says, "But you know none of that for fact."

"True, but there was real fear in Luke's eyes when he told me about what's coming. I know his word probably doesn't hold much weight with you, but I believe him. That group of people heading our way is up to no good, and we'd better stay and fight or go now and leave everything behind. As far as I can see, there are no other options."

Jabil shakes his head, but the majority of his rancor is gone. "Are you going to take this to the elders again? Try to take over yet *another* meeting?"

"I think it's better to be prepared if we have that option, don't you?"

"Fine." He steps to the left and jerks his chin toward the house.

As I walk through the front door, I can

343

see the three deacons and bishop gathered around the two tables in the dim kitchen, where I suppose they've been conducting a meeting in secret. The platters, which I remember being heaped with breakfast a week ago, now hold meager portions of potatoes, toast, and eggs. Even the community's leadership is cutting back, which once again reassures me that they're not expecting their people to do anything they're not willing to do themselves.

I enter the kitchen, and the men look up. "Hello, Moses," Bishop Lowell says.

"Good morning."

A whole bench is empty, but I don't sit down. I lean against the wall with my fists in my pockets. My jeans haven't fully dried from our early morning swim. Behind me, Jabil says, "Moses has something he'd like to say." He may be trying to fight it, but I can hear the contempt in his voice. So I don't really feel like opening my mouth. Let their ignorance get them killed for all I care. But then I remember Leora's face as she stared through the scope at that indistinguishable mass of people, and for her alone I start telling them what I saw this morning and what her father told me last night. However, I leave Leora out of it because I don't want her getting into trouble for tak-

344

ing me to the fire tower unchaperoned.

The bishop and the deacons look at me for a long time after I finish; then they look at each other — communicating through ESP, apparently. Enough time has passed during my speech that steam no longer rises from the platters of food. Then Bishop Lowell folds his square hands and places them beside his mug, like a gavel coming to rest.

"Obviously, I can't ask the people of Mt. Hebron to fight," he says, "but I also can't ask them to leave everything without having seen some evidence for myself that danger is coming."

A toxic mix of frustration and anger surges in my chest. I stride across the kitchen. Placing my palms flat on the table, I lean down and look directly at Bishop Lowell. "Would you even have left Egypt when Moses said it was time?"

"For crying out loud!" Jabil says. "You're not *that* Moses!"

I continue staring at Bishop Lowell. "Am I not?"

The front door opens. Jabil turns toward it, as do I. Leora's standing there, cutting a stark shadow in the sunlit cavity. She comes forward and walks past Jabil. Her hair is as it was before Glacier Falls, slicked back and shackled beneath its prayer covering, like the freedom she experienced in the water didn't happen at all. She looks over at me — her face colorless — before addressing the deacons and the bishop.

"I was there, on the fire tower, with Moses." Her voice remains clear and strong. "I saw it too: the people coming. Everything is just as he says."

Not one of them responds, but their shock is palpable, even to me. Finally Bishop Lowell looks at Leora, paternal reprimand deepening the parallel lines between his brows. "You purposely flouted the rule about being out with a member of the opposite sex after dark?"

"It was actually two in the morning when we met," I say, trying to defend her, but the look Jabil gives me confirms that I sound like a jerk. "I'm sorry, what I mean is that *I'm* the one who asked if she would take me to the fire tower. *I'm* the one. She would've never offered on her own. If you're going to punish someone, punish me."

"Yes, well —" Bishop Lowell unfolds his hands and puts on a pair of half-glasses that are hooked on the front of his shirt. "I think we have more important matters to discuss than curfews." He addresses the deacons. "It would probably be wise to have everyone leave the community for a few days until we know more —"

"We're not talking about a few days," I interrupt. "This might be the end of Mt. Hebron Community as we know it."

Bishop Lowell sighs, his patience wearing thin. "Yes, *you* know that and *I* know that, but there'd be a lot less panic on our hands if we let them think this is only a precautionary measure."

"But don't the people deserve to know the truth, rather than having you all hiding behind doors, discussing their lives?"

Behind me, Jabil growls, "Address my uncle with respect, Moses, or leave."

I flip up my hands. "Okay. I'm not trying to be smart. I'm just trying to understand how a community that — until three weeks ago — worked somewhat like a democracy, has suddenly become this oligarchy, where the decisions for the majority are made by the elite few."

Bishop Lowell takes off his glasses, angling his compact body to face me. "What's happened here, Moses, is that we don't believe everyone who's now part of the community is working for the *good* of the community. We cannot give out critical information to those we can no longer trust."

"This is true, Bishop Lowell," Leora says.

"When Moses and I were in the woods on our way back, we found a cellar concealing rations that were taken from our supplies. They have probably been stealing since day one."

Bishop Lowell shakes his head. "So it is as we feared."

"You knew about this?" I ask him.

"No. Least not entirely," he says. "Jabil's the one who called this meeting. He was the first to notice that supplies were dwindling at a faster rate than we'd anticipated, given we were so closely monitoring our rations. He needs our help understanding how we can uncover who is doing it without making the entire community feel like they're being placed under suspicion."

I say, "I don't think we should even let the community know we're aware someone's stealing rations. It'd be best if we continue like normal and let the thief set himself up for a fall."

"And once he's discovered?" Jabil asks. "What then? Put him in stocks?"

"He'll have to be cast out," Bishop Lowell answers. "We can't build a community on a foundation of lies and distrust."

Leora asks, "So what do we do? How do we help everyone prepare?"

Bishop Lowell rises from the chair and

stands before it, revealing afresh his diminutive height. "What can we do?" he says, as if speaking to himself. He looks up at the three of us — Leora, Jabil, and me — the lines on his forehead dissecting those etched between his brows. "We must stay calm. We must carry on with life the same as before. To leave our homes and the protection of the compound is not an easy decision to make, and on one hand, it seems like the foolish thing to do." He pauses, allowing the room to fall quiet before meeting my eyes. "But if this mob is as you say it is, Moses, then I would rather my community face the uncertainty of the forest than the near certainty of death. I only wish to stave off as much violence and bloodshed as possible. If that means leaving, then we shall leave. The Lord knows all things, and it is to him we must look for our refuge in times like these. No amount of hoarding or fighting will be able to save us. We must trust our God, and if we perish —" the bishop looks up and his blue eyes are brilliant with resignation — "then we perish."

LEORA

I don't say anything as Moses and I walk in tandem down the path leading to the lane. He has no reason that I can see for leaving the Snyders' house. The idea that he might've left simply because he enjoys my presence is frightening and exhilarating at the same time. So I try concentrating on the mountains in an attempt to divert my thoughts.

Yet, looking at them in the distance — each spike and dip defined with snow — I find my mind refusing to be diverted from the memory of Moses holding me on the fire tower as we looked down on the highway. The memory of my behavior makes me uncomfortable, but not ashamed. He held me until my fortifications crumbled . . . until I felt my heart opening up and my body turning toward his. I don't believe he comprehends the magnitude of that scene, as we looked down on our post-EMP world. Or if he does comprehend it, he is at a loss for how to interpret his thoughts and emotions, the same as I.

Only once the silence becomes strained do I realize that Moses — he of the glib tongue — must feel uncomfortable as well.

He bumps into my shoulder with his. "Nice the bishop's so preoccupied with the invasion, we get off the hook for breaking curfew."

His nonchalance gives me a healthy dose of reality. "That's probably the truth . . . for you," I tell him. "For me, on the other hand? Bishop Lowell and the deacons will never look at me the same way again. They'll always just think I'm some rebellious girl who doesn't mind flouting the rules."

"Is that really so bad," he says, "when the rules are so outdated to begin with?"

"Yes, it actually *is* bad. I need them to trust that I have a good head on my shoulders, or else they'll never listen to a word I say."

"Trust me." He grins. "When you speak, they have no choice but to listen."

My face grows warm. "I have to be serious here, Moses. So many things are hanging in the balance."

"Like what?"

"Like if that was really my *vadder* you spoke with at the center, how can he come back here, to the community, when they don't want to let anyone in they cannot trust?"

"But your father's not just some random guy off the street."

"No. But he's also a drug addict."

Moses drags a hand over his beard. "So you know about the drugs."

"I know they're what drove him from our family. Or, I guess, they didn't drive him as much as he drove himself away from us."

We pass the pavilion. Moses looks at the lane as he says, "Melinda came in contact with him, Leora. At the center. She tried paying her way out of Liberty with prescription drugs."

"And he took them?"

Moses nods.

My mouth tastes bitter. I swallow in disgust. "He must be more addicted than I thought."

"I think he's pretty bad."

"Where is Melinda now?"

We are standing in front of my house. The sun beats down hard on my *kapp,* but beyond that, it's almost impossible to feel its warmth.

"Luke doesn't know," Moses says. "I guess she showed up at the center and told him she was willing to do anything to get home. Apparently, after she gave him the pills, he turned her over to someone who could 'help' her, but I'm afraid what that 'friend' might want from her in return."

I wipe tears, angry and sick.

Moses sighs. "I wasn't sure I was going to tell you. Jabil even told me not to. But I thought you should know, since we're going to be leaving soon."

I nod, though I am not sure he has made the right choice, since I cannot handle another stressor in addition to the ones I already have. I watch Anna come out of the greenhouse with a calico kitten draped in surrender over her arms, a stand-in for her favorite orange tom that recently disappeared. My stomach somersaults with anxiety. My sister's been outside, by herself, the entire time I've been over at the Snyders'. I don't know how to keep her safe without telling *Grossmammi* and Seth about the attack so they will guard her as they should. I don't know how to ensure Anna's future while trying to navigate the direction of my own. Therefore I must do what I have always done. Or at least what I have done in the past two years since our *vadder* left. I must put duty before desire and put Anna's needs before my own.

Turning from Moses, I look out over the community: Field to Table, the schoolhouse, the pavilion, the homes that used to be immaculately kept because potential buyers of the log cabin kits, which Jabil and his crew built by hand, liked to drive down the lane and pick out which style they wanted. The gardens in everyone's yards are picked clean of bounty, and I can see — even from here — how the bleak cornstalks shiver and rasp together against the dark backdrop of the forest, how the round bales are lined up against the Lehmans' barn, sustenance necessary for the livestock that will have to be either slaughtered or left behind.

This is not the place where I was born, but it is the place where I imagined, one day, I would die. The place where I've lived through equal parts sorrow and joy. And currently I am forced — we are *all* forced — to give it up and try to seek safety elsewhere because of marauders who may or may not be coming for us. But I agree that we cannot stay here and take the risk that the marauders are real.

"How are we supposed to survive in the mountains?" I ask. "Especially through the winter? How are we supposed to leave everything behind?"

"God will provide. He has to."

I look over at Moses, trying to gauge if he's mimicking one of our community's rote phrases, but his expression is sincere, which irks me. I don't need another Jabil; I need someone who can help me take revenge. "Yeah, well. I'll believe it when I see it."

He frowns. "How is that for a woman of faith?"

"I have a hard time placing faith in a God who'd let my sister suffer."

"Is she the one whose pain you blame yourself for?"

I stare at the Lehmans' red tin roof, which — from this angle — appears white in the sun. "I told you her accident was my fault."

Moses doesn't look at me. I wonder if he's remembering, as I am, that he said almost the same words to me about his brother's death only a few hours ago.

"It's been ten years this summer. I was playing in the hay with a new litter of kittens. It wasn't until I heard Anna scream that I shook the kittens from my lap and ran to the edge of the hayloft. I looked down and saw her tiny body sprawled there, next to our *vadder*'s hoe. She must have hit her head on it. I remember noticing how the blood matched my old dress that she was wearing."

Now Moses looks at me. I am unable to meet his eyes. Having begun this dreadful story — like a broken arm in the midst of being set — I have no choice but to finish the job.

"I was paralyzed by terror. I forced myself to breathe, even though my sister was not breathing. I forced myself to think, even though my sister was incapable of thought. Finally I ran and threw back the door to my *vadder*'s wood shop, choking on my tears. I was so incoherent, my *vadder* didn't wait for me to try to explain but set down his nail gun and ran outside. I started running again and he followed me, and then outran me when he saw Anna. He was able to get her breathing again with CPR, and while he did that I somehow had the presence of mind to run back to the wood shop and use the phone to call 911." At Moses's puzzled look, I explain, "The wood shop was the only place on our farm that had electricity and a telephone."

He nods.

"When I got back, I overheard my *vadder* crying and my *grossmammi* trying to comfort him. She told him it wasn't his fault; that *I* was supposed to be watching her. She didn't realize I was listening."

Time and distance from the event have let me see that *Grossmammi* was only trying to shift the blame so her son wouldn't feel its full weight if Anna died. She was not attempting to place that weight on me. But after my sister's emergency craniotomy, followed by months of rehab, I felt that my *vadder* withdrew from me. That he started blaming me for Anna's accident, which I understood because I started blaming myself minutes after it happened; half of my life has been crucified by guilt.

How different would our lives be if I had been watching Anna that day and therefore prevented her fall? Would my *vadder* still be here? Would my *mamm* still be alive? Would my parents still be in love?

I close my eyes again until the peril of tears has passed and open them afresh to the sun.

"So you see, I feel responsible for Anna in a special way. I let her down once, and I promised myself I would never let her down again."

"Okay," Moses says, clearly having a hard time following my reasoning.

"It seems she was attacked the night we went searching for Melinda."

Moses is quiet; then he reaches out and takes my hand. "You mean . . . raped?"

The barn roof blurs. I turn from him. He holds my hand tighter, rooting me. "I don't know. There was blood on her legs. Scratches on her face. I found her outside. Alone."

"Were there any . . . obvious wounds?"

I shake my head.

"Then could the blood have come from something else?"

"I can't think of what."

"It just seems odd there could be blood like that." I can tell he thinks I'm overreacting.

"It wasn't odd. It was terrifying."

Hearing my frustration, he says, "Sorry for the third degree. I just don't understand how it could've happened when Charlie and I were at the gate."

"Unless Charlie's the one who did it."

"No, Leora. He wouldn't do something like that."

"Maybe not before the EMP. But we're all doing things we wouldn't otherwise."

Moses waits a moment, and then lets go of my hand. "Are you trying to push me away?" he asks.

"I'm not trying to do anything but keep my head above water."

"And you think I might be pulling you down."

"I never said that. I'm just tired of being needed."

"That's because you don't let anybody help you."

"I *can't* let anybody help me. They wouldn't do things the way I would."

"I like you a lot, Leora. But you got some serious control issues." Seeing me flinch, his face softens. He steps closer, tips my chin up until I have no choice but to lift my gaze. "I only say that 'cause over the years I've watched my mom get so eaten up with worry, there's not much of her left." He swallows and looks at me. My soul weakens at the depth of feeling in his eyes. "And, Leora, I sure don't want to see that happen to you. Not if I can help it."

The tables near the schoolhouse are spread with embroidered cloths, redolent of the cedar chips and mothballs in which they were stored. Bishop Lowell's announcement yesterday — to eat any food that could not be transported — made everyone realize there was no point in saving their special table linens for another occasion. Our impromptu feast will be the last celebration we have here for a long time. Maybe the last one ever. Tiny curls of steam rise from the heirloom platters and bowls: corn, green beans, succotash, mashed potatoes puddled with browned butter, sweet potatoes, rolls, even a suckling pig beaded with cloves that Elizabeth Lapp decided to butcher and cook here because that was easier than carting a pig into the mountains.

As I move around the tables, preparing for what could be our last meal on Mt. Hebron soil — folding linen napkins and weighing them down with the cutlery provided — I understand why the pilgrims had their first Thanksgiving before they were certain their spearheading community would survive. Sometimes it is necessary to celebrate life, despite being faced with defeat and death. We have no idea what our future holds, or where we will all be next week, next month, or next year. But today, we are together; therefore we should fellowship in peace.

Ten-year-old Ezekiel Lapp asks if we are ready. At his mother's affirming nod, he hustles inside the schoolhouse to ring the bell. Members of the community, halted in their packing by this sound, soon stream out of their cabins and barns. They converge into a throng of downcast expressions, generated by the quandary: How can we leave almost everything to climb into the national forest surrounding the community? And yet, how can we fight back if we stay?

For the first time in my life, I not only yearn to stare straight into my assailant's face, instead of turning my other cheek to his abuse, but also to defend what I perceive is rightfully mine . . . rightfully my family's. Part of this is because I crave a steam vent for my anger, which is boiling within me, making my insides feel like they are ready to burst. Part of this is because I am also angry at the community for turning themselves over to an unseen enemy rather than attempting to stay and, if necessary, put up a fight. If we each took up a weapon, would

Mt. Hebron stand a chance against this supposed violent gang? The truth is, no one in our community would defend himself, and so we will flee without knowing if we could've remained.

Taking this into account, folding napkins and placing knives, spoons, and forks in the correct order seems trivial compared to what challenges lie ahead, and yet the predictable movements keep me from analyzing to the point of insanity. Anna, sensing that I am not acting myself, remains by my side as the rest of the Mennonites and the few *Englischers* gather around the tables. Two of the women, Esther Glick and Marta Good, grip the chairs with one hand while jiggling their newborns with the other. As I watch them fighting back emotion, I am reminded of the biblical warning that the last days will be hardest for those with babes pressed to their breasts. But I believe it is also hard for those who find themselves falling in love for the first time, when one's heart cannot be given the priority it deserves. I always imagined that, when confronted with the end of life, other desires would fade beyond those needed for survival. This is not the case. In fact, I've found the opposite is true. I yearn to be with Moses, as if he is my North Star in this black hole of madness, but my duty to my family forces me to remain lost.

Bishop Lowell must sense the community's growing discomfort, for he assumes his place at the head of the far-right table. A summer wind blows across the acreage, offering relief as I swelter in my dark cape dress. Behind me, I can hear the swings' ropes creaking in this same wind, and I recall that first day Moses and I sat swing by swing and talked as though I had thoughts worthy of sharing. I set the basket on the table. It has grown too heavy, though its weight has not changed. Anna and Seth stand behind the seats next to me. Jabil and Moses stand behind the seats across from me. I meet Moses's eyes and then force myself to look down the table.

One of the women has placed tea light candles down the center of the tables, reminding me of the runway lights I once saw at the airport in Kalispell. Though it is late afternoon, and therefore a waste to burn candles, it soothes my soul to view such beauty. The minuscule flames waver in the wind, about to be snuffed out. Bishop Lowell motions for us to be seated. I drop my hands from around a tea light to pull out my chair and watch the wind extinguish the flame.

"I called for this celebration today," he begins, "because regardless of what the future holds, I want us to remember that we are a community of people who trust *Gott* to provide, just as he provided for the Israelites in the desert. We are not guaranteed to have it easy, nor that we will even survive. But we are guaranteed that, regardless of how bad it gets, he can take it and use it for good. We must trust him with our provisions and our lives. Therefore, we will not hoard our manna for ourselves but will continue to share with those in need and expect *Gott* to bring manna tomorrow and in the days ahead." The bishop runs his maimed fingers over the tablecloth's pattern. "It has been my honor to serve you these years, and if the Lord wills it, I hope that when we reestablish ourselves as a community — whether it is here or up in the mountains — I will have the honor of serving you again."

Esther's baby begins to *brutz.* Bishop Lowell raises his head and looks at the child. He smiles, the worry momentarily leaving his face. "I would like to sing a prayer over our meal," he says, "to show *Gott* our appreciation for the bounty he has given, even in this season of want."

The bishop extends his hands and hums a

note that is surprisingly steady for someone of his age. The Mt. Hebron Community — composed of the neighbors I have known for years — then begins to sing hymn 131: " 'We thank thee, Lord, for this our food, but more because of Jesus' blood; let manna to our souls be given, the Bread of Life sent down from heaven.' "

As we continue through the simple verses, I can hear our disparate voices uniting into one resonant chorus that rises on the same wind that extinguished the flame. Tears fill my eyes as I listen to Jabil's bass voice harmonizing with my alto. I look over, and our gazes communicate every bittersweet emotion without a word being said. He is my friend, and I care for him, but unless the Lord intervenes and changes my heart, I can never care for him in that way.

The singing stops, and we begin passing bowls to each other. I savor a mouthful of creamed corn and lima beans, a slice of ham with gravy made from canned pineapple, and a sourdough roll slathered with butter, wondering how long it's going to be until I can taste these flavors again. I scoop cranberry sauce onto my china plate and pass the bowl to my sister, whose table manners are superb for someone who cannot communicate well.

I haven't finished my meal when black smoke starts to rise at the beginning of the lane, first as the leavings of a smokestack and then as a cloud. Moses alone is impervious to the inertia that is affecting the rest of us. He leaps up so abruptly, his chair tips back. He runs down the lane with such adrenaline fueling his steps that, for the first time, I see no trace of a limp. Within seconds, our stunned silence dissipates, and everyone bolts into action. Water spills as cups fall over. Napkins twirl to the ground like severed wings. Children begin crying as they sense their parents' panic, and I know this vortex of terror could be the exact thing we were hoping to escape.

I watch, helpless, as Anna rocks in her chair and claps hands over her ears, keening at the riot of sound. I sit beside her and pull her onto my lap, wrapping my arms around her as I would a child. Jabil's wagon wheels fling gravel as he careers past us over the schoolhouse lane. Jerking back on the reins, he jumps out and ties the mare to the hitching post. He touches my shoulder as he walks past. "You and Anna should go," he says. "We have no idea who's —"

"I'll send her with you," I interrupt. "But I'm staying here until everyone's safe."

He nods and turns from me toward *Gross-*

mammi Eunice. In her black cape dress and outdated pince-nez glasses, she appears unruffled by this sudden unrest, just as she's appeared unruffled from the commencement of the EMP. For the past ten minutes, during which the community has been darting to and fro, trying to salvage what they were packing before the ringing of the schoolhouse bell, she has continued to sit and eat. Part of this is probably due to her visual impairment, which barred her from seeing the smoke at the gate and now bars her from seeing the pandemonium erupting around her table. But some of this languor could possibly be because of how long she's lived her life — and how much she's lost during its duration — so she doesn't feel the need to preserve it with the same intensity the rest of us do.

It requires mental and physical effort to lift Anna into Jabil's wagon. Trying to abate her shivering, I wrap a feed sack around her legs and realize it is one of the same feed sacks Old Man Henri used to cover up the shotgun that night we went to the museum. Decades seem to have passed between then and now, and I cannot even remember the person I was in comparison to the person I've become. I am less of a butterfly freed from her cocoon, and more of a predatory bird free-falling from the safety of her nest. Breathing deeply, I help Jabil load everyone left around the table into the wagon, and then we go back for *Grossmammi* Eunice.

She at first refuses to budge because she hasn't finished her pie, but Jabil leans down and smiles, convincing her with a masculine charm that would be impossible for me. She strides across the schoolhouse yard with her thin shoulders back and a china plate balanced in her hands. Batting away Jabil's assistance, she climbs into the rear of the wagon and sits ramrod straight beside the children, who have been separated from their parents in an attempt to let the parents use their wagons to load the last of their goods. My *grossmammi* sighs and blindly reaches for the most heartbroken toddler, Suzie Stoltzfus, who throws herself across her lap. Stroking Suzie's sweaty hair, she takes the spoon and begrudgingly feeds her the last bites of pie.

Climbing up into the wagon, Jabil turns to make sure everyone's safely seated, then glances over at me. I shake my head to let him know I haven't changed my mind. He nods and begins directing the horse toward the old logging trail that wends up into the forest. Bracing my arms across my chest, I watch him go before I survey the abundance of food discarded on gold-rimmed plates, at the heirloom platter with the filigreed edge now broken in half, at the ornate tablecloth I admired earlier tainted with cranberry sauce the color of blood. None of the tea light candles have withstood the unpredictable gusts.

Behind me, but still far too close, I hear the sky being frayed by gunfire. My heart thuds so hard it hurts. I glance at the abandoned feast once more before I sprint across the lane toward the woods, praying that at the perimeter, Moses Hughes — the pilot with a death wish — is alive.

■ ■ ■ ■

CHAPTER 14

■ ■ ■ ■

MOSES

The gunshots echo around me, and it's as though these past three weeks didn't happen — as though *none* of this happened — and I am back in the desert, straining to see black-and-white as I listen for the whiz of the bullet that heralds the moment I die. My fingers shake as I take up a position on the perimeter and level the crosshairs on the man closest to us, shooting from a ditch on the lane.

I remind myself of what my veteran grandpa said when I was debating about reenlisting or staying with him on his Bonners Ferry farm: "Us dreamy types —" he'd bumped my shoulder with his — "we don't do so well on the front lines 'cause we can't see the world in black-and-white enough to do what needs done." But the problem is, even such guileless understanding is no longer simple. I have to see the world as

371

black-and-white again, because I have to be on the front lines again, trying to protect a homestead filled with people I'm beginning to love.

Charlie yells, "Snap out of it, Moses!" Definitely a frontline guy.

I stop remembering then and start thinking. I think of Leora somewhere in the community, the wind pulling a few strands of her dark hair loose from her *kapp* as she runs. For her, a pacifist, I raise my gun and steady it on the log in front of me, but the man in the ditch is already gone. The refugees who've come from Liberty are dispersing in every direction, being driven back by the volley of gunshots hailing from the gang across the road. Most of the gang are taking cover behind their five windowless vehicles. Sean and Old Man Henri are on the scaffolding across from Charlie and me. Sean opens fire on the conversion van and swears, ducks low to wait for the return fire, and then rises to his feet, blinking back sweat.

Some of the Mennonite boys — too young to join the church, but old enough to know better than to fight — climb up the scaffolding to bring us more ammo and even a drink of cool water from the well. I take a cup Leora's brother, Seth, has handed to me from below.

"Need some help?" he asks, jerking his smooth chin toward the perimeter.

Not about to get him mixed up in this, I lie, "No, son. We got all the help we need."

I turn my attention to a heavyset man darting from behind one of the vehicles toward the cover of the ditch. I assume he's trying to get around to our side so he can make his way closer to our flank. But my reaction and speed on the trigger is faster than the speed he uses to cover the short distance. I let two shots loose: the first right on him and the second just in front. The second shot takes him down just short of his destination. I watch as he crawls — still trying to get to cover — but his effort is short-lived.

"Good shooting!" Charlie hollers. "We're holding 'em back, boys!"

Right now, it seems we're not only holding them back, but we're also winning. I do not fool myself. We're outnumbered and only have so much ammo. At this pace, it's only a matter of time before our luck changes and we are taken out and the community is overrun. Old Man Henri jerks back from his position. He cusses and growls, "I'm hit." I can see the wound on his shoulder, and his shirt turning red as the flannel soaks the blood up like a sponge. Sean helps Henri lie back on the plank of the scaffolding. I turn to climb down to help as well, but the Mennonite boys who've been assisting us take hold of Henri and gently lower him from the scaffolding to the ground. They lead him away to what was supposed to be the makeshift hospital, though I doubt any adults are around anymore to assist.

One boy remains with us: Seth.

"I know how to shoot," he calls, but his voice sounds too young to support his claim.

Sean waves a hand, inviting the boy up, even though — behind Seth — I am frantically waving my hands and shaking my head. If anything were to happen to him, Leora would never forgive me. And I would never forgive myself. Seth clambers up the scaffolding's rungs. His suspenders are crisp lines against the blue shirt. He takes Henri's rifle and wipes the stock against his side, cleaning the sticky red with his pants. The image of that boy holding the rifle, his hands stained with someone else's blood — even if it's just Henri's — makes me feel sick. Swallowing the burn in my throat, I call over to him, "You don't need to be up here, Seth. Not if it's against your beliefs. You could get killed."

Seth straightens his shoulders and casts his hat to the side. Tucking down in the hole that Henri was shooting from, he snaps the safety off and looks over at me. "Who says I believe the same as everyone else?"

I nod at him, relinquishing my big brother stance, as I recall how important it was to be taken seriously at his age. "Okay, then. Make your shots count." I point to the spot behind the van where our enemies are gathered. I haven't talked to God in a long time — not since I walked away from every relationship I had before I left for the desert, including the one I had with him. But as this sheltered young man readies to shoot at the enemy through the very hole that Henri took a bullet from, I find myself praying. I pray for the boy's safety; I pray that the shedding of blood won't scar him the way it's scarred me. And then I pray that this community — composed of families I once perceived as eccentric oddities but now perceive as neighbors and friends — can survive against all odds. For I know that, in order to endure this assault, we're going to need a miracle of drastic proportions.

Then, over the chaos and noise, I hear someone call Seth's name from behind the scaffolding. But Seth doesn't hear it. I turn and see Luke — Leora's father, *Seth's* father — shambling toward us. When he sees me, his bearded face cracks into a grin. Sean and Charlie both glance at me and use the moment of stillness to reload, wondering if this rough-looking character — despite his smile — is friend or foe. I am not sure myself. Why on earth did he come wandering in during the fight of our lives? And how did he *get* in here in the first place?

Charlie must decide that Luke Ebersole's not too threatening, because he sets his rifle on the plank and climbs down. "Hold 'em back for a second without me, boys," he says. "Gotta get something from my truck."

From the base of our perch, Luke calls to Seth, "Jabil sent me to tell you he needs help loading the wagon." Seth lowers his rifle and stares back at Luke — a wasted, gray figure of a man — but his face remains impassive. "You should go, Seth," Luke prods. "He needs you right away." The boy appears reluctant to abandon his post, but sweat glistens around the rim of his patchy bowl cut and his face is blanched with fear.

Another barrage of bullets thwacks the wall of the perimeter, making us all duck down below our shooting ports. Seth quickly hands Henri's rifle back to Sean, grabs his hat, and scrambles down the scaffolding. At the base, Luke pats his son awkwardly on the back. "You made the right decision," he says. But Seth, ashamed, doesn't even raise his head to look at his father, and I can tell that he either hasn't made the connection or else he's acting like he hasn't. All four of us watch Seth put his hat on and walk down the lane toward the schoolhouse — not wanting to be part of that world, but also not wanting to be part of ours.

Luke motions to the scaffolding and looks at Sean. Sean looks at me.

"He's all right," I say, unsure of my judgment.

Sean waves him up just like he waved up Seth. Luke climbs the scaffolding and sits with his legs hanging over the side.

"So, you're not a pacifist?" I ask him as he checks out Henri's gun.

"Think I'm a little too far gone for all that," he says.

Charlie, now back from his truck, ignores us while trying to climb up the scaffolding with a large metal ammo box and the four-foot-long metal pipe that he's been lugging around since the EMP. He says to me, "Here, grab this box and give me a hand, will ya?"

I reach down and take the ammo box by the handle and heave it onto the walk plank.

"What else you gonna bust out today?" I ask. "A tommy gun?"

Charlie, still grinning, opens the box and takes something out. I'm not sure whether it should be called a grenade, a mortar, or just an accident waiting to happen. Sliding the homemade ordnance into the back of the improvised weapon, he then uses a lighter to ignite the fuse protruding out the side. "This should give 'em something to think about," he says, winking at me before steadying the beast on the wall. I am seriously thinking of diving for cover, because anything you have to light a fuse on, and then hold, is no better than suicide.

There is a low wallop as the first charge goes off, sending the object flying in slow motion, like a softball through the air. It lands just short of the vehicles, and then skips and bounces on the ground and goes right underneath the closest one. There is a second or two of silence. I turn to look at Charlie — who raises his eyebrow and shrugs, thinking it's a dud — but then the mortar explodes under the car, sending a shock wave throughout the area.

"Meet Bessie, my pipe-bomb launcher," he quips, setting it down beside him and picking his rifle back up. "That thing had over three hundred ball bearings."

"That it?" I dryly reply.

Peering over the wall, I can see that the pipe bomb has lived up to the devastation it was created to inflict. The men who are left are dragging one of their wounded as they retreat from the front to cover farther back. I doubt they were expecting this kind of defense when they tried penetrating our compound, for we have dropped them like flies. There are now about ten of them. We've killed twenty. Maybe more. The smoke pouring out of the burning vehicle makes it almost impossible to tell. I try but can't desensitize myself like I did during that savage fifteen-minute span, seeing these men as fragments of people — skullcaps, tattered T-shirts, and jailhouse tattoos — rather than souls that will one day have to pay the price for the blood they've shed. The same as I will have to pay the price for the blood that's on my hands.

All at once, the bile that has been building in my throat since I watched young Seth preparing to take part in the violence, is more than I can hold back. I lean over the scaffolding. Whatever meager portion of food I consumed during the feast splatters on the ground.

Rising to my knees, I wipe my mouth on the sleeve of my shirt and take a drink from the canteen Charlie tosses to me, swishing the liquid around before spitting it back out.

I rasp, "Ever heard the quote, 'An eye for an eye will make the world blind'?"

"Sure have," Charlie says, even as he turns around to peer over the perimeter, trying to see who's left in the open to kill. "I also heard something like, 'A man's heart is desperately wicked. Who can know it?' That don't make me want to sit around singing 'Kumbaya' and holding hands. Does it you?"

"Of *course* not. But sometimes I wonder if we're becoming the same kind of evil we're trying to fight against, so we're going to end up also fighting ourselves. If that's the case, wouldn't it be better to turn the other cheek, even if it means dying?"

Charlie hocks over the scaffolding before looking at the scope again. "I ain't about to turn no cheek. I'll do whatever it takes to keep myself alive, even if that means picking off a cat."

"A cat?" I look over at him, thinking he's joking.

"Yes. A cat. I shot a cat that I found eating a can of tuna."

"Whose cat?"

"Never you mind whose cat," he says, lifting his jaw at me in defiance. "The point is, we can't be feeding strays. Feline *or* human."

Charlie's making a point, all right. A point not to look at me, despite the fact that I'm staring a hole through his head. "You know exactly whose cat that was, don't you?"

"Don't matter. I didn't eat it, did I? Just tossed it up in the woods, humane-like."

"You shot somebody's pet and you think that's humane? When did you shoot it?"

He shrugs.

"Was it the night we were guarding the gate and everybody else was out searching?"

"My word, Moses. It's like you work for PETA."

"I could care less about the stupid cat. Who I care about is Leora. She thinks her sister was raped that night they went out searching for that woman, 'cause later she found her wandering around in the field with blood all over her pajamas." Now Charlie meets my eyes. I nod at him as his comprehension dawns. "That's right. Leora thinks *you* did it."

"Don't look at me like that, all high and mighty. You woulda done the same. I saw it there beside their greenhouse when I was out making my rounds, eating tuna as happy as you please, tail twitching and all. It had the nerve to growl when I stopped, so I shot it. Never felt a thing. I didn't know your Four-Eyes' kid sister was watching me, or I wouldn't have done it."

"Yes, you would've."

He shrugs again. "Okay, I probably would've. But then that girl came out of the house and started cuddling the cat like it was still . . . alive or something, so I had to pry it from her hands and carry it up in the woods. I felt bad, swear I did. I would've taken the time to bury it and put a little cross and flowers marking its grave if I wasn't supposed to be helping *you* guard the gate from a band of bloodthirsty thieves. So if she hiked up there in the woods after I left and cuddled the corpse some more, that's her own stinkin' fault. We can't be having some worm-infested cat eating our food when we barely got nothing to eat! We're talking *albacore* tuna, not even chunk light! My word, Moses, what was she thinking?"

"She's special-needs, Charlie. She doesn't think like the rest of us."

His chin quivers. This mercurial man who's killed more men than he's got fingers on his hands is about to cry over a cat. "I swear. I didn't know she saw me do it. I'll make it up to her. Taxidermy the fleabag or something. *Then* she can keep it for a pet."

"Probably skip the taxidermy part, but I have to say I'm relieved."

LEORA

I pass the stack of community possessions, so jumbled that it's impossible to tell what belongs to whom: cast-iron skillets, old quilts, a box filled with children's wear, a tray crowded with canning jars, the waning light flashing off the dull gold metal rims and lids. The extent of these provisions makes it obvious the people do not believe the bishop's unflappable optimism that this might be a temporary exodus and, once the danger's past, we can return to Mt. Hebron. Then again, it will be a wonder if — by the end — the EMP doesn't make pessimists of us all.

In three weeks, I have not only become a pessimist; I have discarded my pacifist ideals in pursuit of revenge. The further I drift from this moral mainstay, the easier it is to be pulled by the current of my own self-preservation. Before the feast, when Bishop Lowell said we would continue sharing our supplies with those in need, I knew what I had to do. I overcame any qualms regarding my decision by telling myself that I was just going to reclaim the supplies stolen from us, and I would share them when — or if —

the time came. But I also know my heart would not be drumming in my chest if I truly believed my own reassurances.

My eyes dart across the ground, searching for any inconsistency in the leaves' pattern, which might notify me of the place where, a few hours ago, Moses and I discovered the trapdoor concealing the dugout cellar. I only have minutes to load some of the canned vegetables, cornmeal, and flour into the empty banana box I brought home from Field to Table and store it with the rest of the community's things, hoping no one will notice that these rations are in addition to what was allocated to my family.

Maneuvering around the aspen tree, I see the trapdoor is already open. My pulse quickens. Someone is rustling inside. I draw closer, comprehending — with every step — just how foolish I've been to come out here on my own. I edge around the trapdoor and peer into the cellar. I see a woman's back, her narrow shoulders and waist, her long black braid dangling past a sleeping infant strapped to her spine with a length of floral sheet. Sal. It's Sal. I retreat two paces and trip over the backpack she brought with her the afternoon she showed up outside the community's gates and we let her in.

Sal turns. Her eyes appear as feral as the

night I found her in Liberty, wearing an enormous blue parka and her face petrified. My mind struggles to understand what to say or do. Should I act as if I have just stumbled across this place myself, like I did with Moses, and it's merely a coincidence she's here as well? Sal climbs out of the cellar and slaps at the dirt clotted to the knees of her jeans. But she doesn't bother shutting the trapdoor. She looks at me, and I look at her — both of us trying to guess what the other person is thinking.

The words are readied on my lips: "So, you've been stealing from us, even after we offered you a place to stay? After we offered you food from our own table?" But then I pause and look at baby Colton's soft hair and smooth cheeks. Sal glances up at me again, her eyes shining, and then looks away, as if ashamed of what she's done when I was preparing to do it myself. I picture Anna and the rest of Mt. Hebron's children in Jabil's wagon, fleeing for their lives.

Since Anna's attack, I've known that I would lie, cheat, and steal to ensure her survival. I have already attempted all three and succeeded at one, the first, by avoiding the truth. Both Sal and I are inadvertently tethered to motherhood, though we are too young to handle the responsibilities trailing along with it. The past two years, I have volunteered to be a mother and a father to Anna, but Sal . . . she is *forced* to be both mother and father to her fatherless child.

"You and I aren't too different," I say instead of accusing, reaching across the cellar to touch her back. "We'd both do anything to make sure our families survive."

She pivots to face me. "How's my family supposed to survive, Leora? I am by myself. Even here, in your community, I feel like I'm always by myself. That's why I'm going back."

"To where? Your apartment? You saw what Liberty's like!"

She drops her eyes to the cellar's plywood door. "I've been offered protection."

"By whom? The gang?"

"Yes. The gang," she snaps. "You think you got it so rough 'cause your mom's dead and your dad's disappeared. You've *no* idea what rough really is. My dad's dead, and I never had a mom — or at least no mom that wanted me. I *do* have a Kutenai grandmother, but she cares more about drinking than teaching me about her herbs. I made up that part about being a healer so you'd let me stay. I was raised by my uncle, my dead dad's brother, who was just as much of a deadbeat as my real dad was. *He's* the leader of the gang. *He's* the one offering me protection."

Startled awake by the rage in his mother's voice, Colton begins to cry. Sal loosens the homemade sling, takes him in her arms, and prepares to let him suckle. I look away from her, to give her privacy and because I'm trying to put the puzzle pieces of her life into place. The night we met her on our way to the museum, we were stopped by a gang on our way back through town. The loud-mouthed ringleader of the gang — whom Henri forced to hand over his cigarettes at gunpoint — is *he* the drug-dealing uncle she's talking about?

I ask Sal outright, and she pauses, as if trying to decide if she should tell me the truth. Then she nods. "Uncle Mike raised me from five years old, when my dad OD'd, until I turned eighteen. He thinks this means the rest of my life should be handed over to him like one big IOU. He forced me to sit by the road that night we met, waiting for anybody who might come by and feel bad for a single mom and her baby. You were so easy." Sal sighs. "So eager to help out. It wasn't until I reported seeing you — a Mennonite — in a wagon going down Main Street that my uncle realized you might be from the same community where

Luke hid the drugs."

Hid the drugs? "What . . . drugs?" I ask, reeling. Sal reaches past her anger to balance me.

"Leora, listen," she says. "I appreciate everything you've done, but there are things going on here that you know nothing about. Your dad used to be one of my uncle's biggest drug runners. His furniture business was just a front. But then he got so addicted, he became worthless and my uncle couldn't trust him. After the EMP hit, Uncle Mike's supply started drying up because no one could get the stuff into town from the cities like before. But at the same time, the demand went through the roof because nobody could get ahold of anything. People went nuts. Think fresh drinking water's scarce? Try crack cocaine."

Sal smiles; she actually smiles, like this story has a punch line. Meanwhile my mouth is so dry I can hardly swallow. I haven't reconciled the vagrant Moses talked about with the man who raised me, and Sal's saying a majority of my *vadder*'s life — even before he left — was a lie?

"Your dad was in bad shape," she continues, "and desperate to get ahold of something too, but had nothing to barter, so he 'fessed up that over the years he'd taken some of the cocaine he was supposed to sell for my uncle and stashed it in the community where he used to live — thinking he'd go back for it one day. How he was able to pull that off, I have no clue. But after the EMP, he was delirious from withdrawal and said he couldn't remember where he'd hidden the stash. Uncle Mike was spitting mad and tried getting information out of him by using force, but your dad was so out of it that eventually Uncle Mike figured he really didn't know what he'd done with the drugs, if it was even true that he had them.

"You'd already given me an open invitation to the community, so Uncle Mike sent me as his informant. I was supposed to find out where the drugs were hidden and report back to him. But then there were a bunch of days where I couldn't get out to communicate with him, and he panicked, I guess. Uncle Mike sent those boys up here in the old Suburban to basically bust in and force people to talk, and we both know how *that* turned out. I hadn't said anything about the guys guarding the place, so no doubt they were shocked by what happened."

"But my *vadder* had a driver," I insist, as if this fact alone can undo all the others. "An *Englischer.* Named Ronnie."

389

Sal laughs. "Yeah, good ol' Ronnie. He'd pick your old man up and bring him into town and then come back at the end of the day to take him home again. It was all just for appearances. Your dad had a car that he kept at my uncle's garage." She looks at my face. "What? Did you really think he delivered drugs by horse and buggy?"

I stand perfectly still, as if trying to offset my whirring mind. I don't know what to think. I know nothing about drugs. Not how they are taken or how much they cost. "Why is my *vadder* staying at the civic center? Is that where he lives?"

Sal gives me a one-shoulder shrug. "He does now. He used to have an apartment in the same complex as me. Then he lost everything when he couldn't keep paying my uncle. Honestly, he's lucky he's alive. He's been trying to get clean for a while, I reckon. But now he has no other choice. I didn't find the stash of cocaine until a few days after the teenagers were killed, and it looked like it'd absorbed a bunch of moisture and turned or something. I don't know how long it's been stored like that, but if it's still worth anything, it's probably not much. I've been trying to buy us some time, smuggling out food to the gang and telling Uncle Mike I haven't found anything else, but I'm not sure he believes me anymore."

Sal strokes her baby's fine, dark hair, and I can see her fingers are shaking. I realize that, while I've been judging her, she's been putting herself and her child in jeopardy to keep our community safe. "Your dad's in over his head, Leora," she murmurs. "He used the cocaine he stole as collateral to get more drugs. The word is out about the cocaine and people are waiting for it. Some have already paid, in one form or another. If my uncle discovers the cache is not worth much, your dad's a dead man. And to tell you the truth, the only reason he's not dead already is because Uncle Mike's hoping your dad's head will clear up enough that he'll be able to find the stash himself because, after all, he's the one who hid it."

The two of us wait, listening to the off-kilter creak of Jabil's wagon wheels as he comes through the breach in the fence. I say, "If not remembering's what's keeping him alive, then that's probably exactly why he can't."

"That's the trouble," Sal responds. "I think my uncle's starting to realize that your dad's not remembering on purpose too."

"But where's it hidden?" I ask. "The drugs?"

Sal looks at me in confusion, as if she

can't believe I don't know. Then she points behind her to the cellar. "That's not just flour in those containers," she says. "Some of it's cocaine."

MOSES

I never expected a drug addict to know how to shoot. I also never expected it from a pacifist — or former pacifist. But I was clearly wrong on both counts. Luke Ebersole sends a storm of bullets downrange. His hair keeps getting in the way of his line of sight, and he wipes the oily threads back from his face before firing again. Sometime since I discovered him in the center, he must've tried bathing as best he could, because he at least *looks* cleaner than he did that day, though he smells about the same. But the years of hard living can't be wiped away the same as the filth. They mark him down to the pores, like coal residue.

Thanks to Luke's marksmanship, which came on the heels of Charlie's mortar explosion, the gang has retreated until they're almost out of reach. They're still shooting, but I think they're trying to figure out how to escape and then overtake us from a different approach or at a different time. No doubt Charlie would rather finish them all off and not give them the chance.

Before he gets the opportunity, a yellow Pontiac streaks down the center of the highway and lurches to a stop behind the perforated conversion van. A man clambers out, unfolding his huge body from the car's low-slung frame. His bald, ovule-shaped head catches the light. It takes about five seconds before I place him as the hench-man, working for the gang member we met the same night we went to the museum in town.

Luke gestures to our new arrival. "That guy's part of Liberty's gang. They must've merged with the gang you all've been fighting. I bet the Liberty boys told them what's here."

Charlie barks, " 'What's here'? We got nothing. We're running out of ammo, and we barely got food, so maybe you should tell *that* to the gang, and then maybe they'd leave us alone." Disgruntled, he doesn't look across at Luke, but continues watching his scope.

Luke's hand, which was controlled sec-onds ago, quivers as he picks up the rifle. "I wasn't talking about food. I hid cocaine here a while back. But I was out of my mind when I did it and can't remember where it is. I didn't mean to hurt anyone. I had no idea it'd come to this."

Sean and Charlie stare at Luke in shock. Having known more of his history, I try to clarify by asking, "So . . . you're saying this whole shoot-out's over some drugs you stashed here and the gang's trying to get back?"

Luke turns to the side, away from Sean, and coughs down the front of his shirt. He finishes and wipes his mouth with the back of his hand. "Mike showed up yesterday, along with that guy there —" he points to the Pontiac — "and said I had twenty-four hours to find the cocaine and hand it over, or else they'd burn Mt. Hebron to the ground. I came here to warn the community that I thought the gang was on their way. But then, when I went to cross over the fence in the back, I saw all the commotion and guessed everybody was already heading out."

"You got yourself some impressive powers of observation." But then Charlie stops his grumbling and points. We turn to see one of the gang members stepping out from behind the barricade and darting across the grass toward the pine trees along the left. He's carrying a red container, probably fuel.

"Get that guy," I hiss, the battle with my conscience conquered by sheer instinct for survival. We all open up. One of our bullets hits him low in the leg, but it doesn't seem to faze him. Charlie curses as the man continues his pace like a demented robot, not even favoring his wound. In seconds, the man makes his way into the shadow of our perimeter, so close that he's out of our range. The rest of the gang are sending a wall of lead our way, trying to give their runner some cover. And it's working. There's no way I'm going to stand up to peer over the edge of the wall with bullets whizzing inches above my head. Soon, we can smell smoke and then see the telltale noxious cloud rising over the perimeter.

Luke calls over to us, "He's higher than a kite and can't feel much of anything. That's probably how the gang got him to do it in the first place."

The man has almost made it back to the barricade without the gas can, having surely dumped everything over the logs. Charlie takes aim.

I put up my hand to stop him. "It won't do any good."

He sighs and lowers the weapon. "Now we're even for that cat."

"I think a person's a little more important than a cat."

"Maybe in your book."

Sean says, "Stop jabbering, you two.

Who's going to get the water?"

I say, "That fire's not going out like last time. Besides, they'd shoot us if we tried."

"Great," Charlie says. "We're dead either way you slice it."

Across from us, Luke starts choking on the smoke. Slanting his gun against the scaffolding, he leans over and coughs so hard that, this time, I expect to see blood. There's nothing. He raises his head and meets my eyes. His are a mottled rendition of Leora's. I look back at him without seeing him. Instead I'm seeing his daughter when she reunites with her father after two years apart. Though he's a shell of the man who raised her, he's still her flesh and blood. I know what it's like to lose that fetter to the earth — or to simply cut yourself free from it because you're too ashamed of what you've done. Or of what you didn't have the courage to do. I can't let that level of loss happen to her. She's lost enough.

"I think y'all should go." Nobody responds to me — not Charlie, Luke, or Sean. All three just stare — as if hypnotized — at the flames licking the sides of the logs, at the sound of the wood cracking from the heat. "I'll hold down the fort while you help everyone finish escaping."

"Hold down the fort?" Charlie rolls his

eyes. "Don't talk stupid, Moses. We're about out of bullets, and our cover's in the process of getting burnt to the ground. What're you gonna do then? Throw rocks at them?"

"You said yourself we're dead if we put out the fire, and we're dead if we don't. There's no point in all of us just sitting here, with guns and no ammo, waiting to get overrun." I glance away from Charlie to the other set of scaffolding. "I've already had my string of second chances, Luke. Now I'm giving you one: I want you to get better, to get clean. I want you to reunite with your family. To become a father to them again, like you should've been all along."

Luke Ebersole stares like he can't decide if I'm serious or insane. Brushing a hank of hair away from his face, he says, "Why would you do that? You don't even know me."

I look away from him, and my eyes burn. I tell myself it's from the heat and the smoke of the flames. "I don't know you, but I do know your daughter. And for her, I'd do anything."

LEORA

It's as if I can see my *vadder*'s fate being sealed as Sal picks up the one bag of cocaine, which she's taken from the cellar, and tucks it into her backpack — proof, she says, that she's not telling a lie. For the gang's not going to allow someone who increased his debt with stolen property, which he then had the gall to damage, to just walk away. No, they will find him, I'm sure, and they will kill him. Though I am angry for his abandonment — for the two years my family spent not knowing if he was dead or alive — my stomach lurches at the thought of him actually dying.

My *vadder* wasn't always a drug addict. He didn't always shirk his responsibilities surrounding his children and wife. I remember him sitting at the head of that beautiful table he made, teasing a smile from my *mamm*'s mouth at suppertime as his callused hands passed her steaming bowls. I remember him carrying Anna, then eight years old, back from the pond after she fell skating — his booted feet stamping patterns in the snow as he cradled her, like someone newly born, against his chest. I remember glancing up after my baptism into the Mennonite church and seeing my *vadder* watching me with an incalculable mixture of sadness and warmth, so that I was grateful for the water dripping down my forehead, a screen for my eyes. For the first time since I've learned that he is alive — has, in fact, been living in Liberty this entire time — I feel my heart softening toward him, not because I know I should honor him despite what he's done, but because I realize, despite everything, I love him still.

Sal closes the trapdoor and kicks leaves over the plywood. She tucks strands of hair that have come loose from her braid behind her ears. I can see the crescents of brown beneath her strong, pink-and-white nails where she was peeling back the dirt to reach the cellar, and I know that this telltale dirt was what she was trying to hide from me that day she came into my room to make sure I was all right. I reach out and take that soiled hand.

"Please," I beseech her, thinking if I can protect her life, perhaps I can protect my *vadder*'s as well. "Please stay. You are not alone. We want you here . . . with us."

Sal drops my hand and looks away from me, toward the entrance of the woods. Jabil's so engrossed in unloading the wagon, I am almost certain that he has not noticed us. "I'm an informant, Leora. *Not* your friend. There has always been a deal. If I don't return . . ." She gestures toward the cellar concealing the cocaine. "If I just disappear and leave with you all, they'll come after me . . . the same as they'll come after your dad."

She says this as if she's recited it, but I can see how her eyes gleam in the waning light. We have become friends, despite her many walls and my own; it just makes it easier for her to leave if she says we are not. I search the pockets of my apron, trying to think of something I can offer. I hold my hands up and force myself not to cry. "I have nothing to give."

"You're wrong," she says, and her facade shatters like that heirloom platter at the feast. Tears slide down her cheeks. She smears them away like contagion. "You can give by taking from me." Colton lifts his head from the sling and smiles, sated from his mother's milk. In spite of her pain, I cannot help but smile back. Without looking at him or at me, Sal hooks her hands beneath Colton's arms and gently pulls his legs out of the sling. She hugs the child against her. Tears fall freely now and cling to his hair, dew on blades of ink-black grass.

Straightening, she dabs her nose and places the sweet bulk of him in my arms. Sal chokes down a sob and turns away from the searing image of me holding her son. "Don't try talking me out of this," she says, her voice rigid. "Where I'm going's no place for a child. I'll come back for him when it's safe." Honoring her wishes, I remain silent. Sal loosens the straps of the sling and passes it to me, warm with their body heat. Then she shoulders her pack and slips into the woods, disappearing as the eventide gradually wraps her like a blanket.

I shield Colton's head with my hand to keep him from getting slapped with brushwood as I hurry back toward the opening in the fence, which Jabil cut for easier passage. Behind his wagon, I can see the outline of my people, along with their horses and mules that are packed down with everything they anticipate we'll need to establish a new community on the mountain, if the one in the valley indeed gets destroyed. Some families are already making their way up the old logging path. Bishop Lowell is leading them, his straw hat donned, a walking staff supporting his weary — albeit determined — stride. I think of that verse in Exodus, which he quoted yesterday to encourage the community after they found out about our plight:

And I am come down to deliver them out of the hand of the Egyptians, and to bring them up out of that land unto a good land

and a large, unto a land flowing with milk and honey.

My irritation abates and my heart swells to witness my people's resilience in the face of such adversity. They are in the process of leaving — and losing — so much, and yet, despite this, they are already willing to build again. Leaving does not always equal apathy; in their case, leaving instead of hiding behind firepower is indeed the fearless thing to do.

I look toward the skyline, drinking in my last twilight viewed from Mt. Hebron land. The final rays of sun appear like fingers traced behind the stark cutout of the perimeter, reaching up into the darkening sky. My breath catches, as the peaceful moment is juxtaposed with the understanding that I am not merely viewing the final rays of sun, but also the flames leaping into the air on the perimeter down by the gate.

Seeking an explanation, I turn toward Jabil, who's unloading the last load of supplies at such a furious pace, he doesn't notice me until I yell at him.

He sets down the box and wipes his forehead with an arm equally saturated with sweat. "I see the perimeter. I do. But I can't stop to think about it now."

"What's going to happen to us, Jabil?"

He studies my face, as if resigned to whatever is about to befall. "I don't know, Leora," he says, and I am not sure if he is only speaking about the community or also about him and me.

I leave Jabil to his consuming work and pass through the gap in the fence. The horses and mules paw the earth, their bridles filling the air with a cheerful jingle contrasting our own alarm. Animals and humans alike sense an innate need to escape the fire that has covered the sky with a dense smog of orange-tinged light.

Grossmammi Eunice is standing at the edge of the group with my brother and sister. Anna's face is splotched from crying, the same as mine whenever I'm upset. Seth reminds me of one of the horses, resentful of the restraining bridle of *Grossmammi*'s skinny arm.

I step closer to them. *Grossmammi* lets go of Seth, and as if her fingers are compensating for her inability to see, she touches my face, my shoulder, and then Colton, who is pulling my *kapp* strings. "Where's Sal?" she asks.

"She'll be back. Can you take Colton a minute? It's too complicated to explain."

She accepts Colton, pressing a kiss to his

cheek. He snuggles against her, as accepting of love as any oblivious *kind*. "Stay close," she warns. "We're leaving with the next wagonload."

"I will, but I have to do something first."

Tension radiates from my fractured family with a palpable warmth, and yet *Grossmammi* nods, giving me, her eldest grandchild, the freedom to execute my choices and mistakes, which — as contrary as it is — makes me want to stay. But I cannot. Colton begins to *rutsch* in her arms. *Grossmammi* attempts to calm him by offering him a knuckle to suck. Using her distraction to my advantage, I disappear into the crowd before she or Seth ask what I have to do.

Pebbles fling behind my heels as I hurry down the lane toward the perimeter, which appears more like a torch than an obstruction, and yet it continues to stand. But for how long? I scan every passing face. Though I spot Charlie and Sean in the distance — supporting Henri between them — Moses is nowhere to be found. I am nearly to Field to Table when someone steps from the shadow cast by the awning. "Leora." I jump back at the voice and, by the light of the perimeter fire, see a man reaching out for me.

I do not know if I gasp aloud or only in my mind. I remain immobilized, as drained of my lifeblood as the person's skin appears. He walks toward me, tentative, as if afraid to spook a wild animal. Words will not come. Breath will not come. I am living a nightmare from which I can never awaken and during which I can never scream. The snapshots from our conjoined lives, which filtered through my mind as I stood beside the cellar, are conflicted by reality. My *vadder.* I can smell the smoke lacing his clothing and the acerbic odor of his skin and hair. His eyes — the same shape and shade as mine — are the only thing about him that remains unchanged.

"What are you doing?" My question sounds more like an accusation.

"I came here to help. I came here to . . . to come home."

Eyes burning, I watch a portion of the perimeter collapse. I think of the night I wedged Anna's bloodied nightgown down into the stove, vowing to protect and avenge her honor, no matter the personal cost. I think of *Mamm* pressing my hand while she lay on the couch and telling me to love someone who won't make me cry. Even Seth is vulnerable, as he's longing for a father figure, like Moses, so that he might imitate his life. Father or not, I won't allow this man to come back to our home until he's the kind of man our family deserves.

"Do you know that *Mamm*'s dead?" I ask him. "Because you broke her heart? That I've been trying to keep our family together while *you've* been acting like you don't have one?"

I would think it impossible for him to turn paler if I did not witness the transition with my own eyes. He looks away, his features clenched with pain. "I would've never —"

I interrupt, "Don't tell me you would've never left if you'd known she would die. All that matters is that you *did.*"

"I know that. I know. I'd just like the chance to come home. I won't mess up this time."

"Well. As you can see —" I gesture to the community's vacant acreage — "our home is what we are in the process of fleeing. You can only come back to us when you're well."

He nods, but I don't believe him. Despite the earlier conviction in his voice, I'm not sure he believes himself. Another portion of the wall topples, sending a miasma of ash and sparks high into the air. He touches my arm, and I recoil, my mind not comprehending that this displaced person is the same one who used to let me ride his shoulders as he walked through town. "The wall's not going to hold," he says. "They're going to be here soon. You should go."

"Aren't *you* going to go?"

"Moses told me to. Said he could hold everything down on his own. But I'm tired of leaving, Leora. You and I both know I've abandoned my post long enough."

I brace my eyes against rising tears. "Where is he?"

My *vadder* looks toward the perimeter. At the base of the scaffolding, which I thought was abandoned, a single man stands. "I have to go," I say. "Right now." My *vadder* nods and retreats into the shadows.

I watch him go, turn and walk away like he's always done, and then sprint the distance between Moses and me, as if leaving a ghost in my wake. Moses's corn-colored hair appears singed by the heat of the fire. His profile is so stoic, it is as if someone has already died. He must sense my approach, for he turns. His lips form my name, but I can't hear anything. I step closer, and the two of us stand in front of each other — a soldier and a pacifist — backlit by the wall of flames. And yet I'm not sure either of us can be categorized as easily as before.

"You shouldn't be here," he says.

"I had to come," I murmur, tasting salt. I

reach out and take his hand. He flinches, and my fingers braille the blisters bubbled across his palm. "Please don't do this, Moses," I murmur. "Don't stay here. Alone. . . . You can't hold them back yourself."

"No," he agrees. "I probably can't. But I think I can at least hold them off long enough for everyone to escape." He withdraws his hand and moves closer, his eyes wide and staring at everything but me. "All this time I wondered why I didn't die in the desert. I wondered why I didn't die when I crashed in your field. Now I know. I was given a second chance because I was meant to come here and give your father a second chance too."

"He lost out on second chances when he left us!"

"Maybe so. But think of your family. Doesn't your father deserve a second chance for them? Don't *you* deserve a second chance as well? A chance to stop living with all this guilt and worry . . . to stop always having to prepare yourself for the worst?"

"The worst already happened, Moses. You know about —"

"Anna?" I nod. He continues, "Anna wasn't raped. She wasn't. Charlie confessed to shooting her cat. He threw it into the woods, and she followed him and picked it up, not understanding that it was dead. That's where the blood came from."

"A *cat*?" I cry. "A dead cat is what made me question my pacifist beliefs?"

"If it wasn't the incident with your sister, Leora, it would've been something else. You were just searching for a reason to question. Besides, you can't doubt something you don't believe in. In the end, your faith will be stronger for having been tested."

"Maybe so, but God could've avoided the testing altogether."

"Yes, he could have. Your sister also could have not fallen that day. Or I could have shot that kid and saved my brother's life. But sometimes life isn't as cut-and-dried as we'd like it to be. We just have to know that, regardless of what happens, God can work all things together for good."

"Listen to you. When you came here, you said you weren't a man of faith. But now your faith's stronger than mine."

Smiling at me, he reaches for my hand. "Strange as it is, that's because of you. Isn't that proof in itself that God has a plan? Maybe not just for you and me . . . but for us?"

He pulls my hand closer. I swallow my reserve and lean against Moses's chest. He wraps his arms around me. Another log topples from the perimeter. I sense the vestiges of my own perimeter crumbling, and I give myself over to it — to the healing love I refused to embrace because I felt more in control, living behind my fear. I lift my face up to Moses's. Reflected in his eyes, I see the flames' red glow. His head leans down toward mine. We kiss. A declarative. A pronoun and a verb combined, so simple, and yet each syllable possessing its own language.

He draws himself away and meets my eyes. "Leora, please. Go."

"Promise me you'll come find us."

"I promise." He dries my tears with his thumbs. Unsnapping his holster, he places his revolver in my hands. "I want you to have this, just in case."

"You still believe in weapons?"

"Using weapons doesn't negate faith. But if you're putting faith in your weapon rather than in God, that's where the trouble lies." He presses his hand on top of mine until my fingers wrap around the gun.

I nod, head down to hide my tears, and slip the revolver into my apron pocket: a welcome weight, an extension of my free will. But how can I leave him standing here in front of a crumbling wall, outside of which the marauders are waiting to overtake our utopia?

"I can't do it, Moses. I can't leave you."

"There are no other options. You must."

A staccato beat of hooves on gravel. I dry my eyes on my sleeve and look up the lane. Jabil is astride his horse, the tired mare's sides heaving and frothy with sweat. "Come, Leora," he calls as he pulls back the reins. "We're the last ones."

Pressing the revolver against my thigh, I look at Moses once more before accepting Jabil's hand. He grips my wrist and lifts me without effort onto the bareback mare. He nods at Moses, and Moses nods in return, though both men are grim. Without a word, a promise is being spoken, and I can tell that I am the transacting cargo they want to keep safe.

Jabil says, "Hold tight," and drives his heels into the horse's sides with a vehemence so rare for him, I know the abuse stems from his urgency to reach safety.

The wind whistles in my ears as the mare lunges through the darkened maze of Mt. Hebron Community, which I could navigate blind . . . which I might never see again. Tears stream past my temples and saturate my hair. I rest my face against Jabil's back, not for comfort, but because my hands are wrapped around his waist and I have no other way to stifle my weeping. I inhale his sweat, my salt mixing with his own. Jabil says nothing, but his spine is ridged with strain. He doesn't steer the mare around the gravestones but drives her forward, among them, as if death itself can be trodden upon.

Before we pass through the fence, I turn and look down the valley that cradles my home but is in the process of being enveloped in flame. Only God himself knows if, like the legendary phoenix, my faith, my love, will one day arise from the ash.

A NOTE FROM THE AUTHOR

I guess you could say I had a slightly different childhood. When I was six and my brother ten, our family stood in a field at the camp where my parents were caretakers, and my parents told us that this was where we would meet if we were separated when the world "blew up." From this field, our family would travel by foot to our friends' elaborate, fairy-tale home and live in the blue room hidden behind their bookshelves.

My parents did not mean to instill fear in us. Now that I'm a parent, I see that they were trying to assuage their own fears by coming up with a plan. But I was born with an overactive imagination, and therefore this plan planted in me the seed of fear — and subsequently, a driving need to control my environment.

I wish I could say I uprooted this fear once I became an adult, but after I had my firstborn daughter, my fear grew worse, for not only did I have to control *my* environment; I also had to control hers. When my eldest was six months old, an unnerving exchange with a logger deepened the roots of my fear and caused me to ask whether I would ever use lethal force to protect myself and my family. I believed I would, even though, growing up, I sensed my own father would adhere to his pacifist heritage if placed in such a situation.

The final puzzle piece for my book, *The Alliance,* slid into place when my father told us that we needed heirloom seeds to last us until the next harvest season. I remember standing in my darkened kitchen and repeating that phrase to myself — *the harvest season.* Initially, I believed this would be the title of the book, but over time, I knew a community having enough food to last until the next harvest season was only a small element of the story. The larger element came from the protagonist, Leora Ebersole, and her driving need to control her environment, even after society crumbles around her, because she believes if she controls her environment, she will be able to keep her orphaned family safe.

With every one of my books, God's been faithful to allow me to experience some portion of whatever topic I'm addressing. *The Alliance* has been no exception. My family and I moved from Tennessee to Wisconsin shortly before I finished the rough draft. Eight weeks later, my husband went in for a CAT scan, which revealed a tumor near his brain stem. He had surgery the next morning, and all through that night next to his hospital bed, I feared for my family. I feared for our two young daughters — our firstborn was two and a half and our second, four months old at the time. I feared that I would be a widow, living on a grid-tie solar-powered farm six hundred miles away from our immediate families. In a matter of hours, one of my worst fears had come true, and I didn't know how to handle it.

However, all through my Garden of Gethsemane night, during the hours my husband was in surgery, and in the critical weeks that followed the craniotomy, I felt God's presence as if he was sitting beside me. I then understood that God had allowed me to face one of my greatest fears so that I would learn that inner peace can never be acquired through my futile attempts to control my environment — and therefore keep my family safe. Moreover, I can only achieve inner peace if I continually surrender my life and the lives of my family to the One who called us into being.

So I pray, dear reader, that you will discover the author of the peace that passes all understanding and daily surrender your life — and the lives of your family — to him.

DISCUSSION QUESTIONS

1. Have you ever given much thought to the dangers of an EMP? How likely do you think it is that something like this might really happen? Is it something you should prepare for, and if so, how might you prepare? How do you balance being prepared with being controlled by fear?

2. How do Leora's beliefs change throughout the story? Was this progression portrayed realistically? Do you think Leora will ever come back around to her pacifist beliefs? Why or why not? Have your own convictions changed from childhood to adulthood? What caused them to change?

3. Moses feels anger toward God, believing that God has spared him while letting others around him suffer and die. Has there ever been a time in your life when God's plan felt like a punishment? How would

you encourage Moses to move past his anger?

4. How does Moses's faith change throughout the book? How do you think he will continue to grow or change spiritually in the next book?

5. Describe Leora's feelings toward Anna. Is Leora right to feel guilty about Anna's accident? Have you ever struggled with a similar situation? How did — or might — it affect your outlook and decisions?

6. How do Leora's feelings toward her father shift over the course of the story? How do you think Leora should have reacted to her father's return?

7. Were you surprised by the identity of the person stealing food from the community? What did you think of the way Leora reacted? Where would you like to see this thread go in the next book?

8. When Moses and Jabil go into town in search of a tractor, Moses vacillates on how the community views their plan. Though they do not plan to pillage or harm anyone, they are prepared to steal to

better themselves and the community. If placed in the same position, would you be willing to break the law in order to save yourself or your family? Why or why not?

9. In what ways are Moses and Jabil similar? In what ways are they different? If placed in Leora's position, which man would you find it easier to trust with your heart? Why?

10. Leora admits, "I yearn to be with Moses, as if he is my North Star in this black hole of madness, but my duty to my family forces me to remain lost." Could the two coexist, or must Leora make a choice? Faced with a choice between love and a responsibility to your family, how would you decide?

11. Why does Leora think her grandmother might not be as anxious as everyone else despite the upheaval they're experiencing? How have you seen this illustrated (or contradicted) in people you know? In general, why do you think we are so fearful for our lives and those of the people we love?

12. Which characters, if any, would you like to know more about? What would you like

to see happen to them as the story concludes in the next book?

ABOUT THE AUTHOR

Jolina Petersheim is the bestselling author of *The Outcast,* which *Library Journal* called "outstanding . . . fresh and inspirational" in a starred review and named one of the best books of 2013. That book also became an ECPA, CBA, and Amazon bestseller and was featured in *Huffington Post*'s Fall Picks, *USA Today, Publishers Weekly,* and the *Tennessean. CBA Retailers + Resources* called her second book, *The Midwife,* "an excellent read [that] will be hard to put down," and *Romantic Times* declared, "Petersheim is an amazing new author." Jolina's nonfiction writing has been featured in *Reader's Digest, Writer's Digest,* and *Today's Christian Woman.*

Jolina and her husband share the same unique Amish and Mennonite heritage that originated in Lancaster County, Pennsylvania. After years of living in the mountains of

Tennessee, they moved to a farm in the Driftless Region of Wisconsin, where they live with their two young daughters. Follow Jolina's blog at www.jolinapetersheim.com.

The employees of Thorndike Press hope you have enjoyed this Large Print book. All our Thorndike, Wheeler, and Kennebec Large Print titles are designed for easy reading, and all our books are made to last. Other Thorndike Press Large Print books are available at your library, through selected bookstores, or directly from us.

For information about titles, please call:
  (800) 223-1244

or visit our Web site at:
  http://gale.cengage.com/thorndike

To share your comments, please write:
  Publisher
  Thorndike Press
  10 Water St., Suite 310
  Waterville, ME 04901